To my wife, Karen, who was a source of inspiration and encouragement throughout the writing of *The Redemption Codes*.

And to my friend, Dick DeBock, who was instrumental in editing comments and chapter headings and a steady voice throughout the process.

CONTENTS

Chapter 1: A Tragedy...1
Chapter 2: The Gambler..4
Chapter 3: Failed Mission..14
Chapter 4: A Bittersweet Reunion...16
Chapter 5: Jerusalem, Israel...21
Chapter 6: The Professor Is Dead?..33
Chapter 7: Creedmoor Industries LLC..46
Chapter 8: Bootlegger's Cabin..51
Chapter 9: Bad News..57
Chapter 10: Epitome of Evil...60
Chapter 11: Is the Code Real?...65
Chapter 12: Not the "Appointed Time"..82
Chapter 13: Money and Power...86
Chapter 14: The Routine...88
Chapter 15: Have You Found Them Yet?..99
Chapter 16: Kind Words...102
Chapter 17: Plaintext..105
Chapter 18: The Meeting..109
Chapter 19: Black SUV..115
Chapter 20: He Saved My Life...121
Chapter 21: Failure Continues..133
Chapter 22: Shaken to the Core...136
Chapter 23: Shimon Arrives...143
Chapter 24: Duplicity..163
Chapter 25: The Chase Begins...166
Chapter 26: Escape To Israel...174
Chapter 27: The Missionary...177
Chapter 28: Economic Disaster..186

Chapter 29: King David Hotel 200
Chapter 30: Correlations 214
Chapter 31: It Gets Ugly 218
Chapter 32: The "Appointed Place" 245

Epilogue... 251

Chapter 1

A Tragedy

The squeak from the back screen door opening startled the old man awake from his customary afternoon nap. *It's about time I fix that door.* It never closed all the way, and the old man's cat, Tiger, had scratched so many holes in the wire mesh that the old man was forever chasing away flies. "It's probably Lisa. I wonder why she is coming in the back door?" The old man lived for the day of the week when his favorite granddaughter visited. Actually, she was his only grandchild, but he never tired of reminding Lisa that she was his favorite.

He was pretty sure it was not Tuesday. He was prone, after all, to forget what day it was. At his age and alone, the days all seemed to run together—except Sunday and Tuesday. Sunday was church, the place where the old man most felt at home. On a clear Sunday morning, he would walk the quarter mile to the neighborhood church with its red brick, white steeple, and stained glass. If the weather was bad, he drove his '94 Carolina-blue Cadillac.

Church had also become a place to socialize, maybe even flirt a little with the widows. It was only a flirt—never serious. Though many had wanted to make it serious through the years, he could never find anyone who could hold a candle to his wife. She had died several decades ago, but the pain had never completely gone away.

Everyone loved the old man, and for him, the feeling was mutual. He had reached an age where an afternoon with his granddaughter or a hug and a smile from a friend was all he needed out of life.

And Tuesday. Lisa always visited on Tuesday—the day he got to spend time with the most special person in his life. In Lisa's early adolescent years, time was occupied with small talk and his joy in seeing her mature into a young lady. But the talks took on a more serious tone in the past year. She could trust him. She could ask the hard questions and advice about a serious boyfriend, a class at the university, or a career decision, and the grandfather's answers always came from a potent combination of unconditional love and profound wisdom. She could show pain, knowing that he had experienced his share of pain too. But most of all, with her grandpa, she could show unbridled joy.

He went through the untrustworthy calendar in his mind. "Well, maybe it is Tuesday, but this is much earlier than she normally visits." As an aspiring graduate student, Tuesday was Lisa's heavy class day at the university, and her last class was not over until late afternoon. It had recently been their custom to share supper with whatever food Lisa decided to bring that day.

Now the old man could hear footsteps against the wood flooring of the hallway leading from the back door. It sounded like one person, but the footsteps were slow and measured and from someone much heavier than Lisa. And by now, he would have already heard those cheerful words, *"Grandpa! Grandpa!"*

He called out anyway. "Lisa, honey, is that you?"

There was no answer as the footsteps stopped. The old man knew how this was going to end. For months, he had mentally tried to prepare for this day. He quickly opened the antique drawer beside the recliner and dialed the number on the phone hidden under the pull-out section. As soon as it rang, he quietly slipped the receiver back on its cradle and closed the drawer.

A large man with black gloves raised his gun. The worst scenario the large man had planned for was that the old man would be home. But he did not have a choice. His assignment was clear. *Get the information today! Steal it. If the old man is home, you know what you have to do. This is bigger than you. This is bigger than the old man or the professor. The future of the United States depends on this.* The large man was following orders as he had been trained to do.

The large man with the black gloves turned the corner of the hallway past the kitchen, aimed his pistol with its silencer, and, with military precision, pulled the trigger.

Chapter 2

The Gambler

Blackjack had become an obsession with Neil. Like so many other facets of his life recently, gambling was one more on a long list of vices he was not particularly proud of. One thing you couldn't argue, though, was that blackjack was something at which Neil was very good. And as a struggling graduate student, the money from the blackjack table allowed him to make ends meet and stay current with a pile of student loans.

A dysfunctional family life had left Neil with only a few places where he felt at home. One had been the mathematics lab, the other a blackjack table. Today, like most days recently, it was the latter.

Neil Coles was a tall, classically handsome young man with a disarming smile and a confident demeanor. Despite his sedentary hobby, he was in relatively good physical shape. When he sat at the blackjack table, his long waistline made him appear even taller than his six-foot-two-inch frame. Broad shoulders and long arms had held him in good stead as a competitive swimmer. He played basketball and soccer as a kid, but it was swimming that came naturally to him. Throughout the adolescent years, he won swimming competitions on natural ability alone. It was the sacrifice, hard work, and long training hours required to excel at the college or Olympic level that had always held him back.

Not achieving athletically had been more disappointing for his mom than for him. She knew he had the talent to compete at the highest level, but unfortunately, he just did not have the drive or the commitment. From time to time, he felt remorse that he had not given her a few more happy moments seeing him compete before she succumbed to the cancer.

For all the natural ability he had as a swimmer, it was in math class where Neil really shined. He knew from an early age that he was blessed with a talent for math. It just came easy to him. "That gift must have come from your father's side of the family," his mom would sometimes remark.

That is something Neil would not know or, for that matter, care to know. His father was a no-show his whole life, and by now, Neil had learned to live with it. If it weren't for his sister's insistence, Neil would not even acknowledge his father's existence.

After the death of their mother, his sister urged them to reach out to their father with the hopes of keeping the semblance of a family together. For Neil, that time had passed. As far as Neil was concerned, his father had forfeited any opportunity for a family. After all, he needed a father during all the good and bad times growing up—to play catch with him or to watch him swim. But more than just for himself, Neil knew there were many times when his mom was lonely. He could see it in her eyes. For that alone, he could not and would not forgive. Reaching out now to a father who had never been there was not going to happen, not now, not ever. Period. End of story.

Neil's math skills did not go unnoticed, even at an early age. In high school, he routinely corrected his teachers and, on more than one occasion, proved that the math textbook had printed an incorrect answer. He could translate a problem into an equation faster than it took most students to write their names on the top of the paper. He never missed a math question on a standardized test from elementary to high school, and the math portion of his college boards was like a walk in the park. Neil could answer double-digit multiplication numbers in his head. And though it was never verified, rumor was that in one class, he accepted a challenge from a professor that he could beat the class record of repeating a string of numbers after hearing them once. He repeated twenty-eight numbers—the previous class record had been twelve.

When the opportunity to enter MIT presented itself, Neil jumped at it. If it hadn't been for his sick mom, Neil would have graduated from MIT, probably at the top of his class. He had that kind of gift. He would have been wooed and recruited for employment like a modern-day free-agent athlete.

That plan all changed when his mom was first diagnosed. She insisted throughout the early stages of the cancer that Neil remain at MIT, but Neil would have no part of that. If there was one characteristic of Neil, other than his extraordinary math skills and newfound propensity for winning at blackjack, it was his steadfast devotion to his mom. She had carried the burden of raising a family alone, and Neil was not about to abandon her at the time of her greatest need.

It was his sophomore year when he transferred to the Chapel Hill campus of the University of North Carolina. In the area of study where Neil excelled, UNC was not in the same league as MIT, but it had the one characteristic Neil wanted most. It was close to his mom, whom the doctors diagnosed was fading faster than originally thought. He found time to visit her every day, without exception, right up to that last day when the ravages of the disease took its final toll. She died in Neil's junior year.

Along the way, Neil learned his *gift* offered rewards in the most unexpected ways. This first came to light on his seventeenth birthday, the winter of his freshman year at MIT. Two of his friends, armed with fake IDs, loaded into his buddy's car for a trip to the casinos of Atlantic City.

At that time, Neil was not much of a gambler or a partier, for that matter, and he resisted their overture to join them. It was his best friend who concocted a scheme to get Neil to agree to go. He showed Neil the art of card counting. Neil was instantly hooked. "*Math as a sport,*" Neil would often say, "*is a beautiful thing.*"

It was in the casino that Neil first learned that he could convert a gift into a hobby and a hobby into a moneymaking enterprise. He did not tell his mom about the trip. She would not have approved. He finally justified that the money he made in the casino was better than drawing on his student loan, which would take him forever to repay.

That first trip put two thousand dollars in Neil's pocket. Future trips netted Neil all the money he needed to pay his tuition, books, and more. But as he later learned, all gifts that are abused come with a price; for him, now it was a lifestyle of overindulgence, partying, and alcohol.

Today, Neil turned twenty-five. By now, his friends had grown weary of his excesses. Although he found himself once again in a casino, surrounded by smiling people having the time of their lives, Neil felt alone on his birthday. *Who am I kidding? This lifestyle can't go on forever. It is time to grow up to do something productive with this God-given gift.*

All night in the casino was starting to take its toll. Too much concentration mixed with too much alcohol without any food caused his head to ache. Sleep was what Neil desired the most. There would be no more partying tonight as he headed to his hotel room alone.

A hot bath would be a welcomed end to the night. But Neil never made it past the bed. He was unconscious within seconds, fully dressed, and sprawled across the bed.

How long he had been asleep when the phone rang, he did not know. He knew it was not long enough to fully dissipate the effects of the alcohol or lessen the throbbing in his head.

The phone rang again. At first, the ring somehow crept into his dream, but soon, the subconscious gave way to the conscious. He finally raised his head high enough to see the clock. It was six thirty in the morning, Las Vegas time.

Who could be calling? Who even knows where I am? Who even cares? Not even my sister called to wish me a happy birthday. "Hello," he managed.

The sobs and muted sounds instantly pierced his soul to the quick. He knew something was very wrong, but his consciousness had not yet fully kicked into place.

"Who is this?"

There was a silence. *Maybe a wrong number.* He wanted to hang up the phone, but he couldn't.

Finally, *the* voice said, "Neil, this is Lisa. My father has been killed."

This must be a dream. No, a nightmare. That is Lisa's voice. If there was one unmistakable voice he knew for sure, it was Lisa's. "Oh my god! What are you saying? The professor is…"

Neil was at a loss for words. His hand started to shake. Finally, he said the only thing that made sense to him at the time. "An accident?"

"No, murdered."

"My god!"

"The police…are you okay? Are you at a safe place?"

"Yes, the police are on their way."

"And you?"

"I am. What do I do, Neil?"

Neil was not equipped for this news, physically or mentally. And most recently, he was unaccustomed to making adult decisions.

"I don't know. I'll stay on the phone until—"

"They're here. I'll call you back." And with that, the phone went dead.

*****

Neil was not hungry, but he ordered some coffee from room service. The combination of the coffee and the events of the past few minutes had its intended effect of sobering him. His mind tried to shake the effects of the alcohol and comprehend what he had just heard. *Who would want to hurt Professor Lange? My god, who would kill him?*

Professor Lange was the head of the mathematics department at MIT when Neil first met him. In a situation eerily similar to what Neil faced, the professor took a job at the University of North Carolina so that he could be near his father, who had suffered a stroke and whose health, like Neil's mom, was deteriorating.

Physically, the professor was not an opposing figure. A man of normal size, slightly balding, his blond hair of youth had turned prematurely to a shiny gray. His students affectionately referred to him as the old man, which you might mistakenly assume from his hair. Actually, he was in good physical shape, which belied his fifty-two years, thanks to a healthy diet and half-mile morning swims.

For those who knew the professor, it was his mind that set him apart from all the rest, even from other elite mathematicians and scientists. Considered one of the foremost authorities on quantum mechanics and chance mathematics, Professor Lange possessed the unusual combination of being both extremely brilliant and extremely creative in his approach to his research. For those in the know, it was not if, but when, he would receive a Nobel Prize for physics.

Neil's mind wandered back to the first time he met the professor. Meeting Professor Lange was like a young baseball player meeting Babe Ruth or Ted Williams, an artist meeting Rembrandt or Picasso, or a musician meeting Beethoven or Mozart. In the world of mathematics, it was the closest thing to meeting a celebrity, especially for an underclassman.

The professor was brilliant, to say the least. But Neil saw something more in the professor than his intelligence. In the world of academic arrogance and elitism, the professor stood out as a genuinely good and kind person.

Neil soon observed that he cared about his students and treated them with dignity and respect. That was what made this news seem so impossible. *Who would hurt such a good man?*

The relationship and admiration worked both ways. Early on, the professor recognized in Neil someone like himself at that age, someone who had the *gift*. Their relationship quickly took hold and grew fast, the teacher and the student.

Over time, the professor represented for Neil more than a teacher or a model worthy of emulation. Whether Neil was conscious of it or not, the professor represented the only father figure he ever had. And for the professor, though he would never admit it, Neil represented the son he never had.

The phone rang again.

Before he could answer, "Neil, the police are here. It is awful. They just took him away. Can you come? He would want you here."

The sobs started again. "Can you please come? I don't know where to turn."

Lisa didn't have to beg. That was the least he could do.

"Yes. I'll get the first flight out. I'll be there as soon as I can."

"Thanks, Neil."

Before he could say any of the things that were running through his head, the phone clicked again. Neil sensed that his life was about to change dramatically.

If only he knew how much.

*****

Neil threw some clothes into a suitcase before he took a long, hot shower. He packed the only suit he owned. His remaining clothes and belongings would remain in the hotel storage until he returned.

It was almost dark by the time Neil arrived at the Las Vegas—McCarran International Airport. He had been fortunate to book the last seat on a nonstop flight leaving for Raleigh, North Carolina.

As the 727 taxied to the runway, what Neil wanted more than anything else was to be left alone. He needed time to sort through the range of emotions that were flooding his head. Even the bright lights of the Las Vegas strip, which had always captured his imagination, held no allure for him tonight.

He avoided making eye contact with the flight attendant or the man beside him. The man could not have cared less. He was part of a group leaving Las Vegas after a few days of recreation. Although it was early evening, the group had obviously spent the better part of the afternoon at the bar. The agony of hearing their endless stories was only outweighed by the volume in which those stories were told.

The flood of emotions at times almost overwhelmed Neil. He could not make sense of the death of his mentor and friend. *Who would kill the professor? A student? No. He was adored or at least respected by all of his students. Was it a robbery?* Those who knew the professor knew that he was not a man who obsessed over personal things. One look at how he dressed could tell you that. *But who? Who would do such an awful thing?*

Confusion gave way to sadness, and sadness to remorse. His last conversation with the professor had been somewhat combative, and Neil had said some things that he later regretted. The professor had chastised his student for not utilizing his gifts. *You have gifts that could benefit mankind. You are wasting them.* Neil had walked out of the room. He could not argue with him. He knew the professor was right.

Remorse gave way to regret. He could not get the thought out of his head that he had disappointed the professor. Time ran out before he had a chance to tell the professor he was right.

And Lisa. It wasn't just the emotion of his dead friend and mentor that he had to confront. He would see Lisa again—the first and only one he ever loved.

Seeing Lisa again would be bittersweet. There was no doubt that it would remind him of everything he had done wrong over the past year. After all, it is one thing to destroy your own hopes and dreams; it is another to destroy the only truly good thing that ever happened in your life. *Maybe I am no better than my father.*

His mind flashed back to the day he first met Lisa. The professor had invited a few of the students to his house. Neil knew that the professor's wife had died a couple of years earlier and that he had not remarried. The professor was a handsome man but had always resisted the advances of his fellow female professors. He never mentioned his family, and Neil assumed the professor lived alone. When he arrived at the front door that night, he was met by the most beautiful woman he had ever seen. Tall and slender traits he found came from her mother, as did blond hair, which she inherited from her father. But her face, Neil would later say, was like that of an angel.

"Professor," he remembered saying. "You never mentioned that you had a daughter."

"You never asked," the professor quipped. "And had you asked, I would have probably denied it."

It would take Neil more than a week to get the nerve to ask Lisa out and another week before she got around to answering. His first mistake in that regard was asking the professor for permission. He learned early on that the professor was extremely protective of his daughter. A trait Neil discovered was born from the untimely sickness and death of his wife. The professor realized that people you love can be gone faster than you think. So he held on to Lisa tightly.

After a few tries, the professor finally relented. Neil only hoped that it wouldn't be that hard to convince Lisa.

He didn't remember much about that first date other than he was nervous and lacked the confidence and brashness he normally possessed. He and Lisa sat on the swing on the front porch, talking late into the night. He let himself smile now, remembering that the professor would periodically clear his throat, just as a friendly reminder that he was inside, like a shepherd keeping watch by night.

Their relationship grew over the next few weeks and months. He realized early on that what started as an infatuation was turning into something that, at least in his mind, was love. He longed for one chance to talk to his mom about Lisa. He knew she would have approved. After all, they were very similar, at least in the ways of the heart.

He discovered that Lisa was much different from her father. Where the professor excelled in the sciences, Lisa excelled in the arts. Where the professor spoke to make a point, Lisa would ramble on and on. For the professor, life was black-and-white. There was no room for the grays. For Lisa, life was all grays. Everyone she met had some redeeming quality, and if they didn't show one, she would impute one for them.

He would never forget when they had encountered a homeless man on the street. At Lisa's insistence, he gave the man a few dollars. The man said thank you. Lisa was impressed. *Oh, what wonderful manners he has.*

Neil often wondered whether Lisa's loving nature and carefree view of life came from her mother. Clearly, in his mind, that was where her beauty came from, a matter he often reminded the professor.

Why did he let her slip through his hands? To Neil, that was a rhetorical question. He clearly was the problem. He had screwed up opportunities and, along the way, alienated the two people he loved the most.

The flight attendant interrupted his loathing. "Can I get you anything?"

"Nothing, thank you."

The flood of emotions was starting to grip Neil so tightly that he could hardly breathe. The level of immaturity he displayed the last few months stood in sharp contrast to what he would need to deal with the events coming over the next few days. This was going to be the hardest thing Neil had to do since he buried his mom.

His mind drifted again back to the mystery of the professor's death. He heard that the professor had recently taken an unusual leave of absence from the university. Rumors flew around as they always do in these situations. Neil knew it was not for medical reasons. The professor was in excellent health for his age, or any age, for that matter. *But why did the professor leave the university so abruptly? Was there a connection to what happened today?* The professor certainly did not frequent places he should not. His routine was the same every day—gym, class, lab, and home. *I guess I'll find out soon.*

He closed his eyes, but sleep escaped him. For the next few hours, he was a prisoner of his thoughts, remorse, and regrets.

Thankfully, the 727 finally hit the runway, and the pilot announced that they had arrived at the Raleigh-Durham International Airport on time.

Chapter 3

Failed Mission

The instructions to the large man with the black gloves had been clear. Get in and get out without causing attention and preferably without collateral damage. But most importantly, get the information from the old man.

Things had not gone as the large man had hoped. He was trained to carry out difficult missions, and that included planning for the unexpected. He had no conscience when it came to killing the bad guys. Over his checkered military and paramilitary career, he had killed more than he could count. But killing the old man weighed heavily on the large man's mind. He was not convinced the old man was part of this plot—*maybe I just killed an innocent victim.* When he became anxious, he shook his head violently back and forth, the manifestation of an uncontrollable tick. *I'm going to hell for this one.*

He took a deep breath as he pulled the cell phone from his pocket and punched in the special number he had memorized. A brood of a man with large hands and a muscular body, he had been trained not to be afraid of anyone. Today, he was afraid. His hands started to shake as if in concert with his head.

"Do you have the material?" demanded the man who answered the phone call.

"I could not find the—"

"You did get the old man's computer?"

"Yes…sir."

"The charts. Did you find any charts?" the man snarled.

"No, sir. There were no charts, no graphs."

"E drives?"

"No, sir. I looked in every desk and drawer in the house."

"Where there any programs open on the computer?"

"Yes. There was only one program open."

"What was it?" the man demanded, becoming more agitated and impatient with each question.

"Solitaire."

"The only program open on his computer was Solitaire?"

"Yes, sir."

"Was the old man there?"

"Yes, sir. I did what I had to do."

"You made it look like a robbery?"

"Yes, sir. I was careful not to leave any clues."

"Did anyone see you come or go?"

"There was no one around the old man's house or in the neighborhood except for a cat. I parked several blocks away and entered through the back door. The mission was accomplished as planned, sir."

"Deliver the computer to the warehouse. I will have technicians there ready. The old man is hiding the information somewhere." And with that, the phone clicked.

The large man with the black gloves and the uncontrollable tick had an uneasy feeling that the mission had failed. He knew it was not his fault. He exactly did what he was instructed to do. But that would not satisfy this man, this monster.

The shoulders of the large man slumped like a chastised animal. *What will happen next?* he wondered. He was afraid to even imagine.

Chapter 4

A Bittersweet Reunion

Neil loaded his suitcase into the trunk of the rental car. It was still dark outside, and it felt like the temperature was just a few degrees above freezing. Fall was definitely Neil's favorite time of the year in North Carolina.

A sign by the rental car exit soliciting donations reminded him that Thanksgiving was just a few weeks away. He had been so preoccupied with his lifestyle that he had failed to realize that the holidays were just around the corner. A picture of his smiling mom and sister around the table on Thanksgiving flashed across his mind. Mom had a way of making the most of the holidays, even in the days when she did not feel well.

He pulled a jacket from the suitcase and reached into the pockets to see if he had left some gloves. They were not there, but it didn't matter—it would not be that cold. As the car was warming inside, he turned off the Airline mode on his cell phone and retrieved the number Lisa had called from. *That's strange. The number is not there. Wait, that's right. She called me on the hotel phone. That's interesting— how did she know where I was staying?*

It did not matter. If there was a telephone number he remembered, it was Lisa's. He assumed her number had not changed in just the few months he had been away. It was busy. He tried the home number. After just one ring, it immediately went to the answering machine. The unmistakable voice on the answering machine was that of the professor. Neil could barely stand to listen. He made a mental note to erase the professor's message. Since he had not spoken to Lisa since he left, he decided to leave a message that he was on the way.

As he pulled out of the airport onto Interstate 40, the sun was just starting to peek over the horizon. At this time of day, with just a few cars on the highway getting an early start to the workday, he definitely would be at the professor's house in less than half an hour.

Unlike most of the professors who lived in nearby Chapel Hill near the University of North Carolina's campus, the professor lived in a quaint, older section of Raleigh, three-quarters of an hour from campus. The professor chose Raleigh so he could be closer to his father, who insisted on living alone even though his health was deteriorating rapidly.

Although Raleigh had experienced tremendous growth in the last decade, due in large part to the fact that it was home to many of the major hi-tech companies that had grown as that sector of the economy had grown, in many ways, it still had the feel of a small town, and like the professor, the town and the neighborhood were simple and unpretentious.

Against the backdrop of a world that felt to Neil like it was spinning out of control, the professor's home looked just like he remembered. The muted red brick and small white columns accented the Colonial-style home that appeared to be one story from the street. From the rear, it was actually a two-story house with a daylight basement opening to a sloping backyard. In the spring and summer, a vegetable garden took up most of the backyard. Gardening had become one of the professor's only hobbies. It always seemed to Neil that the garden never produced any significant amount of produce. For that, the professor always blamed the deer and rabbits.

A single light shone next to the front door. The wooden swing still hung on one end of the front porch that spanned the entire width of the home.

What immediately struck Neil as he drove up was the lack of a police presence, or police tape, for that matter. It had taken him less than a day after he received the phone call from Lisa. Surely, there would be some sign that a crime had been committed.

The professor's gray Volvo was parked in its customary space in the driveway. Although the house had a two-car garage, Neil was sure that space was full of books and research, with just enough room left for the yard equipment. Lisa's red Jeep was nowhere to be seen. There wasn't enough room on the driveway, so Neil parked the rental car along the street.

Neil took a deep breath of the cold morning air as he got out of the car and started the short walk up the straight, narrow sidewalk to the front door. Remorse, regret, sorrow, you name it—they were all competing for his emotions.

It was early, so Neil decided to knock rather than ring the doorbell. Within seconds, Lisa appeared. Her natural beauty captivated him like it always had before. She obviously had been crying. Her eyes were swollen, and it appeared like she had not slept since the crime occurred.

They embraced, her body enveloped by his large frame. He wanted to hold her forever. There was no place for words.

Finally, she whispered, "Thank you, Neil. You were the only one I knew who could help us." She appeared even more fragile than he had expected.

"I am sorry. I wish there was something I could say that could… you know that I loved the professor. He was like a—"

"I know, Neil. My father always looked at you as more than a student. You were like family."

She gazed into his eyes for a brief moment. "Come in. There is a lot we need to talk about, and we don't have much time." Lisa closed the door behind him, taking a quick glance toward the street.

Neil instinctively went left to the parlor in the front of the house. It was a place of many fond memories. He sat down on the couch where, on past occasions, he had waited for Lisa to get dressed for their date. It had always been worth the wait. Before relations with the professor had become strained, he could count on the professor to entertain him during those times. But now was not the time to reminisce.

Lisa disappeared momentarily before returning to the parlor. When she returned, she slumped in the chair beside two large suitcases resting against the couch. Again, Neil thought things seemed awfully strange. There were no signs that the police had put up crime tape or, for that matter, been here at all. Things were not adding up in Neil's mind. *Maybe the professor had been killed on campus or somewhere else. And what about those suitcases? They appeared packed as if someone was ready to leave at a moment's notice.*

"Neil, my father never stopped caring for you. You represented his, I guess you would say his academic legacy. When you told him that there was no future in mathematics for you, that you wanted to find a profession where you could make a lot of money. Well, it took him some time to get over that. He said that you have a gift—a gift from God, and you are wasting it. He never lost hope that you would one day appreciate that gift and find a way to use it for a greater good."

"I know I let him down. And I know that I hurt you too. You must believe me. At the right time, I was coming back and trying to make it right."

"When you ran out of money or when you had enough partying?"

Neil had no response, at least one that would not appear shallow. Lisa was right. He had been so caught up in the lifestyle that only a major event, like the death of his friend, was going to shake him out of it.

"I know it's too late to make it right for the professor, but maybe..." He stopped. This wasn't the right time for this conversation. There would be another time to try to mend that fence. Neil stood up and paced up and down the length of the parlor, trying to collect his thoughts.

"I just don't understand, Lisa. Who would want to kill the professor? He was admired by everyone. He had no enemies. Do the police have any clues?"

"I will tell you everything, but I need to know if I can trust you." She looked deep and long into his eyes. The look of sorrow momentarily disappeared, and in its place was a cold, rock-solid focus and determination. Neil had played enough poker to know the importance of what the eyes revealed. *Always look at the eyes. They will tell you everything. The eyes do not reveal the soul; they reflect it.* He sensed there was something in Lisa's eyes that transcended sorrow. He could not put his finger on it, but for a brief moment, he felt like he was at the beginning of a great mystery that was going to unfold in front of him and that, in some way, whether he liked it or not, he was going to be a player.

"Lisa. Why are you asking me if you can trust me? You know who killed your father?"

"I know that there is something at work here that is bigger than all of us. And we are all in danger. Serious danger."

CHAPTER 5

Jerusalem, Israel

Around the oval table, located in a small conference room on the third floor of the mathematics wing of the Hebrew University, sat five of Israel's finest and most progressive thinkers of the twenty-first century. As was their monthly custom, they gathered to debate, argue, and sometimes almost fight over the significant issues of their day. While they disagreed more often than they agreed, there was one unmistakable truth about which they did not disagree and rallied together around. It was the glue that held them together. And that was their unwavering dedication to the independence and sovereignty of Israel.

All issues, in their final analysis, were viewed through one lens: Was it in the best interest of Israel and her people? If it wasn't, forget trying to get the support of this group. If it was, the argument eventually centered more on the means and methods of achieving the desired outcome.

The group tried hard to seek solutions and strategies to the country's pressing problems, apart from the pressures of conciliation, which seemed to be in vogue with many Israeli politicians and a population that had grown weary of war. They never compromised what they thought was for the best long-term benefit of Israel, even if it meant that peace for their country might be delayed. That is why politicians were never invited, and the meetings were always held in secret.

The group was made up of a mathematician, a nuclear scientist, a political scientist, a military strategist, and an economist. There was no doubt that they were all experts in their respective fields, but when an argument started, those lines of expertise became blurry. Every member had a strong opinion about everything, even if it was outside their respective expertise.

The unmistakable leader of the group was Rabbi Benjamin Breuer. Now in his late fifties, the rabbi was at the top of his game, enjoying the admiration and respect of government officials as well as the general population of Israel. If there was an issue that impacted Israel, domestic or international, it was unlikely that the prime minister would make a decision until the rabbi had been consulted.

As a boy growing up in Brooklyn to Orthodox Jewish parents, those who knew Benjamin would have said that he was the farthest thing from what you would call a serious sort. His friends would have laughed at the notion that Benjamin would someday be in a position of responsibility. In the adolescent years of his life, he was not considered a deep thinker, and as a teenager, Benjamin opted for an even mix of partying and women, with just enough academics to get by. For Benjamin, life was meant to be consumed, like fine wine and cigars, both of which he developed a taste for at an early age.

After graduating from New York University, he knocked around at various odd jobs in the city. He really had no idea what he wanted to do. No thing or nobody captured his complete attention. He just drifted along with the ebb and flow of life. His philosophy was simple: *Party until your anchor snags a rock.* It made no sense to anyone but him.

In the most unusual way, his anchor finally did snag a rock. The occasion was the wedding of his best friend. Benji, as his friends called him back then, was the best man. The maid of honor was an old friend of the brides from high school who had moved to Israel to attend college.

It was one of those magical nights where Benji seemed to float on a cloud. He could not take his eyes off the beautiful girl with dark black hair, smooth olive skin, and a reluctant smile that melted all of Benji's pretensions. He was not ashamed to say it then or for many years after they had been married; for Benji, it was love at first sight. She, on the other hand, was much too coy to admit that at first, but later in life, she conceded that was how she had felt too.

First, there was a date, then another. Six months later, to the surprise of everyone, they were married.

Benji's family pooled their resources and gave the couple a honeymoon trip to Israel. Little did he know that a brief visit would spark another love affair, this time for a country. And like before, this, too, was love at first sight. After the honeymoon, they returned to New York only long enough for Benji to gather his belongings and say his goodbyes. Israel would be their new home.

Like his new wife, Benji enrolled in graduate school at Hebrew University, where he studied mathematics. After obtaining his doctorate degree from Hebrew University, he enrolled in one of the most influential rabbinical colleges in Israel. There, he studied and earned a degree in Hebrew languages. Although later ordained as a rabbi, he chose to return to Hebrew University to teach mathematics. In time, he would become more recognized as a mathematician than a rabbi, but the moniker of rabbi remained with him.

In between raising a family, his wife continued her studies in archeology. Like Benji, she, too, earned her degree and accepted a teaching position at Hebrew University. In time, she would be considered one of the foremost biblical archeologists in the world.

It was five years ago when Rabbi Benjamin Breuer's life took a dramatic turn. Almost overnight, it seemed, he went from relative obscurity to Israel's favorite son. He was not just the toast of Jerusalem; he was the toast of the country.

Looking back, it was more a provincial discovery than one you could mark up as purely accidental. His wife came across a reference by a rabbi from the eighteenth century who questioned whether there might be hidden messages in the Torah. For many in the faith, the Torah had always represented both a sacred and a mystical quality. Of course, this was right up the rabbi's alley—part Hebrew language, part mathematics. What started as a fascination ended two years later with the first publication of the discovery. Mathematicians rarely earned front-page news, but in a land where many still embraced the traditions and teachings of the faith, this was no ordinary news.

The rabbi discovered that there were, in fact, hidden, encoded words in the Torah, and they could be located through a process that he called Equal Letter Sequence or ELS.

The professor tried to downplay the discovery. By his own admission, rabbis had theorized for hundreds of years that words and messages were encoded in the Torah. The rabbi later found that many early rabbis had even written extensively about it.

The difference was that they lacked the means to find those encoded words. Rabbi Benjamin Breuer had the one resource they didn't—a high-speed computer.

Many graciously hailed it as further evidence of the existence of God. Others saw it as a mandate for the God of the Jews. After all, what better way to support the position that God really did come down on the side of the Jew and not the Muslim. After all, it was the Torah, not the Koran, which was used to uncover these hidden words.

For those in Israel who continued to fight a public-relations battle in the world community, such rhetoric made their job even more difficult. Their adversaries saw the Jew occupying a land that was not rightfully theirs. Now they saw them using this discovery to legitimize their existence and their religion. For some in the government, it was a political land mine.

But for the average Jew on the street, this was Israel's own discovery and a source of national pride.

Confident that his discovery only scratched the surface of what the codes could reveal, the rabbi sought to attract the best minds he could find to join him. That became the *raison d'être* for the collection of Israel's finest, who joined the rabbi each month at the oval table in the small office on the third floor of the Hebrew University.

*****

The rabbi always prepared a written agenda for the monthly meetings. It had become a source of amusement to the other members of the group that the rabbi continued the practice. On many occasions, they would start talking about the first item on the agenda, never even making it to the second item, much less anything after that. After all, these were confident and opinionated professionals that the rabbi had assembled.

Today, there was only one item on the agenda. Advances in code research had stalled, and several respected mathematicians in the United States attempted to discredit the rabbi's findings. Many in the academic world called it "contrived science," "a silly waste of time," and that was what could be printed.

As was the rabbi's prerogative, on occasions, he would invite his son, Shimon, to attend the monthly meeting. Shimon, like his father, had chosen a life at Hebrew University. Dr. Shimon Breuer was the head of the Hebrew language department.

Although Shimon was not involved with the original "codes" discovery, those who knew were aware that his father consulted him quite extensively recently about where the direction the research, both in Israel and the United States, was heading.

As odd as it may sound, in the twenty-first century, Shimon was far more Orthodox, not to mention more Zionist, than his father. He wrote extensively about the need for the Jewish community to resist buying into the secular direction the country was moving, even when it meant that the prospects for peace might be compromised. This often put Shimon at odds with certain members of the Israeli government, particularly dealing with the trading of land for peace or the addition of new settlements.

Today, the rabbi also invited Shimon's longtime friend, Steve Gold, considered one of Israel's most astute young businessmen. A Jew by birth, Steve was the opposite of Shimon. He had little interest in the things of God. He had a lot of interest in financial things.

Although they were opposite in many ways, Steve and Shimon had remained friends throughout childhood and college. Recently, many of Shimon's Zionist positions had caused them to drift apart. Shimon was more dogmatic in his beliefs, while Steve was more pragmatic. After all, Steve had to navigate a business climate that was made up of both secular and religious Jews. Over time, they realized that there was not much that they shared together. That was until the codes had been discovered.

The code research brought them back together. For Shimon, the codes provided a vehicle to recapture those who were straying from the faith—those who considered being a Jew more of a cultural or national identity than a religious one. It was a confirmation that the old writings truly were sacred and true, not to mention their mystical or supernatural quality.

Steve, on the other hand, promoted the codes as a way to forever legitimize the Israeli state. If the codes could legitimize the birthright of the Jew, how could you argue against the Jews' sovereignty of Israel? There were other "benefits," you might say, that Steve hoped could be found in the codes, but he did not share those with the rabbi or Shimon.

*****

The Rabbi called the meeting to order and distributed the agenda.

"Short meeting. Are you worried we might not finish before lunch?" mused the economist by the name of David Goldstein, a rotund-looking man with a large mustache and consistently red cheeks that made him appear like a walrus.

The rabbi ignored the wisecrack and began. "Gentlemen, I am becoming more and more concerned that the code research has hit a roadblock. There have been published reports in the United States that suggest that the math and methodology used in my initial findings were flawed at best, sloppy at worst—that the research was a clever way to promote Zionism."

"That is the world's response to every creative product that comes out of Israel," replied the economist. He stood to adjust the belt that appeared too small for its intended use.

"You are right, of course, but math is no respecter of political positions. Either it is scientifically supportable, or it is not," replied the rabbi.

THE REDEMPTION CODES

Uri Weiss, the military strategist, was a short, muscular man in his late forties. Uri had been a senior officer in the Israeli Defense Forces and was always consulted by the prime minister in defense matters. "Let the doubters remain the doubters. We know the truth, and eventually, even in Israel, the truth will set us free."

"With the rhetoric that has been coming from the academic community recently, I fear they are creating doubt about the credibility of the codes," said the rabbi, shaking his head as the weight of the recent criticisms was starting to take their toll.

Shimon, who always addressed his father as Rabbi in public, stood up. "Rabbi, don't you think that scientists always find it difficult to recognize the existence of God? God is competition with a humanistic view of life. If the codes prove there is a God, their whole argument and worldview become compromised. They have a huge stake in this battle."

"That is not necessarily their motivation," said the nuclear scientist by the name of Yitzhak Lieberman. He was a very large man with a deep voice that fit perfectly with his stature. "When it comes to research, they are not going to give anyone a free pass. I think it is legitimate scientific inquiry to question these things, particularly when you make the claims that your father has made."

"They passed scientific inquiry a long time ago. They have resorted to name-calling," responded Shimon.

The scientist waived down Shimon in a condescending way. "Your instincts are to protect your father's good name, Shimon. But that is not how it works. Good research can stand up to the scientific scrutiny. Bad research cannot. Don't take it personally. They are not trying to harm your father."

It was the economist's turn to respond. His cheeks turned brighter red, and his voice became louder. "I agree with Shimon. We must not ignore these charges. If we do, at a minimum, we are going to lose the public relations battle. Rabbi, it's your discovery. What do you suggest that we do?"

"There is a mathematician and scientist in the United States. His name is Dr. Lange. He was the head of mathematics at MIT for many years. Now I believe he moved to another university. He is well respected as a scientist, extremely independent, and one who does not have what Shimon would call an 'agenda.' Perhaps we could employ him to independently review my findings. His conclusion would carry a lot of weight in academia."

"What if he downplays the research like so many of the others have?" questioned Shimon.

"I have my reasons to believe that he is the right person to review this work."

"And those reasons are?" questioned the nuclear scientist.

"That, gentlemen, will be disclosed at the *Appointed Time*."

"Then arrange for us to meet him in New York," said the military strategist.

"Rabbi, we have never agreed so easily with one of your recommendations," said the economist.

The rabbi resisted the temptation to smile. He knew there were other more controversial issues to be discussed. "I am sure you all know Steve Gold. He has requested to attend our meeting today. He has a proposition that he would like to discuss with the group," said the rabbi.

Steve was an excellent public speaker and generally adept at getting his way. But today, he would have to be at the top of his game. These weren't just some of the most respected people in Israel; they were also some of the most intelligent, not to mention some of the most opinionated.

"Rabbi, I appreciate the opportunity to present an idea to this… group." He hesitated. He was going to say *esteemed group*, but pandering would have set the discussion off on the wrong path. This group was too smart to be pandered to.

"It has come to my attention through contacts with the prime minister's office that the research done on the codes has been of interest to the president of the United States."

"Yes?" said the rabbi, his bushy eyebrows raised. "Go on."

"Well, as I understand it, the prime minister told the president that we were continuing the research and an effort to…ah—"

"To what, Steve?" questioned the rabbi impatiently.

"In an effort to be able to…well…that hopefully, the codes might reveal information that would allow us to make long-term strategic moves."

"Which is another way of saying that we hope the codes can tell us the future," responded the rabbi, sensing that his blood pressure was rising.

"Well…"

"No. No. No," said the rabbi, pounding his fist on the table. "The codes are not a fortune cookie."

"Rabbi. The prime minister approached me as well about the codes. He wants to ensure that they would be used in the best interest of Israel," said the military strategist. "He sees it more as a strategic benefit for Israel."

"The prime minister sees everything as a strategic benefit," said the rabbi.

"Do you blame him? I am sure that I don't need to remind you that we are surrounded in every direction by our enemies."

That was one thing that the rabbi knew all too well. Israel's independence always seemed to hang by a thread. Every advantage the country could get from a strategic standpoint was pursued. After all, that was the value of this group the rabbi had assembled.

"I am curious how the president of the United States got involved," said the rabbi.

"In a conversation the prime minister had with the president, he suggested that there might be strategic benefits that could be obtained from the codes," said Steve.

"Benefits for Israel or the United States?" asked the rabbi.

"Both. You know we are strategically aligned. Any benefit to Israel would benefit the United States and vice versa."

Steve continued in spite of the verbal responses and eyes rolling to his last statement. "The president wants to have an American participation in additional research on the codes."

The rabbi had an uneasy feeling he was about to lose control of his own discovery. "That is interesting. On the one hand, we have American scientists who are taking shots at the discovery. And on the other hand, we have a president who wants to control additional research because he thinks there could be possible, as you say, 'strategic gains.'"

"And you assumed it would be different?" piped up the economist sarcastically.

"Don't you think that is presumptuous to think that the codes can give us that kind of, you know, forward-looking information?" asked the rabbi.

"Not if God desires our independence and sovereignty," said Steve. "It would not be the first time that He has chosen to intervene in the affairs of our people. Yes?"

Shimon was amused at Steve's newfound religion but did not say a word.

"Rabbi. The prime minister contacted me also," said the political scientist, appearing to be uncomfortable with what he was about to say.

Ben Cohen, a slightly built and balding man in his early forties, was born and educated in the United States. The political scientist was the least self-assured of the group and, at times, seemed to be overmatched by the rest of the group, which caused many of the group to suspect that he was a surrogate for the prime minister. It was uncanny how much the prime minister knew about the activities of the group, and some thought the political scientist was the source.

"Well, speak up," said the economist.

"He asked if such…ah…strategic information could possibly come from the codes."

"We have gone from fortune cookies to fortune tellers," said the rabbi. "Well, what did you tell the prime minister?"

"I reminded him that there were many other factors that come into play when you are dealing with the future."

"Such as?" asked the rabbi.

"Such as free will."

"You make a good point."

"But I did not rule out the possibility that the codes can reveal more than they have so far," continued the political scientist.

The military strategist interrupted the rabbi before he could say anything else. "Rabbi, the prime minister is intent on pursuing this.

We can argue if you wish, but the prime minister has made up his mind."

"Then we will pursue it," said the rabbi. "Right? You agree? We all agree? We will pursue it. If the codes will tell us more, then they will tell us more. But we must control the research."

"Honestly, I don't believe that we have the resources necessary to go further than we have already gone. I know that is not what you want to hear," said the economist a little sheepishly.

"I agree," said the nuclear scientist. "Plus, you know that the president is going to want to have a say in who controls the research."

"But this is my…this is Israel's discovery."

"Then you convince the prime minister that we can advance this research," said the economist.

"That is a losing argument," said the military strategist, standing up again as if to secure a position of strength. "The prime minister has already authorized Steve to enter into discussions with an American defense contractor who has an extensive background in secret codes in an effort to secure a joint venture."

"Is that true, Steve?" said the rabbi in disbelief.

"Yes. That is true. That is why I asked to attend the meeting today, Rabbi. It is not my intent to circumvent the very one who made this all possible."

Shimon stood up, pointing his index finger in the air like he had a loaded gun. His face was bright red, and his voice grew louder. "Rabbi, this must be stopped at once. This is a sacred discovery, not to be manipulated for personal gain. What keeps the research from stopping at strategic or military decisions? Why not see what the stock market is going to be tomorrow? Or determine who is going to be elected as the next prime minister?"

"You raise valid concerns, but your father does not have a choice, Shimon. The prime minister sees this in the best interest of the sovereignty of Israel," said the military strategist.

"Then we should at least control the research," said Shimon. "The American would report all findings to us, which we would then report to the prime minister. The prime minister could tell the president which discoveries have been made that affect the United States."

"Shimon is right. Steve, tell the prime minister that we must control the process. It is our discovery," said the rabbi.

"I already had that discussion with the prime minister. He has instructed me to be the liaison with the American contractor. But he agreed that I should get my directions from this group. He has confidence that you will do what is best for Israel."

"So we can disagree all that we want. It doesn't matter. The prime minister has already made up his mind," said the rabbi.

"I am afraid that is correct," replied Steve.

With that, Shimon stood up and walked out of the room. For a period, there was complete silence. The rabbi was a proud man, and everyone knew this decision was difficult for him to accept.

Finally, the economist spoke. "Steve. What can you tell us about the American Corporation?"

"They were recommended to the president by the secretary of defense. They are a military subcontractor, intelligence, not procurement, and a very secretive group. Not much is known about them."

"So we don't even know if they have Israel's best interest in mind," said the rabbi.

"We have to trust the prime minister in that regard," replied Steve.

"Their expertise is in breaking codes. They were the group responsible for solving Bin Laden's codes and narrowing down where he was hiding. Several military people have gone to work for them recently. The president is rewarding those efforts with this assignment," said the military strategist.

Shimon walked back into the room. "It is one thing to decipher codes made by man. It is quite another to decipher codes made by—"

"Perhaps you are right, Shimon. We will rely on Steve to monitor the situation. We will give them the benefit of the doubt for the time being. I have serious concerns that I will express to the prime minister," said the rabbi.

"You have doubts that they will be successful or that we can trust them?" asked the military strategist.

"Both."

CHAPTER 6

The Professor Is Dead?

Neil's mind was racing. His friend and mentor is dead, and the woman he cares about just told him they are in serious danger.

Lisa reached out and touched his hand. She always had a way of making everything seem all right. Making everything seem all right now was beyond even her magic.

"This may be difficult for you to understand, Neil, at least at first. Soon, you will know everything that we know and understand what's at stake here. The bottom line is, well, we could use your help."

"What are you trying to tell me? You need help doing what, and who are the 'we'?"

"This is going to take some time. If you are going to get involved, you need to know everything. There should be no secrets."

Lisa walked to the window in the parlor and took a brief glance toward the street. She took a deep breath and returned to the seat across from Neil.

"Here is the story. My father got involved with a project. There were…uh…people—not good people—but people with bad intentions who desperately wanted my father to work for them on the project. They offered all kinds of incentives and pressed him for weeks to join the team. But he refused. Needless to say, this made them extremely angry."

"Angry enough to kill your father?"

"And everyone else my father cares about."

Neil stood up and paced again, his hand running through his hair. As he sat down, Lisa could see that his face had turned ashen. He rubbed his temples, but it did not seem to help push back the ache or lessen the anxiety. "The professor was involved with quantum physics. I personally worked with him on several projects. They were important, maybe even cutting-edge, but the outcomes and breakthroughs were certainly not worthy of being killed. What could he have possibly uncovered that put him in that kind of danger?"

"What you did not know about my father was that he lived two professional lives. At the university, he worked on the projects you were aware of. At home, he worked on another project—a project with far-reaching consequences. I do not think I would overstate by saying it is a project of potentially cosmic proportions. Neil, he thinks there is a breakthrough that could change the world. The ramifications of this research—political, economic, spiritual—are beyond belief."

"And this project is so important that someone would kill him?"

"Yes."

"And the professor was aware of this?"

"My father was aware of the dangers but committed himself to keep pushing forward with the research."

"This is too much, too fast, Lisa. You are telling me that the professor had information that was so valuable that someone would kill for—not just pay for but kill for."

"Yes. That is exactly what I am saying."

Neil stood up again. Even though the room was cold, perspiration was now forming at his temples, and his head was throbbing. "I don't know why you are telling me all of this. Shouldn't you be giving this information to the police or the FBI or…or the CIA? My god, why me? What can I possibly do that they can't?"

"Why you?" For the first time since Neil returned, Lisa appeared to be exasperated. "Honestly, my father thought you might not be able to handle this information. I convinced him that even with all of the immaturity you have shown recently, you might be able to help us."

"You know I would do anything for the professor. But why not at least tell the authorities that your father was in danger?"

"You will understand the answer to that question in due time."

"So what do you want from me? To finish the project? What project? I don't even know what I am asking."

Lisa started to answer when the back door opened. To Neil, the sound of the door with its creaking hinges was unmistakable. He had often brought Lisa home later than he should have, and they would enter through the back door. That sound had become the professor's alarm clock. Neil could never forget that sound.

"Who is here?" Neil appeared nervous and jumpy.

Lisa stood up immediately. "I'll be right back."

Neil was confused and afraid, neither emotion he had much experience with. He tried to cycle through all the projects the professor had been involved with. *A project so valuable that someone would kill him.* The weight of the world felt like it was on his shoulders. His best friend and someone he loved very much was dead. *Secret projects. Cosmic proportions. Something that could change the world.* He hadn't bargained for this. He just came to console the woman he cared so much about.

Lisa walked to the back door, where a man stood in the opening.

"Neil is here," she said.

"Yes, I know, and you are sure we can trust him?"

Lisa did not answer the man's question. Instead, she walked back into the parlor.

"Neil, I haven't been totally honest with you. For me to trust you means that you must be able to trust me. I promised no secrets."

"What are you saying?" Neil asked, his face reflecting the accumulation of one surprise after another.

Before Lisa could answer, the door to the parlor opened, and through it walked what Neil thought was a ghost.

"Professor?"

"Yes, Neil. It's me."

"But I thought you were—"

"Dead?" Lisa spoke up. "I had to tell you that to get you here. I am sorry for the false pretenses. But soon, you will understand the importance of what's at stake here. In the end, I hope you will forgive me."

"So there was no murder? That explains why there was no evidence of the police."

Lisa slumped in her chair. For the first time, he saw that deep, raw emotion he expected from the beginning. Neil looked at her and then at the professor. He thought he had asked a rhetorical question. After all, the professor was standing right in front of him—alive and well.

The professor's eyes reddened, and tears began to well in his eyes. Neil looked back at Lisa. She, too, had begun to cry.

"Neil, in due time, you will understand the magnitude of what is involved here. To answer your question, well, I'm sorry to say, but there was a murder yesterday," said the professor, trying to gain some composure.

"But who?"

The professor paused. "My father."

Before Neil could even comprehend what he had just seen and heard, the professor regained his composure. In a moment, he went from a grieving son to a man who was clearly in charge of the circumstances.

"Neil. I will fill you in on the details, but we can't stay around here any longer. Park your rental car at the park. The one that is about two blocks south of here on Douglas Street. Lisa and I will pick you up there. We need to leave this area immediately. We are not safe here."

Neil did as he was instructed and drove to the park, where he and Lisa had spent many afternoons swinging, talking, laughing, and kissing.

Before Neil could remove his bag from the rental car's trunk, a gray Volvo with the professor driving turned the corner from the house into the entrance to the park.

"Do you think my rental car is safe here overnight?"

"Overnight, maybe, but it will not be there when we return. It will be towed away," Lisa responded.

"But—"

"Don't worry," the professor interrupted. "You are better off without it for now. They probably followed you here anyway. It would not be safe to drive it."

Neil's heart began to beat faster. He had been mischievous at times. Even a few casinos had removed him when he got carried away, but never the object of someone that wanted to hurt or, worse, kill him. Whether he liked it or not, he was caught up in a dangerous game of keeps.

"Where are we going?" asked Neil as he placed his suitcase in the trunk and tossed his travel bag onto the seat next to him.

"I rent a house in the mountains that I have reason to believe they have not been able to track, at least not yet. There, I have all of my computers and research. It's a little hike through the woods, but we will be safe there for a while. Hopefully, by the time they find it, we will be finished with our work and on our way."

"On our way to where?"

The professor ignored the question as he turned at the corner of the park and headed down a one-way street in the direction Neil knew was a shopping mall. A black pickup truck pulled out of an alley behind them.

"Professor, I think that truck is following us."

"It is. He is one of us. He is a friend of the family whom my father hired to help protect us. There will be others that follow us. It is his job to distract them long enough for us to get out of town safely."

The professor picked up speed as he raced in the direction of the mall. It was still early morning, and the parking lot had not yet become crowded with shoppers. The professor turned the corner and headed down an alley behind the mall, barely missing a trash truck. At the perfect time, he made a sharp U-turn and headed up the down ramp of the parking deck connected to the mall. He had obviously practiced that maneuver before. Only a car of this size could have made the turn. He continued in the opposite direction up two levels.

"Aren't you worried that a car will be coming down while you are going up?"

"Not to worry. We have people directing traffic up there. Well, actually, they created a small incident to give us enough time to get up the ramp."

"Now when we get to the third floor, we will abandon the car and walk," directed the professor, confident and in control. "Just be prepared to follow me. Look calm, you know, as if you were shopping. We will take the stairs from the third floor back down to the first floor, through a back door, to the underground garage. Lisa's Jeep will be waiting there. That will take us to my cabin in the mountains."

"I have my suitcase in the trunk."

"Leave it. Don't you think it would look strange with a suitcase in the mall?"

"But—"

"I have extra clothes you can use."

Neil did exactly as he was instructed. It was clear the escape had been well planned, and he was determined not to do anything to upset it.

*****

The plan had been executed to perfection. Everyone who appeared to be a menacing character turned out to be part of the professor's getaway team.

Safely in the Jeep, the professor started the three-and-a-half-hour drive to the cabin in the mountains. There was a long silence as the professor focused on the carefully planned escape route while Lisa acted as the lookout.

After about half an hour, the professor finally appeared to relax a little. "I bet you never expected this kind of adventure when Lisa called you."

"In all due respect, I expected to attend a funeral, just not my own."

The professor managed a brief smile. "Neil, I must confess that my instincts were to write you off. It was Lisa who insisted that at some point, you would recognize that your gift would mean more if it was shared with humanity rather than wasted. It was Lisa's idea to get you involved in this project."

Neil took a quick glance at Lisa, who was still preoccupied with her role as the lookout.

"Honestly, I am glad she did. I think there will be a point where your assistance will be valuable. Neil, we cannot finish this without your help."

"I really don't know what to say, not that I had a choice in this matter."

"You gave up that choice when you arrived at my house."

"Tricked to come to your house."

"Yes, I admit that I tricked you into coming under somewhat false pretenses," said Lisa, momentarily looking up from the I-40 traffic. "But I knew you could help us."

Right now, Neil had mixed emotions. For sure, he was confused about what was happening all around him, but he was glad that Lisa still cared.

"I don't know if I can help because I don't know what's going on."

"I understand. Up to this point, we have kept you in the dark. Let me give you some background on what is happening and what is at stake. After I am finished, if you want to leave, that will be your decision. But Lisa is right. We do need your help. And by the time we are finished, I know you will feel good about your involvement."

The professor adjusted the mirror. Looking around, he felt confident that the escape had been pulled off exactly as planned.

"Neil, before I get to the good stuff, I need to give you a little personal history." The professor paused and swallowed. This was tough. The memory and images of his father flooded his head. "Well, I guess it starts with my father. I know you met my father, but I bet that you did not know he is the reason I became a mathematician. In fact, everything I ever achieved, I owe to my father. My mother died when I was young. My father raised me and my sister."

Neil thought to himself, *I know what it's like to have a mother die as a teenager. It is uncanny how many similarities the professor's background has been to mine.*

"My father was a Baptist minister. We moved from one church to another as I was growing up. Like many preachers' kids, I rebelled from my father and from my father's religion, or should I say, from his faith."

It's good to know that someone as stable as the professor had also been a rebellious youth.

"I know what you are thinking, Neil. But my rebellion was not in the sense of a wild lifestyle, partying and doing things like what you are going through. That would have bothered my father, but he would have known I would eventually mature. No, I rebelled in the worst possible way."

"Worse than partying and doing things?"

"I turned away from the church. Science became my religion. I think, at first, it was purely rebellion. But once I got into academia, I was surrounded by a culture that hated God and religion and everything it stood for."

"That must have been tough on him."

"It was extremely tough. I think that the pressure of a rebellious son, particularly one who was starting to make a name for himself, made it hard for him to confront a congregation, week in and week out. So tough that he eventually got out of the ministry altogether."

"Did you stay in contact with him?"

"Oh, yes, we were never estranged. We just never talked about it. I think he knew deep down that someday I would see the light. He was patient that way. He had so much confidence in his faith. He thought that someday I would see it the way he did. It wasn't until Lisa was born that we started to have conversations about God, the meaning of life, and life after death. Babies have a way of forcing you to confront the important issues of life."

"In all due respect, Professor, I don't understand the connection to what happened."

"You will. Just be patient. Hear me out."

"I am trying. Your father's death, clandestine meetings, and car escapes have made me a little on edge."

The professor continued. "Well, after my father left the ministry, he opened a Christian bookstore. He liked books, and he loved to read, and I think it was a good fit for him. He would never admit it, but I think he was always on an odyssey to, well, win my soul. And he knew that to do that—to win me over—he would have to battle for my soul on my turf."

"Science and mathematics," interrupted Neil.

"Exactly. For years, he submersed himself in every science journal and classical Christian apologetic he could read."

"Apologetics?"

"The study of the proof that there is a God by logic and rational arguments," answered Lisa.

"Oh. It sounds like you are saying you're sorry."

"It comes from the Greek word *apologia*, which means to give a reason or defense," answered Lisa.

"You're into this, Lisa," said Neil, mildly sarcastic.

"You will be too. You haven't seen anything yet."

"In the course of studying science and religion, he came upon a discovery made by a rabbi in Israel. The rabbi discovered that when the Torah, the first five books of the Bible, was written out end to end in its original Hebrew language, certain encoded words would appear at equal spacing. The rabbi hypothesized that the Bible might have been written as a code. In fact, it is now often referred to as the Bible Codes."

"The Bible as a code?"

"Actually, the idea of the Bible as a code has been around for hundreds, maybe thousands, of years. Even Einstein and Sir Isaac Newton surmised that the Bible might contain certain 'codes' that were somehow embedded into the language."

"Think of it this way," said Lisa. "The Bible might be the equivalent of a computer program, and by unlocking the secrets of the program, you could unlock the secrets and mysteries of the Bible."

"You're getting ahead of me, Lisa. Let me continue the story."

Neil's mind was trying to comprehend what he just heard. *The Bible as a computer program?*

"My father sought to understand this discovery as a way to bridge the gap between science and religion—between his world and my world."

"And to bridge the gap between him and you—and maybe ultimately you and God."

"You are perceptive, Neil. I could not have said it better. Anyway, he studied this for months before he confronted me with the idea. He said he wanted to make sure that it was credible before he talked to me about it. In his mind, he knew he had only so many chances to bridge that gap. If he was wrong here, he knew I might become even more disillusioned with the faith."

"How did you respond when you first heard of it?"

"At first, I blew it off as a crank concept, a hoax."

"I can understand why. It sounds like a hoax to me."

"But my father was extremely patient. He did not try to force me to accept it. And then he took what he said was a monumental risk. He challenged me to prove that the codes were not real but fake."

"Mathematically?"

"Yes."

"And?"

"And I did. I did attempt to prove they were not real."

"And?"

"Well, life wasn't so good then. Lisa's mom got sick about the same time my father first exposed me to the codes. I hadn't yet submitted it to any scientific or mathematical scrutiny. On the surface, I continued to discount it. As she got sicker, I struggled with a whole range of emotions.

"Near the end, right before she died, I got to tell you that I read the Bible a little. I was searching for answers. And as I read, it kind of spoke to me."

"What...it...who spoke to you?"

"It was a combination of things. But as I look back at it, I think God was trying to speak to me."

"No offense, Professor, but that sounds more like faith than science."

The professor continued the story, ignoring Neil's comment. "After my wife died, I took a six-month leave of absence from the university. For the first month, all I could think about was my wife.

I did not have the energy to do anything but grieve day and night. Thankfully, my father helped me through this ordeal. He was able to take care of Lisa.

"After a month, I pulled out my computer and started experimenting with some things my father said about these codes."

"And?"

"To my amazement, words which had been hidden for thousands of years started to be revealed to me. The more I got into it, the more real patterns started to present themselves. I got excited about what I was seeing. I realized that the odds of what I was finding were too high to be there by chance.

"Well, after a couple of months, I decided to tell my father what I had found. I had to be convinced this was something worth pursuing."

"But I don't understand. Your wife died while you were teaching at MIT before you left MIT to go to the University of North Carolina. I have known you for several years."

"I know what you are thinking, and the answer is yes. I have been working on this for several years. At first, the research was more casual, like a hobby. Only recently has the research taken on a more serious tone."

"I am surprised that I did not know anything about this."

"I never discussed this with my colleagues, and I never allowed this research to be on any of the computers on campus. The only one who knew about this research was my father. Lisa was not even aware of this until recently. In your case, Neil, soon, you will know everything that I—" The professor paused in midsentence. A truck entered from a side road and slowed up behind them. The professor's heart began to beat fast. Thoughts raced through his mind. *How could they have found us? Don't be paranoid.*

The truck pulled out from behind and passed the professor. A young man was driving with a young girl seated next to him with her arms wrapped around his neck. Behind them, they towed a small fishing boat. The professor breathed a sigh of relief.

"Enough of the story for now, Neil. The next few days might be a little hectic. I suggest that you spend the rest of the trip resting. You're going to need all of the energy you can muster."

Lisa smiled. "What he is really trying to tell you is that we are at the part of the trip where my father gets lost, and he needs to concentrate."

The remaining part of the drive went relatively quiet. A highway patrolman followed them for a little while but appeared to lose interest and turned around in the median.

After making a series of turns from small rural roads to even smaller rural roads, the professor finally interrupted the silence. "We are almost there." And with that, the professor slowed almost to a stop. "I sometimes have trouble knowing exactly where to turn."

"There are no paved roads to your cabin?" asked Neil incredulously.

"Yes, there is a road leading off of the highway that runs in front of the cabin. But we can't take the chance of being seen from the highway, so we will reach the cabin from a small road they use to load logs."

"Hold on!" Lisa shouted. And with that, the Jeep hit a log that had fallen across the path and came to a quick stop.

"From here, we walk," said the professor.

"How far?" asked Neil, knowing that he had already exceeded his allotment of adventure light years ago.

"I think it's about a mile or so. To be honest, I have never come this way before. Lisa, reach into the box and get the flashlights. At some point, Neil, you might want to take off those fancy shoes. We have to cross a stream."

"Professor. It must be thirty degrees outside and falling."

"Suit yourself. If they get wet, we will put them in front of the fire."

With that, the professor opened the back door and pulled out a pair of hip boots from underneath the seat.

"Sorry, I have only one pair."

Lying next to the boots was a rifle. Neil stared at it as if he had never seen a rifle before. The professor lifted the bungee cord that was holding the rifle in place. Neil did not have to ask. He already knew that whoever the parties in this game were, they were obviously playing for keeps.

CHAPTER 7

Creedmoor Industries LLC

The brochure handed out by commercial real estate agents to visitors and prospective Fortune 500 tenants was filled with glossy photographs and a slick narrative.

The Research Triangle Park, also known as RTP, is a 6,800-acre international research and development park. The park is home to all the major players in the high-tech arena, IMB, Cisco, Ericsson, Motorola, and others. You name the company, and if they are an international player in information technologies and communications, they most likely have a presence in the Research Triangle Park.

The park is located just west of the Raleigh-Durham International Airport, just off I-40 between Raleigh and Durham, North Carolina. Although the park started as a modest commercial development in the late 1960s, as the Information Age grew, so did the development of the park. Aided by government tax incentives, an inventory of smart college graduates, and a desire to compete with Silicon Valley, there was an unrelenting growth of new companies coming to the park every year. And with every new company came new buildings, each one larger and grander than the last. There were so many additions to the park that the local planning department added a special staff just to accommodate the new building permits. During the go-go period of dotcoms, for the hi-tech company, it was *the* place to do business.

THE REDEMPTION CODES

The "Triangle" reference was added when the initial developers realized the park was located at the cross section of three major universities: University of North Carolina in Chapel Hill, North Carolina State in Raleigh, and Duke University in Durham.

Located in the rolling terrain at the northern end of the park, among seventy huge, multinational companies that called the park their home was the Creedmoor Company. In the directory of companies, which are distributed to visitors of the park, the Creedmoor Company was mysteriously not listed. In fact, little was known about the company other than it was an approved defense contractor that specialized in telecommunications for the Armed Forces.

Beyond that, there was not much else known about the company. The tax records showed the owner as Creedmoor Industries LLC registered in Billings, Montana, a privately held company that exempted it from a certain amount of both government and Wall Street scrutiny and oversight.

Creedmoor's high national security clearance provided the owner of the company the ability to build the entire facility without the watchful eyes of the local building authorities. No city inspector ever laid one foot inside the facility during construction. With the exception of the technicians who now worked in the facility, only a select few generals from the Pentagon had been inside the facility.

From the street, the building had a modest, eccentric architectural feel to it—if you could even call it an "architectural feel." A small reception area, no larger than the size of a double-wide trailer and not much taller, was in a small building detached and in front of the main building. It was the only building in the complex that faced the street and the only building that had any windows. There were no parking spaces anywhere near the small building, which suggested that there were not many visitors or, at least, visitors were not encouraged.

Behind the small building was the main building. The main building looked more like a small warehouse, no more than ten thousand square feet. There were no windows in the main building that appeared to be about thirty feet high, and the only door was located on an elevated dock area on the side of the building facing away from the street. Although the dock area appeared to be built to accommodate deliveries by trucks, there were no truck-size doors on the dock area and no pavement leading to the dock for trucks to unload. Like the front building, there were no parking spaces near the dock door.

Behind the main building was the parking lot that accommodated ninety-nine parking spaces. A narrow, one-way entrance led into the lot. There were no lights in the parking lot that was surrounded by a ten-foot-high security fence covered by three strands of razor wire. Two cameras were located on each corner of the fenced parking lot and the main building.

A young, somewhat absent-minded girl in her early twenties sat at the receptionist's desk. She had been on the job for three weeks. When she was hired by a young man who described himself as the human resource officer, she was told Creedmoor was a start-up company and that it would take time before there were customers coming to the facility. She did not really know what a start-up company meant, nor did she really care. In fact, she was pretty sure she was never told what the company did, and if she was told, she since forgot.

There were many mysteries about this company she worked for that she couldn't explain. For one thing, when she was hired, she was told never to enter the main building and that she was to park on the small grass strip next to the street in front of the smaller building. She tried to imagine how so many people could fit into such a small building. She couldn't do the math, but she knew there were a lot of cars in the parking lot for such a small building. She laughed when she pictured that maybe they stacked the desks on top of one another. She often wondered what went on in the main building beyond the door. It didn't matter. She tried to open it once, only to find that it was locked with cameras everywhere.

And there was the thing about the other employees. They were all dressed in white lab coats and came and went at random times. Except for the occasional cold-calling salesperson, there were no phone calls that came through the main switchboard. She thought this odd for any new company, particularly for a company of Creedmoor's apparent size. And when she did see the occasional visitor, they never came to the receptionist area to check in.

THE REDEMPTION CODES

She didn't really care about any of this. They offered to pay her more than two dollars per hour higher than she was making at the diner. And with a small child at home who always seemed to be sick, it was the health insurance that really mattered.

With not much to do, she would find herself staring outside. She always tried to observe visitors and imagine what business they might have with the company she worked for. This afternoon, she observed a white van entering, the same one that had left a couple of hours or so ago.

The large man, returning from the old man's house, turned into the Creedmoor entrance. There was no building or monument sign for the company, only a diminutive sign that read *Deliveries Only*. The security guard, recognizing the unmarked white van, raised the security gate. The guard did not make eye contact with the driver, but with one motion, he waved the van through the gate. As instructed, the large man parked the van in the parking lot alongside several black SUVs.

Reaching into the sliding door of the van, he removed the computer and headed for the door on the loading dock. Before he reached the door, it opened, and the large man disappeared inside.

Inside, he was met by two technicians dressed in white lab coats.

"Mr. Haggerty wants to see you," said one of the technicians who was taking the computer from the large man. "You are to wait here."

With that, the two technicians disappeared down a long hall through several sets of doors to a set of wide stairs that led to a level below ground. Arriving at the underground level, the technicians passed another set of doors before they arrived at an elevator. One of the technicians supplied a visual eye scan to the security system. Opening ahead of them was one set of elevator doors. Entering the elevator, one of the technicians pushed the button marked with an arrow pointing down. There were not the usual floor designations. This elevator only had two stops.

The door closed, and the elevator proceeded down the equivalent of two stories. Built into the side of a large hill, the descent below the main building gave the feeling that you were entering deep into the caverns of the earth.

The elevator opened to a large room the size of a ballroom with high ceilings, high-intensity lights, and bright, white walls. The room was modestly decorated and very cold. In the middle of the room where the elevator opened was a collection of several high-speed computers. It was there that the technicians carried the computer. They were met by two other technicians who carried the computer to a large table. It was apparent that each of the technicians knew what was expected because there was no banter between the technicians, and little emotion was expressed.

Ringing the large room were thirty-nine smaller rooms, each with a short hallway to the main room as if spokes on a wheel. None of the smaller rooms had access to one another, only to the main room. The first five to the left of the elevator were larger than the remaining thirty-four. In each of the five larger rooms were six technicians. Two technicians were working in each of the remaining thirty-four rooms.

Each room was marked on the door with a name spelled in Hebrew with the English word underneath. The first room to the left of the entrance was marked *Genesis*.

Chapter 8

Bootlegger's Cabin

The decision to park on the back side of the mountain from the cabin made sense from a security standpoint. The Jeep would not be seen from the main road leading through the mountains to the small town. Getting to the cabin from this side was another thing altogether. The professor was totally unfamiliar with this side of the mountain, its terrain, or any other obstacle that stood between them and the cabin, for that matter.

There was no path leading to the cabin from this direction. Knowing that the cabin stood on the top of the mountain meant that the group would at least start walking up, hoping that there would be some landmark along the way that the professor recognized.

It was cold and dark, with the only light coming from the two flashlights that the professor and Lisa carried and an almost full moon. Not expecting a hike through the woods of North Carolina when he left the bright lights of Las Vegas, Neil only had a light jacket, and his fancy dress pants were constantly snagging on the thick brush. The professor and Lisa, who packed in anticipation of this hike, were a little better prepared. There were times when Neil heard, or at least thought he heard, the rattle of a diamondback. The professor said nothing to dissuade Neil's concern because he thought he heard them, too, and he knew the diamondbacks were prolific throughout the mountains.

The group was making steady progress through the thick brush until it reached what appeared as a gully. The professor was pretty sure that it was the same stream that circumnavigated most of the mountain. It had been widened a decade or so ago to help move water away from certain areas of the mountain and avoid erosion. The stream was usually peaceful and home to tadpoles and frogs, but because of recent heavy rain, this peaceful stream had turned into fast-moving rapids. The ominous sound of the moving water punctuated what was otherwise a silent night.

"If I am correct, there is no way around this gully. I do not believe that it is very wide. But with the rain over the past few days, I do not know how deep it is."

Neil stepped out without hesitation. "I am the best swimmer. Let me go first."

"Okay. But cross over at ninety degrees. Somewhere, this gully ends at a ledge of the mountain, and the drop-off is sixty or seventy feet. If the current is as strong as I expect it is, you could get swept downstream, and I just don't know how close that ledge is from here."

The water level almost came to Neil's waist as he started to wade across the stream. Neil did not even think about removing his shoes, which were now already muddy from the wet clay of the mountain. Neil confidently turned to tell the others that it was okay to proceed when he stepped into a hole, and for an instant, was totally submerged. He almost instantly popped up and instinctively started to swim to the other side. Safely across the stream, he waved for the others to follow.

Climbing the bank of the stream, the professor remarked, "I guess it has been raining for several days for the water to be this strong."

"Great. That is a remarkable insight on your part. What other surprises do you have in store for us?"

"None. Ah, well, as bad as the stream."

"You don't sound confident."

"There is one more part."

"Where can I drown or get bitten by a rattlesnake?"

The professor ignored Neil's sarcasm. "The cabin sits on a high point of the mountain. The grade in front of the cabin is a relatively gradual slope, but—"

"But the back is steep. Is that what you are saying?"

"Well, yes. That is exactly what I am saying."

"Can we at least cross to a section of the mountain where the grade is not so steep?"

"No, Neil. It drops off on all three sides. Two of the sides are actually steeper. I think we are better to climb up the backside."

After many more treacherous steps over one rock after another, under all of which Neil was convinced lived a six-foot rattlesnake, the professor broke the silence. "We are almost there. I would say ten to fifteen minutes, tops. Unfortunately, it is almost vertical from here."

The professor was right. Above their heads, the cabin appeared like a silhouette against the gray sky.

"How do we climb this steep terrain without ropes?"

"Neil, the side of the mountain we will climb caved about ten years ago after a tropical storm came through this area. The trees fell over, decayed, and died. But the roots and stumps are still there. We will use them to climb up."

First, the professor, then Lisa, and finally, Neil all made the slow climb up the bank of the mountain to level ground. At the top, Neil took a deep breath. The hour and a half it took the group to make it to the cabin seemed like an eternity to Neil. At several times, he felt it would be a minor miracle if they all made it through alive. And by the time they did make it to the cabin, he was not sure which was worse, the thoughts of deadly snakes navigating the stream or the last almost vertical climb up that last bank. He was tired, wet, and cold.

From the outside, the cabin appeared small, but inside, it was larger than Neil had pictured in his mind. Entering the cabin, it was only slightly warmer than the outside temperature, which by now had dropped to well below freezing. A large fireplace with a hearth made of stone from the local riverbeds dominated the open room, which served as a living room, dining room, and kitchen. Firewood had been neatly stacked beside the hearth.

"Lisa, there are matches in the side drawer. Grab some old newspaper and a fire starter from the basket. Neil, unfortunately, the fireplace provides the only warmth for the cabin."

Within minutes, the fire was blazing. None too soon for Neil who had now started to shake uncontrollably from the cold.

Lisa had packed a change of clothing and took off to change.

Neil, unable to bring his suitcase, brought only a few items in a duffel bag. To make matters worse, the mishap at the stream caused him to drop his bag. He was able to grab it before it went downstream, but its contents were now soaking wet.

"Lay out your wet clothes on the clothes rack over there," the professor said, pointing to a wooden rack next to the side wall. "I have a robe in the bathroom you can wear until your clothes dry."

Lisa returned from the one and only bathroom located behind the main room next to the single bedroom. Neil gave her the sign of approval as he walked through the bedroom toward the bathroom, which was located at the opposite end of the room.

The bedroom appeared very modest to Neil. Other than the bed and a small nightstand, there was no other furniture or pictures adorned the wooden walls. It was obvious the professor did not spend much time in this room.

As Neil got close to the bathroom, he felt a draft of cold air. It appeared to be coming from the direction of a large metal door located between the bathroom and the door leading into the bedroom. Being wet and cold was trumped by his curiosity as to what was behind the door. Neil's curiosity was a trait that had not gone unnoticed by the professor and one, Neil thought, made him a better mathematician and scientist.

He hesitated a second before he opened the large metal door. It was a heavy door, so he used his shoulder to push it open. Inside, the room was dark and damp, and Neil could not see anything. Although it was colder than the bedroom, he did not believe it led to the outside, and there was no evidence of a sky. It did appear there was a roof or ceiling of some sort. For all he knew, the room could have been as small as a closet or as big as a house. He reached back to find what he hoped was a light switch but instead rubbed his hand on what felt more like a stone wall. The light from the bedroom provided little help to the mystery of what was inside the room. *This is probably a room to stack wood for the fireplace*, he thought, but there did not appear to be anything on the floor.

Neil's preoccupation with finding a light obscured the silhouette of someone who had entered the dark room from another direction. Before he knew what happened, a large hand reached across and grabbed Neil by the shoulder. Neil instinctively retreated, falling backward through the opening in the direction of the bedroom. Standing over Neil was a hulk of a man, bending his head to avoid hitting the top of the door frame.

Hearing the fall, the professor rushed to the room. Neil was lying on the floor, shaken but unhurt.

"I see you have met Biltmore," the professor said calmly.

Neil was relieved to hear the professor identify the huge man. "If that is what you call it."

"The folks in this area refer to him as Old Henry. He is my handyman, security guard, fishing guide, close friend, you name it. I should have mentioned him to you before we arrived. Biltmore, this is Neil Coles. I've told you about Neil. He will be staying with us the next few days."

Standing up now, Neil reached out his hand. "Do I call you Henry or Biltmore?"

Before the big man could respond, the professor answered, as if Biltmore was not even there, "With everything in the mountains, there is always a story, Neil. When I first saw how big and strong Henry is, I told him that he was built stronger than the Biltmore, you know, the mansion built by Vanderbilt in Asheville. The name stuck with me. I don't think he minds if you call him Biltmore."

"At least, I hope not. He could rip me apart as easily as you rip open a bag of potato chips. I'll try to stay on your good side, Biltmore," Neil said.

"Don't worry about Biltmore. I have never met a kinder, gentler person in my whole life."

With that, Biltmore turned and walked back into the darkness from which he came, not having spoken a single word.

"You had better change before you get sick," said Lisa. "I will make us something to eat before we begin."

Before we begin what? There has already been more adventure than I can handle in one day. Neil did not have a clue what was ahead of him.

Chapter 9

Bad News

Rabbi Breuer was deep in thought, sitting at his modest desk at Hebrew University, and did not notice that Steve Gold had entered the room.

"I am sorry to bother you, Rabbi. Your secretary was not at her desk, so I took the liberty to come in."

"Steve, you look like you just saw a ghost."

"May I?" he said, gesturing toward a chair in front of the desk.

"Please."

Steve knew that the rabbi was not typically fond of small talk, so he started right in. "Rabbi, as you know, it has been a couple of weeks since I updated the group on the progress of the American Corporation."

"Yes, and from your expression, it appears that you have nothing encouraging to report."

"I have bad news to report, very bad news."

"Okay, what is it, Steve?"

Steve blurted out, "The American professor's father has been killed!"

"What?" Now it was the rabbi who turned pale. "Professor Lange's father?"

"Yes."

"You mean killed as in murdered?"

"Yes, sir. Unfortunately, I do."

"By whom?"

"The police report indicated that it was a robbery."

"Oh, and what was stolen?"

"As far as the police could tell, only a computer." Steve knew that the rabbi was way ahead of him and had already reached his conclusion.

"Damn that American. That was never part of our agreement with the American Corporation. Never was there to be any violence. Never!" The rabbi pounded his desk loud enough that the sound echoed down the hall.

Steve could not argue with the rabbi. "I am truly sorry that I ever let you or the prime minister convince us to seek assistance from the Americans on the code research. We would have been better off without their help. And now bloodshed."

Shimon walked into the office. It was the one day in the week that the rabbi always set aside to have lunch with his son. Shimon instantly recognized the concern on his father's face.

"They have killed the professor's father," said the rabbi.

"The 'they' being the American, I presume," said Shimon nonchalantly as if this news was not a surprise.

"Yes. Or at least that would be the logical assumption."

"What would possess them to do a thing like that?"

"It is my conclusion based on the rudimentary facts as Steve has presented them that they had reason to believe that the professor's father possessed certain developments in the research which the American found challenging."

"Or rewarding," said Shimon.

"That is why they took his computer," said Steve.

"But the father is not a scientist. He is an old man, and his stroke has made it difficult for him to even speak. Why would they think he had anything to do with this or any information that would prove beneficial? It is the professor who would have this material," said the rabbi.

"Unless they thought the father was hiding the information as a cover for the professor," said Steve.

"Stealing would be one thing. Murder is quite another," said Shimon.

"I don't care if the professor's father knew the exact day of the Messiah's arrival. Killing is unacceptable," said the rabbi.

Shimon turned to Steve. "Do you know what they were looking for?"

"I assume since the police report indicated that a computer had been stolen, that was where they thought the information was hidden," replied Steve.

"How did the police know a computer had been stolen?" asked the rabbi.

"The report indicated that the professor's sister met the police at the father's home," replied Steve.

"Did the Americans find anything from the computer?" asked Shimon.

"We may never know the answer to that question. We are dealing with powerful forces."

"Where was the professor?" asked the rabbi.

"Apparently, he has moved out of his home to another location," replied Steve.

The rabbi stood up. "We will discuss this at our next meeting."

Shimon and Steve knew that meant it was the end of the discussion.

CHAPTER 10

Epitome of Evil

It had been an hour since the technician with the white coat had told the large man with the black gloves to wait.

The large man paced back and forth in the small lobby. "What could be taking so long? How long does it take to go through the old man's computer? I told Mr. Haggerty that I searched the old man's house, and there was nothing. I did what he asked me to do. I didn't want to kill the old man, but I had no choice. I have been a loyal employee. Surely, he wouldn't—"

Larry Haggerty's identity could be summed up in his insatiable drive to be both wealthy and powerful. This drive was the one characteristic that distinguished him from all his competitors and adversaries. He was not particularly well educated, at least by the standard of graduating from a prestigious university. And according to his resumé, there was no mention of Haggerty ever finishing college. Studying and going to class was just not his thing. He was too impatient for either. He figured there must be other ways to get ahead, and climbing the corporate ladder was not one of them.

He did not come from a wealthy or powerful family either. In fact, little was known about his background. He would never speak about his past, and no one even knew if he had a family.

His power would not come from the political arena either. He was not the type to make it in politics, and he did not like politicians unless they could help him. He was too unpolished for that world.

THE REDEMPTION CODES

No, it was clear to everyone, including himself, that he was going to make it in the world of making money. Lots of money. And from the money would come the power. You could ride his coattails if you wished, but his ambition would steamroll you if you got in his way. He was someone you just didn't want to mess with.

Haggerty was relatively short, under six feet, with dyed black hair cut short and a pasty complexion. His physical features were somewhat unassuming, that is, except for one characteristic: his piercing dark eyes. People who met him swore the eyes were almost black. When he talked to you, it was as if he could see through you, and he never appeared to blink. He never referred to someone as a friend and was not known to have either a social or romantic life. It was no wonder that he never had a date. He could be intimidating if not just downright scary.

After a failed attempt at college, Haggerty joined the army. There, he showed an aptitude for deciphering codes. But like college, he quickly lost interest and got out at the first chance.

His first real job was as a private detective. But chasing wayward husbands quickly became boring to him. And it seemed he spent more time trying to get paid than doing the work in the first place.

Once he got so frustrated at not getting paid that he published the pictures of the husband in a compromising position with his nurse on the Internet. The ironic thing was that the husband was his client, who had hired Haggerty after he suspected that his wife was cheating on him. The husband was one of many along the way who paid dearly for making Haggerty mad.

The one aspect of being a private detective that Haggerty liked was trying out the latest in surveillance gadgets: the fountain pen with the tape recorder or the tie clip with the miniature camera. He practically spent every paycheck buying the latest gadget.

He decided that if that was what he enjoyed, there might be a business opportunity. And he was not particularly impressed that technology was keeping up with the criminal. So with the help of a money partner, he bought a company that made surveillance equipment.

One opportunity led to another, and the business exploded. He offered to buy out his partner, but the partner refused. Within a month, the partner died in a traffic accident. Many suspected that Haggerty was somehow involved, but no one could prove it. The widow gladly sold her interest to Haggerty.

Haggerty soon realized that the private detective and the local cop could not afford what he was making. The big money would be made on the international scene.

With the end of the Cold War, many had lost interest in that business, but Haggerty was a contrarian by nature, always swimming against the tide of prevailing thought. When others were winding down research, Haggerty was ramping up.

Like every success story, Haggerty could trace his big break back to the period shortly after the terrorist attacks in New York, Washington, and Pennsylvania on September 11, 2001. Success, he learned, is sometimes no more complicated than being in the right place at the right time with the right product.

The Pentagon realized that it needed to upgrade some of its intelligence-gathering equipment, particularly in the area of voice recognition and photo dating. In this case, there was not the typical government bidding. By now, Haggerty had influence in high places. Haggerty got the contract at his price.

The Pentagon's investment immediately paid off. The surveillance equipment that had been used to capture Saddam Hussein was Haggerty's equipment.

After that success, when the Pentagon needed a special kind of surveillance equipment, they called Larry Haggerty. He became the toast of the Pentagon. Every general would gladly accept a telephone call from Larry Haggerty.

Following a series of successes after another, it was when Haggerty first learned about code research. The word had come from the president through the Pentagon that the Israelis had discovered a code in the Torah that might have national and international implications.

Like every other situation where Haggerty saw an opportunity, he acted quickly and decisively. He convinced the Pentagon to let him lead the research on behalf of the Pentagon for the president. He would build a specialized facility and staff it with the brightest mathematicians that money could buy, including two of the head code crackers in the Pentagon, and house some of the best and fastest computers in the private sector, hence the birth of Haggerty's brainchild, the Creedmoor Company.

Things had not gone as planned, though. It was several months into the research, and progress on the research had been slow. In Haggerty's world, this was unacceptable. People would pay.

*****

The technician finally returned and instructed the large man to follow him. Navigating through one locked door after another, they arrived at an empty office next to what the large man assumed was Mr. Haggerty's office. The technician instructed him to wait there and, immediately, turned and walked away.

Passing the office, he could see Haggerty in an animated discussion with someone. But there was no one else in the office, and there did not appear to be a phone in sight.

"Yes, I will do your bidding. We will discover the secret of the codes. If not, we will obtain the information by other means. After we obtain the information we are looking for, the research and all associated with the research will be destroyed forever. No one will ever equate the codes with God or the Jews. But my price is…"

The large man could not hear any more of the conversation. There was only silence. It was as if the door had been closed midway in the conversation, even though he could see that it had not. An eerie cloud of darkness seemed to surround him. It was as if evil incarnate was in the room.

There was a motion, and the large man stood up as Haggerty walked into the room. Haggerty did not greet him warmly.

"We have taken all of the information out of the old man's computer. There was nothing of value. We will no longer need your services." With that, Haggerty turned and walked out of the room.

"You have got to be kidding. I just committed a crime. I could go to jail for the rest of my life. No, we appreciate your sacrifice for the company. No, thanks. You're a good employee."

The large man's instincts told him to leave at once. *I need to get out of here.* He stood up and headed for the same door where he had arrived. The large man would not make it. He was dead within seconds, his large body crashing to the floor.

CHAPTER 11

Is the Code Real?

The fire in the fireplace finally started to warm the cabin. Lisa prepared dinner from the little amount of food Biltmore had left in the refrigerator and pantry. Neil eagerly consumed every bit. He couldn't remember when he had last eaten. The lights and sounds of the casino that had been so much of his life seemed like an eternity ago.

Neil and Lisa sat alone at the small, wooden, circular dining table. The table occupied most of the space between the small kitchen and the seating area in front of the fireplace. The professor was not hungry and excused himself. The shock from the death of his father was taking its toll on the professor. He felt remorse as he realized that the exhilaration of the escape had not allowed him a proper mourning.

Biltmore disappeared after the incident with Neil, a practice the professor said was common. "Biltmore will disappear for hours, sometimes a whole day. But he has an uncanny knack for being here when I need him."

Neil pushed away from the table. "Thank you, Lisa. I needed that."

He moved from the small dining room table to a sofa in front of the fireplace. Lisa sat down beside him. Neil longed for the time when he and Lisa would sit together for hours. On many of those occasions, the conversation would be about the most trivial of matters. This time, the conversation would not be about trivial matters. Life had suddenly become a lot more serious.

"Lisa, I need to ask you a question."

"I bet I can guess, but go ahead anyway."

"Do you believe in the codes?"

"I figured you would get around to asking my opinion."

"Your opinion is and always will be important to me."

Lisa smiled sheepishly. "Do I believe in the codes? For me, it is not about believing, like faith, or you might say blind faith. My father says there is more than enough mathematical and statistical evidence to support it. Yes, I am convinced. You'll see soon."

"You are convinced because your father is convinced."

"Well, yes. But after all, you said yourself that he is the smartest person you know. And I might add, when it comes to this, he started out very skeptical."

"I hope my skepticism does not come across as if I don't have an open mind on the subject."

"If you want to know how I really feel…"

Neil sat forward in his seat. "Yes."

"I believe there is more than just the math and all the stuff you and my father will work on."

"What do you mean?"

"I think there is more to this discovery, like on a deeper level. As maybe my grandpa might say, a spiritual level."

"A deeper level?"

"I think God foresaw a way to reveal Himself to this generation in a way that only this generation could understand and appreciate."

"You mean technologically?"

"Yes. That is exactly what I mean. Maybe God reveals Himself to this generation through computers."

Neil shrugged. If there was anyone on the face of the earth that he trusted, it was the professor. He would still withhold judgment until he had seen more.

"But even if I didn't want to believe, Neil, how do you explain people willing to kill for this information?"

THE REDEMPTION CODES

People willing to kill for this information? Lisa was right about that. This was obviously a game with high stakes. He wanted to ask more when the professor walked back into the room. It appeared that his eyes were red.

"We don't have much time, Neil. We must get started. If we don't find the hidden meaning of the codes, my father's death will have been in vain."

The professor motioned for Neil and Lisa to follow him. Neil quickly darted into the bathroom. His clothes had not completely dried, but they would have to do for now.

The three headed through the master bedroom to the large metal door and hall where Neil had first encountered Biltmore. The professor reached into a drawer beside the hall and pulled out a flashlight. Lighting the path, Neil could see that the hallway was much longer than he had expected.

"Follow me."

After walking what seemed like the distance of half a football field, the hallway abruptly ended. There appeared to be two ways to go. The professor shined the light on a small opening in the wall just above the floor on the left side of the hallway.

"I will lead the way from here," said the professor. "We have to go single file. You follow me. Lisa will take up the rear. Watch your head. The opening is small."

With that, the professor crawled through the small opening. Neil and Lisa followed. The floor and walls appeared smooth but unfinished. Within a few yards, the opening got larger, and they could stand up again. Although the path now seemed to be high, it was narrow. They walked single file for another twenty yards.

"Careful now. There are some steps ahead of us."

The steps appeared to be cut into the side of a mountain. Neil wondered whether they were outside. Looking up, he could see no sky. It was cold and damp but not as cold as when they scaled the mountains. *Maybe we are in a cave.*

"We are almost there. Stay here."

The professor walked a few steps to his right and pushed down on the handle of a large metal door. From the sound of the door opening, Neil knew they were about to enter a room. The professor took a few steps and was out of sight of Neil and Lisa. The professor searched for the silver handle connected to the electric box. Finding it, he grabbed the handle and lifted it. The lights instantly flashed bright.

What opened up in front of Neil nearly took his breath away. It was a large room, probably the size of a small high school auditorium. The walls were lined with cedar from floor to ceiling. There were no windows. The only light was provided by several fluorescent lights hung down from chains secured to wooden trusses that spanned the entire length of the room. In the middle of the room were a series of fold-up tables like you would find at a church picnic. On the tables were a row of personal computers. Around the computers were several charts sitting on easels.

Neil was used to seeing computers everywhere. They were a part of his everyday life. Many of the projects that he worked on with the professor required the use of high-powered computers. He just did not expect to see so many of them lined up inside a room next to a cabin at the top of a mountain.

Neil did not move for several seconds. He tried to absorb the detail and magnitude of the setup. The technology in front of him stood in sharp contrast to the casual surroundings of the cabin and the simplicity of the mountain man, Biltmore. This could have been expected in the finest universities in America, not in a cabin in the mountains of western North Carolina.

His eyes surveyed the room. A large fireplace burning strongly appeared to provide the only warmth for the large room. But what caught his attention were the models that lined the left side of the room opposite the fireplace. One appeared like a colored DNA strand like you would find in a science class. There was a Christian cross. Some of the models he did not recognize.

In addition to several charts on the easels, there were also hand drawings. There was a tree, a rainbow, and a wheel. Next to each figure, there appeared to be a Bible reference.

Finally, the professor broke the silence. "So you approve?"

Neil did not answer; he just shook his head.

"Neil, we have everything here we need to solve this mystery. Now we just need your brainpower."

Neil ignored the compliment. "What is the meaning of the models and the drawings, Professor?"

"I think somewhere in those collections of symbols or another symbol yet to be found lies the key to what we are searching for. But you are getting ahead of me. We must first start with the basics. Let me show you how these hidden codes are revealed—what the rabbi in Israel discovered."

The professor went to the first computer and turned the monitor so Neil could see. "It basically works like this." The professor turned the computer on and entered a password.

"The Bible, or should I say the Torah, the first five books of the Old Testament, was originally given by God through Moses. Perhaps a better way of saying it is that people of faith believe that God dictated it to Moses, letter by letter. After generations of passing it down orally, it was finally written in Hebrew, the language of the Jews. Right to left, unlike English sentences, which are left to right. No spaces between sentences and no punctuations."

"One continuous run-on sentence," quipped Neil.

"In a manner of speaking, yes," replied the professor.

"The exact way God dictated it to Moses," said Lisa.

"The Torah, as tradition goes, has been preserved in that fashion for six thousand years. Those scribes whose job was to pass down the Torah took their job extremely seriously. Not a single letter could be placed out of order. The legendary warning to the scribes was strong. *Should you, perchance, omit or add one single letter from the Torah, you would thereby destroy all the universe.*

"When Christ came along, He repeated the same message. *I tell you the truth: Until heaven and earth disappear, not the smallest letter, not the least stroke of a pen, will by any means disappear from the Law of Moses until everything is accomplished.*

"It is that discipline of not making an error in copying the Torah, for generation after generation, which gives the Hebrew we use today its credibility for being the basis upon which the codes could be revealed in the twenty-first century." The professor's eyes sparkled. "The story goes that part of the reason that the Jews were God's chosen people was that He could trust them to pass down the written word, without mistake, from generation to generation. Obviously, there were no books or printing presses.

"If God hides the codes based on a manuscript several thousand years ago, you can see how they would never be revealed today if the original manuscript had been changed along the way. You will see what I mean when we get into it. Changing just one letter can make a significant difference.

"Well, for centuries, it was speculated that God hid messages within the Scriptures. As I told you, even Einstein conjectured that such a hidden message existed, and before him, Sir Isaac Newton. However, though both Einstein and Newton attempted to find the codes, neither could go through the task of uncovering it. It was too time-consuming. It wasn't until the computer came along that the task of sorting the text could be done. What would have taken Newton years could now be found in seconds."

"How are the hidden messages revealed?" Neil asked.

"I'll answer that, but first, let me start with some history about how the codes were discovered, and that will explain how the codes are revealed."

Neil wasn't about to argue. He remembered that the professor had a methodical way of teaching. And make no mistake about it; the professor was the teacher, and Neil was clearly the student again.

"About five years ago, a rabbi from Jerusalem started experimenting with the Torah using original Hebrew. He discovered a process called Equidistant Letter Sequences, commonly called ELS. The first thing he did was to lay out the Torah, as it was originally written, in one continuous line, all 304,805 letters. Next, he started experimenting with word groupings, in other words, finding names written at equal intervals."

"There would be the exact same number of spaces between each letter of the name which was discovered?" asked Neil.

"Yes, that was the essence of ELS."

"And what did he find?"

THE REDEMPTION CODES

"One of the first word groupings he discovered involved the assassination of Yitzhak Rabin."

"Israel's prime minister," Neil interjected.

"Correct. When the computer searched for the name 'Yitzhak Rabin,' it appeared once at a skip or ELS of every 4,772 letters. When he found that the name appeared every 4,772 letters, he created a grid by dividing the Torah into 64 rows of 4,772 letters per row. Remember, there are 304,805 letters, 64 times 4772."

"By doing that, the name was spelled out vertically, I assume," said Neil.

"Exactly. The grid the rabbi created started to look like a crossword puzzle."

You could hear the level of excitement building in the professor's voice.

"But that wasn't the best part. When he created the crossword puzzle, matching words and phrases also started to appear. Let me show you how it looks."

The professor grabbed a piece of blank paper from the desk. He wrote 'Yitzhak Rabin' vertically on the paper. "This was the rabbi's first discovery." Then the professor wrote the words 'assassin will assassinate' horizontally so that they intersected with the vertical words. "That was the rabbi's second discovery."

The professor could see that he had gotten Neil's attention.

"Wait. It gets better. The name 'Amir,' the person who assassinated Rabin, also appeared, as did the month and year of his assassination. All on the same crossword puzzle."

"Let me see if I understand. They would find a name, create a grid based on the interval between letters of that name, and from that grid, or as you call it, crossword puzzle, related words appeared."

"Basically, that's it. And the related words always expose the main events or characteristics associated with that person or event."

"I assume that was not the only discovery made?"

"No. Emboldened with their early discovery, they tested it on other major events. They discovered KENNEDY, ASSASSINATED, DALLAS, and the year of the assassination—all clustered together," said the professor.

"Another one was HITLER, EVIL MAN, NAZI, and SLAUGHTER—all clustered together," added Lisa.

"Neil, we could go on, Shakespeare, Newton, Einstein, Watergate, the Oklahoma City Bombing, 9-11. All of the major events in our history have been found. And more importantly, whenever they found a name or event, they also found a cluster of related events that support or verify the original name or event."

"Professor, I hear what you are saying, but—"

"You appear to have some doubts, Neil."

"For one thing, the Torah is pretty large. Couldn't this have occurred in other large works of literature, like *War and Peace?*"

"It has been tested with Tolstoy's *War and Peace*, and I tested it with Shakespeare's plays and several other large works of literature. A match has never been found with any other piece of literature. I decided to verify the information originally found by the rabbi. Everything he had originally discovered was exactly as he had claimed. I then decided to quantify the *P* value. You still remember what a *P* value is, Neil?"

"The value of something happening by chance," said Neil confidently. He knew the professor was messing with him.

"Yes, I am glad you have not forgotten everything I taught you."

"The lower the *P* value, the more likely that an event could not occur by chance," continued Neil.

"When I quantified the rabbi's research, I was astonished to find *P* values so small they would be reserved for only the most obvious predictions—a prediction so obvious, in fact, you would not even bother testing. I would have a better chance of finding a coin that had been hidden by someone on the streets of New York City than that this information occurred by chance.

"The rabbi was definitely on to something. The odds of this information occurring by chance were too great. Take the discovery of Yitzhak Rabin. The odds are 3,000 to 1 that the name of the assassin could be found in the same place as Yitzhak Rabin. If you apply additional collaborating information, like the location where he was assassinated, the odds go through the roof."

"When you ask me if I believe in the codes, this was what I was trying to say. You can believe from the standpoint of faith if you want to, but the math speaks for itself," said Lisa.

"Neil, these odds take their way out of the realm of chance. There is no question in my mind that these codes were planted. It is one thing to find names and events. But when you find supporting names and events within the same cluster of words, well…"

The gravity of this information showed on Neil's face. "You're saying that God planted these codes in the Torah."

"Yes, that is exactly what I am saying. That is why my father said this discovery was bigger than us."

"But for what purpose?"

"Maybe God wanted to reveal Himself one last time, in a kind of a twenty-first-century way. Maybe that was His way of reaching this generation—through the computer," said Lisa.

"Maybe Lisa is right," said the professor. "For me, I cannot answer that question. At least not now." There was an expression on the professor's face that Neil had only seen one other time, right before a major discovery at the university.

"Professor. This is impressive information. And by no means am I attempting to minimize this discovery. But there is one thing I don't understand."

"And what is that?"

"As impressive as this might be, why would someone want to kill your father over this? You said these discoveries were made by a mathematician in Israel. Where is the connection to your father?"

"Only if the codes could reveal something more than just historical information. Mysteries which, if discovered, could make the discoverer rich and powerful."

"I still don't understand."

"During the trip here, I promised you an explanation. Here it is."

Neil sensed he was about to learn more about this mystery. Whether or not he was prepared for what he would hear, only time would tell.

"After I found out about the codes, I decided to put it to the test. Like you, I had my doubts and needed to prove it to myself, which I set out to do. It was what I did with that information I now regret." The professor rubbed his chin. "I should have kept this information to myself, at least until I had a better understanding of the ramifications of this discovery. Instead, I published my findings in the *Journal of Mathematics*."

Neil knew that in the elite circles of academia, the professor was considered one of the top mathematicians in the world. And in that world, there was no room for science and religion to coexist.

"Were you thought of as a crackpot by your colleagues?"

"Yes, to some degree, that was uncomfortable. I had to be absolutely sure my analysis was supportable. I had spent years developing a reputation for hard analysis. I wasn't about to let some quackery destroy it overnight. If anything, my testing was more thorough than any I had ever done. I was determined to make absolutely certain I was right.

"When I published my findings, I became front and center on this whole discovery. I became the Poster Boy for the codes, whether I liked it or not. That triggered the series of events that followed."

"From the academic world?" questioned Neil.

"Actually, there wasn't much backlash at all from my colleagues. Believe it or not, many understood and respected the analysis. They might not have liked the ramifications of the research, but they kept that to themselves. No. It was far more sinister than that."

"More sinister?"

"I was contacted by the rabbi from Jerusalem who originally discovered the codes. He asked if he could meet with me. He was coming to the States, and we agreed to meet in an office in New York. He wanted to hear more about how I came to my conclusions. Well, at the time, I thought that was strange. After all, he was the one who discovered the codes. All I had done was to test the probability of this happening by chance and then to present my findings in a more scientific or scholarly manner."

"Don't you think he was just seeking validation?"

"I told him that my conclusion was that these so-called hidden codes did not occur by chance. I ascribed odds to the discovery that related words, like I showed you, could occur randomly in the text based on Equal Letter Sequences. Nothing more. He just wasn't satisfied with my explanation. He kept pushing me. He wanted to know how far I had taken the study. Had I discovered anything more?"

"What was he after?" asked Neil.

"Neil, at first, I took his question of whether I had found something new, different, or insightful at face value. But I couldn't get it out of my head that there was more to his probing. Then about a week later, I received a call from a man who claimed that he represented a consortium made up of the rabbi, several scientists from Jerusalem, and a "think tank" from the United States. He asks to meet me. Says it is urgent. I agreed. He flies down from New York. I figured that my father would get a kick out of how far this had progressed, so I arranged for the meeting at my father's house.

"The man arrives at my father's house dressed like a banker. Well, my father more or less takes over the conversation. The stroke had caused his speech to be slow, and maybe, at times, his thoughts appeared a little disjointed. The truth is that my father knew exactly where this whole charade was heading. He presses the man to know why they are so interested in my research or what their motive is.

"It is obvious to both my father and me that the man came with one purpose and one purpose alone, and that was to convince me to work on this project for the consortium. He had a job to do, and he sold hard on my joining the team. But then the man made the ultimate mistake."

Neil leaned forward, unaware that his body language reflected his hunger to know everything about this whole mystery.

"The man makes a closing pitch. He says that his group believes that the information found in the codes and the discoveries that will come out of that research will be the best thing for humanity and that it will prove, once and for all, that there is a God and perhaps bring the world into a new age of enlightenment.

"Well, there is one thing I learned at an early age. Don't BS or lie to my father. He had a sixth sense in that regard. But to my father's credit, he didn't say anything. Well, the man stands up, shakes our hand, and leaves. Tells me he will be waiting for my response."

"What did your father say after he left?"

"As was his style even before the stroke, he spoke slowly and weighed every word. In short, he said that their motivations were not as pure as the man made it out."

"I assume that he didn't buy the part about a new age of enlightenment."

"No. But then he said something that I will never forget. Something that I did not expect."

"Yes?"

"It was one of those poignant moments between a son and his father. He reached out and took my hand. He paused before he spoke. Then he said the words I will never forget. *'There is something yet to be discovered that is bigger than what has already been discovered—bigger than us, son. And that is the reason why you are involved.'* My father realized that day that my involvement was more than a way for him to reach me on my turf. There was more, much more."

"Much more? What do you mean much more?"

"That is the part of the story that has not yet been written. You will play a part in that story, Neil."

Neil was confused by what the professor was saying. "The story, where did it go from there? How'd you leave it with the man?"

"My intuition told me at that point we had a tiger by the tail. They were not the kind of people who went away quietly. They had a mission they thought I could help them, and they were dangerous. To me, that trifecta was a blueprint for disaster. Unfortunately, I was right on all three."

"And what was their motive? Let me guess. They saw that this discovery could somehow make them a fortune."

"At first, I wanted to give them the benefit of the doubt. After all, the profit motive has been the fuel that has driven this nation and has been the source of many discoveries that we all enjoy today. No. It was more than making money that motivated them. They wanted the ultimate prize."

"The ultimate prize?" asked Neil, a look of bewilderment on his face. Money had been Neil's ultimate prize for the past few months.

"Yes, the ultimate prize. Whether it's in your profession, a relationship, everywhere—it's the same. The ultimate prize is always the same: power and control."

Power and control. That sounded more sinister than Neil had even thought.

"The next day, I get a call from a senator."

"A United States senator?"

"Yes. A real United States senator. He starts out in a pandering way. 'Oh, Professor, I am glad you are willing to consider this opportunity. The United States needs to get out in front of this issue. These discoveries could mean a lot for our culture, our way of life.' I knew this senator was not looking to promote a reversion to a God-centered nation. He was as progressive as you can be and get elected in this country."

"What did you tell him?"

"I told him I needed a little time to think about it. The next morning, I received a note from the dean of the mathematics department. He needs to speak with me. Before I could even get a word out, he says that he received a call from the administration."

"The president of the university?"

"No. The president of the United States."

"The president of the United States?"

"Yes. The message was that the university was to accommodate any change in schedule that I needed to make myself available to this 'think tank.'"

"What did you say?"

"I was not prepared for what was happening. I just kept remembering what my father said, *This is bigger than us.* I had intended to go in to request a leave of absence. I knew there was one thing I needed to do, and that was to get away long enough to study this situation for myself. I told the dean I would give him an answer within a few days. That would give me time to think through this whole series of events. I waited a couple of days and then went back to the dean and requested a leave of absence to work on this project. Not where—just to work on the project."

"He assumed you were going to work with the consortium?"

"Yes. That night, I packed my bags and left for the cabin we are in now. I knew my career at the university was probably over. But I had to take the chance. The words from my father still rang in my head. *There is a reason why you are involved, son.*"

Neil stood up. It was starting to make a little sense.

"So you know who killed your father."

The professor nodded, the pain clearly etched on his face.

Then the professor turned to Lisa. "Sweetie," using a term of endearment that Lisa remembered him using that painful day he had to tell her that her mom was going to die.

"I have struggled with whether I should tell you this. I decided that you need to know this. Neil needs to hear this too."

The professor turned his chair to face Lisa.

"The day before your grandfather died, he and I had a long conversation. He was confident that we would make some discoveries with the codes that would prove to be earthshaking. I remember how excited he got as he told me this. Then he got somber. He said the temptation is to personally benefit from these discoveries. But if you do, he said, you will be no better than the other guys. You need to know that I promised him that any discovery we made would only be used for the good of all of mankind, never for our personal profit."

Though neither spoke, both Neil and Lisa shook their head.

"You need to know something else." The professor swallowed. "Lisa, your grandfather knew he was going to die."

"What? How could he possibly know that?" questioned Lisa, a look of disbelief on her face.

"He gave me a copy of a letter that he wrote. It was sealed in an envelope. He asked that I not read it until after he died. I read it tonight while you and Neil were having dinner."

"A letter to whom?"

"It was addressed to a Mr. Larry Haggerty from the American Corporation that had become active researching the codes. It was the corporation that the so-called think tank had been a front for."

"What did the letter say?"

"He told Mr. Haggerty that there had been a breakthrough in the codes that might be of interest to them—the breakthrough that they were waiting for. He ended the letter by telling them that this information was not for sale now. If and when he decided to sell it, it would be available to the highest bidder at an extremely high cost."

"I don't understand why he wrote that letter. That does not sound like something Grandpa would say."

"Your grandfather knew they had been working hard on this research, had not made a breakthrough, and were getting desperate. They had spent a lot of money, had made a lot of promises, and had nothing to show for their investment.

"He also knew that they were afraid that I would find the information before they did. They are a bad group and will do anything to eliminate the competition. In plain English, if they did not discover this information soon, they were going to get it from me, even if they had to kill me. It was just a matter of time."

"Wow!"

"*Wow* is right, Lisa. Your grandfather made the ultimate sacrifice. He died knowing that would be how we could live. If he had not written that letter, they would have assumed that I had the information and come after me, probably sooner than I realized and definitely sooner than I could plan for. This bought us just enough time to get out of town."

Codes. Death. Sacrifice. Neil's head was spinning. Just when he thought he had a handle on the situation, there was something new to consider.

Lisa's eyes moistened. "I guess what you told me should make me feel better. But it hurts to think of what he did for us."

"He did it because he loved us. We can't allow that love to go wasted. We'll use it to motivate us over the next few days and weeks."

"Professor, what are they going to do with your father? Who is going to bury him?"

"My sister will take care of the arrangements."

Neil shook his head. He was having a hard time understanding how someone could commit that kind of sacrifice for another. Neil felt genuinely sorry for the professor and Lisa, an emotion he had not felt since his mother died.

Lisa wiped the tears from her eyes. She had always loved her grandfather. Tonight, that love took on a whole new dimension.

"Lisa, though it is hard to understand if he could tell us anything now, it would be to assure us he is in a better place. I think if he were here tonight, he would encourage us to make this discovery and use it for the good of all, which brings us to the present."

"Yes, the present."

"In all due respect, Professor, I still don't see how I fit into this or what I add."

"I, we need your help. There is more to be discovered. You didn't think we were finished?"

"You verified that the codes are real. That they are not there by chance. What else are you looking for?"

"There is more to the story. I told you that both the group from Jerusalem and the liaison from the consortium were leading me to tell them whether I had advanced the discovery, whether I had found more than just the kind of information I showed you earlier. At first, I didn't understand what they were asking. But the more I got involved, the more I realized what they were after. You see, God had placed clues in the first few books of the Bible that would someday be discovered. But that was not the gold mine, what I call the holy grail. Yes, it was nice to see those messages revealed, but that wasn't the end of the story. No, there was more. They knew it, and I knew it. The difference was that they thought I had already found what they had been looking for."

"So it's a race," said Neil.

"Yes, exactly. Now it is a race. They find me, or I find the real hidden messages. Neil, where you come in, I have confidence in your abilities, and Lisa has faith we can trust you."

Neil did not acknowledge the compliment. "What exactly do you mean by the holy grail?"

The professor ignored the question. "We need to get started. We have a lot of work ahead of us."

The professor stood up, stopped, and turned back toward Neil. "In a way, I'm sorry Lisa got you involved. There are no guarantees this whole thing will have a happy ending for any of us. But as regrettable as her decision was, you really don't have a choice anymore. When you left with us, your fate was sealed."

CHAPTER 12

Not the "Appointed Time"

The rabbi and the other members walked down the hall from the rabbi's office to the conference room. An air of seriousness replaced the usual friendly banter.

The rabbi insisted that Steve be present. Shimon invited himself.

There was only one topic on the agenda distributed by the rabbi: *The future relationship with the American Corporation.*

Everyone had been brought up to date on the revelation made by Steve. There was no debate that what happened to the professor's father was terribly wrong. But a consensus on where to go from here would not be easily achieved.

The group took their customary places at the table with the rabbi at its head. It did not take long for the discussion to begin.

"We should move very deliberately. Perhaps there is more to the story that we do not know. Pulling the plug on the Americans' research so early would not be in our best interest," said the economist, biting on an unlit cigar.

"I agree. We must make sure that this does not happen again," said another member. "There is too much at stake to give up now."

Shimon stared at his father. The one thing he knew and respected about his father was that he would never compromise his beliefs.

"Gentlemen. Listen to yourselves. How can something good come out of something so bad?" asked the rabbi.

"Casualties always come from war. You remind us of that all the time, Rabbi," said the military strategist. "Isn't this research partly an attempt to legitimize Israel's existence? We battle with guns every day to accomplish those same goals. And there are casualties."

"We are not at war with the professor or his father," said the rabbi, his voice growing louder with each word.

"Yes, but wasn't one of the benefits of the research to ensure Israel is always identified with the research. What if we back out now and the American makes future discoveries? Not only do we lose control. We give up our rights to any future benefits," said the economist.

"We lost control once innocent people started getting killed," replied the rabbi.

"Have not the codes already benefited Israel? Have they not already revealed the unmistakable handprint of God for our unbelieving youth?" said Shimon.

"What good is there in a believing youth if there is no country left for them to live in?" said the military strategist.

"The code research doesn't guarantee Israel's future. God and guns guarantee her future," replied the rabbi.

"But knowing when and where to point those guns, wasn't the idea of the codes to give us a tactical advantage?" replied the military strategist.

"Aren't we getting ahead of ourselves? Perhaps the codes have told us all they intend to tell us anyway," said Shimon.

"Shimon is right. There is no guarantee that the American will advance the research any further than it already has. There has not been one significant discovery since the partnership was formed, only some trivial historical references. Isn't that correct, Steve?" asked the rabbi.

"Yes, sir. That is correct."

"Gentlemen. Does this make sense to you? We have entered into a partnership with someone who is willing to steal information rather than obtain it through hard work and research and, along the way, kill innocent people," said the rabbi.

Deep down, they knew the rabbi was right. The blood of the old man was already on their hands.

The rabbi stood. This time, it was not to make a point. Periodically, he would stand to help relieve the debilitating pain he was experiencing every day.

"I have listened to this banter and realize once again that we are more identified with our talk than our actions. Doesn't it bother anyone that the research has not progressed beyond the original discovery?" asked the rabbi.

"Are we not capable of advancing the research ourselves? Certainly, we can do no worse than the Americans," said Shimon.

"There is only one who has the combination of skill and creativity necessary to advance this research," said the rabbi.

"Professor Lange?" said Steve.

"Yes. That is the reason I scheduled the meeting with him in New York."

"Then, is he not our adversary?" said the economist.

Shimon looked over at Steve, who appeared to have a nervous expression on his face. No one in the room was aware that Steve had visited the professor and had so aggressively recruited him on behalf of the American Corporation.

"The professor is a good man, a brilliant mathematician, and someone I consider worthy to work on the codes," added the rabbi. "After all, it was the professor who defended the code research against a growing peer pressure."

"At your request, no?" said the economist.

"No. By the time that we met, he had already presented his case to the review board."

"Then what's his angle?" murmured one of the members. "Do you expect us to believe that the only thing the professor cared about was whether the research had statistical credibility?"

The rabbi was uncomfortable with the direction this conversation was going. "I think if the professor had any desire to advance the research, well, it is my belief that it would be handled carefully and professionally."

The military strategist appeared irritated. "What are you trying to tell us? Do you know something about the professor that you would like to share with us? How can you be so confident that the professor does not have ties with…?"

"That is ridiculous. You do not know what you are saying."

"Contrary, Rabbi. The burden of proof is on you to convince us why he can be trusted."

"This conversation is coming to an end. I have heard enough. Killing his father was a mistake. That is only going to deepen his resolve. It certainly is not going to make him give up."

"And if he makes certain advancements to the research, what do we do then?" asked the military strategist. "Do we give him a parade, or does he become a *de facto* enemy of the State?"

The rabbi waved his hands in total disgust. "This meeting is officially over."

"But what do we tell the prime minister?" asked Steve.

The rabbi stood up, which was a sign that the debate had come to a conclusion.

"We tell him the truth. The Americans are not capable of advancing the research any further. Perhaps no one is capable of that, at least not now. It is not the *Appointed Time*."

Chapter 13

Money and Power

The technician with the white coat cautiously walked into Haggerty's office. He waited for his presence to be acknowledged before he spoke.

"We threw the body into the incinerator. I will have the van stripped and cleaned. There should be no evidence he was ever here unless he was seen by the lady up front."

"Don't worry about her. As soon as we get the information we are looking for, I will take care of her."

The technician turned to leave.

"Remind your people of the financial reward that awaits them. After you have encouraged them, then tell them that Mr. Haggerty is not pleased with the lack of progress. It has been several months since the Jews provided us with their original discovery. As far as I can tell, we are no closer today than we were then."

"You have been gracious to pay for the best mathematical minds there are. They will find the key that unlocks the secrets."

A slim man in his early thirties popped out of an office next to where Haggerty was meeting with the technician. With one hand, Haggerty gestured for him to wait before speaking as he pointed his finger into the technician's chest. "You are dismissed, and tell your people that I am running out of patience."

The young man waited for the technician to leave the room. "Mr. Haggerty, a Mr. Steve Gold is on the phone."

"Is it the secure line?"

"Yes, sir."

Haggerty walked to where the phone rested on the table. Before he picked up the phone, he drank from a golden chalice sitting on a table next to the phone.

"Mr. Gold."

"Mr. Haggerty. The rabbi has requested that I deliver an important message to you."

Haggerty paused for a moment. "And that message is?"

"They have requested that I deliver it in person. I will be in your office the day after tomorrow." Steve Gold hung up the phone.

Haggerty knew by now they had found out about the professor's father. He also assumed that would probably mark the end of the rabbi's involvement. He assured himself that was okay. He no longer needed the rabbi. After all, this was not about religion. This was not about showing the world there was a God or proving that Israel would survive. This was about money and power. Steve Gold knew it. He knew it. At this point, to the victor be the spoils.

Chapter 14

The Routine

The three had settled into a routine by the second day. They would work from dawn to lunch, take a break for lunch, work to dinner, take a break, and work until the early morning hours.

Neil learned the history of the area where they worked. During Prohibition, it had been a whiskey mill run by Biltmore's grandfather and uncle. It offered the perfect cover for the bootleggers hiding from the law. Today, it offered the perfect cover for the professor's operation. The cabin was hard to get to, as Neil could attest, and the side benefit was that there were several places to hide, both under and above the cabin. Although the thought was disconcerting to Neil, he also learned that there were many ways to escape quickly. And though he was not amused, Neil also learned that there was a direct path from the cabin to the work area that did not require kneeling and ducking. The professor admitted that he brought them through a maze of tunnels the first time for a dramatic effect.

It did not take long for Neil to pick up on the process. Several additional historical events and names were discovered during the first day. Neil had come to appreciate what the professor had long known; these words were not there by chance. Both Lisa and Neil observed that the professor seemed detached from Neil's discoveries and rarely looked up from his concentration to acknowledge Neil's excitement at every new discovery.

Neil finally spoke. "I don't understand one thing, Professor."

"And what is that?"

"If the American Corporation has the same, if not better, computers as you, a group of the brightest mathematicians in the world, an unlimited budget, and obviously a strong desire to find out how these codes work, no offense, but why did they need you?"

"Neil, there is a simple explanation. They thought that I knew something they didn't, or at least that I had already discovered something."

"I can understand why they would think that. You are one of the most brilliant mathematicians on the earth."

"Thanks for the compliment. But I meant it in a different way. It started from a talk that I made at a conference after I wrote the article for the *Journal of Mathematics*. After the article was published, I was invited to speak about the codes everywhere I went. At first, I was a little self-conscious about it. After all, I had not discovered the codes. I merely attempted to verify their credibility using statistical probabilities.

"Well, at one of the talks I was invited to make in Washington, there were some very powerful people in the audience, a US senator and a general from the Pentagon. To be honest, during the question-and-answer period, I got a little carried away."

"By getting a little carried away—"

"There was a question from a journalist in the audience. He wanted to know what all the hoopla was about the codes, so what if they told us things we already knew? I can still remember him saying, '*The history books already tell us about the past, why do we need the codes?*'"

"Did he attempt to discredit your analysis or…?"

"Oh, no, he was not qualified to discredit the analysis. I think he was from the *New York Times*. Someone told me later that he was the Religion reporter. Basically, his angle to the rabbi's initial discover was a 'so what.'

"Anyway, I answered that he was right, at least as it related to the outcome. The codes had, to date, only pointed out historical facts—things we already knew about. But I remember pausing, almost as if I was telling myself to keep my mouth shut."

"But obviously, you did not."

"No, I did not. I did not listen to my conscience tell me that I had already said enough. I knew that I had crossed the line, so I kept going."

"No offense, Professor, but you are killing me here. What did you say?"

"I said that in order for the codes to reveal their maximum power, they couldn't just reveal the past. They needed to be forward-looking. I think I used the word *prophetic*."

"Prophetic as in show us the future?"

"Yes. We know what the codes have revealed about the past. You were able to discover more of those historical events today. I know I appeared disinterested in your discoveries, but I have found many myself."

"But it's the future."

"Yes."

"What you were referring to earlier as the holy grail?"

"Yes, that is exactly what I was referring to. The real holy grail is discovering what the hidden codes reveal about the future—the future of the world and all of its mysteries."

"So in a nutshell, our mission is to use the codes to foresee the future."

"No. Our mission is to determine if—and that's a big *if*—the codes can reveal the future. But we can't answer the *if* until we find out the *how*."

"In all due respect, isn't it ultimately to determine what the codes say about the future?"

"Yes, in a manner of speaking. If we discover the *how*, we will not stop until we find the *what*."

"I am a little confused. If we don't know what the future looks like, how are we going to know we found it?"

"I can't answer that. In my heart, I just believe we will know when we find it."

"What in your heart you will know. I am sorry, Professor, but you have lost me."

"I believe if the codes can reveal the future, we will know it. It will be as clear as day."

"How so?"

"In the discoveries we have made with the ELS, the historical discoveries, the spacing has been fairly far apart. Still not there by chance, but still far apart. I do not believe that will be the case about the future. I believe the spacing will be close, unmistakably close."

"What leads you to believe that is the case?"

"A hunch, just a hunch."

Neil stood up to stretch his legs. He knew that for at least a few minutes, he had the professor's attention.

"Let's say that we discover that the codes reveal the future. And let's say we didn't like what the future looked like. Then couldn't we, as a society and as a civilization, change our behavior? After all, don't we have 'free will'?"

"Well…"

Neil continued, "And if we could change the future that had been revealed by the codes, that would mean that God did not have enough power to foresee the future. Then logically, wouldn't that mean that what the codes revealed was just one of many paths available for the human race?"

"We are learning more and more how to predict the weather, but I don't think we will ever be able to change it. If we cannot change the weather, do you really believe that we are going to change what God foreordained?" asked the professor.

"Just prepare for it, like the weather," said Lisa.

"Good analogy, Lisa," said Neil.

"Thank you."

The professor ignored the flirtatious exchange.

"Neil, let me give you another example. My father used to tell me stories about how the Bible described the end of the human race. It is spelled out in detail—in black-and-white in many books of the Bible. Does that mean that humanity has changed its way because it knows the outcome of those who choose evil over good? If people do not believe what the Bible says about the future, why would they believe what the codes say?

"Remember when I told you after my wife died that I picked up a Bible and started reading it?"

Neil nodded.

"I was amazed at how many times Israel was warned by God to do this or not to do that. There always were consequences when they did not do what God had instructed, and when they did, they were always blessed. Maybe that is what the codes will reveal—warnings, which we can choose to accept or reject. Then there would be no conflict with our free will."

Neil stood and walked to the fireplace, where he put another log on the fire and poured a fresh cup of coffee. "So back to your story, Professor. It sounded like you realized at the conference or later that you had said too much or, as you said, 'crossed the line.'"

"I absolutely believe there were some in the audience who construed my comments that the codes could be used like a cosmic crystal ball. They figured if the codes could reveal the future, they wanted to be in a position to capitalize on it. For example, if you knew which horse would win the race before the race started, you could bet on that horse. Multiply that exponentially, and you can see how my comments were taken by some in the audience. The ramifications of manipulating the world powers had even more alarming possibilities. The codes could give the one who discovered it ultimate power and control."

"And you think that there were people in the audience who speculated that you had already uncovered this 'holy grail' of the codes?"

"At first, I think they accepted at face value that I had tested the codes, determined they were credible, and wrote about them. But when I took the leave of absence and later disappeared, well, then I believe they were not sure. My disappearance gave fodder for their conspiracy theory."

Neil walked back from the fireplace to where the professor was sitting. He stood next to the professor, bending to make eye contact.

"Professor. I need to know something that has been bothering me for a while."

"And what is that?"

"Do you know more about the codes than you are telling me?"

"If you are asking, have I uncovered the secret to the predictive powers of the codes, the holy grail, the answer is no. If you are asking whether I have uncovered more than I have shared with you, the answer is yes."

"Then you have not been honest with me."

"Neil, I have been honest with you. I believe the codes will be revealed to those who seek them over time at different levels. The first level is what you heard from me and what you discovered for yourself today. I know we don't have much time, but I did not want to go further until I felt you understood the codes at this level. I speak of this level as self-revealing. If you did not see the value of the codes at that level, it makes no sense for you to seek them at a deeper level."

"And you are satisfied that I understand and appreciate the value of the codes at that level?"

"You tell me."

"Well, of course. The messages are unmistakable, at least those that reveal historical events."

"Good."

"So you will tell me what you have discovered, Professor."

The professor stood up. "Follow me".

They walked to a table on the left side of the room, where there were several models on the table.

"Neil, I determined early on that the codes revealed in the Torah were a breakthrough of divine proportions. They revealed facts about the world in detail, which certainly could not be there by chance. And I proved that statistically.

"In some regards, that was enough for me. It helped me, as a scientist, to, well, reconfirm God—the same God Whom my father had found through his faith. You see, I had always said that faith was important, but if there was a God, He would reveal Himself to me at my level."

"In a scientific way."

"Yes, in a scientific way. When I would say this to my father, he would always say the same thing. 'Son, if you want proof there is a God, just look at nature. Look at the sky, the moon, the sun, the galaxy. Look at the intricacies of a human eyeball.' That was enough for him, but I was seeking more, or at least something different."

"I don't understand where you are heading with this, Professor."

"Well, after I recognized the divine origin of the codes, I wanted to learn more. I knew there was more to the codes. I could feel that there was a revelation that God would show me if I just knew where to look. But I knew I would not find what I was looking for at the level I was searching."

"So what did you do then?"

"I started reading the Bible, day and night."

"What were you looking for?"

"A sign."

"Thunder and lightning kind of sign."

"Well, that would have been okay. Frankly, I didn't expect something that dramatic. I was trying to justify with science what my father already knew by faith—that there is a God Who is ready to reveal Himself to us whenever we are ready. I was searching for that revelation. My thinking was that if God wanted to reveal Himself to me, He would do so with a sign or symbol. God had often revealed Himself throughout the ages by signs and symbols."

"A sign or symbol, huh?"

"I believed this sign or symbol would lead me to a deeper level of the codes. Or maybe a better way of saying it, the sign or symbol would reveal a deeper level."

"In what way?"

"I'll explain that in a minute."

"Okay, I guess."

"Well, I started by looking at every sign and symbol God used in the Bible. Here, on the table, are a few God used."

"He used a DNA strand?"

"No, not exactly. But I thought of it as a symbol of life. At this point, I want to be creative…do not exclude anything."

"I'm sorry, Professor. I still don't understand why these signs or symbols are important in what we are looking for."

THE REDEMPTION CODES

"Neil, I would stare at these symbols for hours. Somewhere, somehow, I felt like these symbols would lead me to where I needed to go. But I could never make the connection. Then it finally hit me."

"It hit you. What hit you?"

"I will ask you the question that it took me a long time to answer: What characteristic about these symbols is the same for all of them?"

One by one, Neil picked up each of the symbols that were lying on the table. "They are not the same color, not the same shape, not the same size." Neil continued to stare at each of them. "I don't know what value there is for me to waste everyone's time. I give up."

"They are all three-dimensional."

"Yes, and?"

"You see it?"

"See what?"

"Everyone who has investigated the codes for years has always looked at them from a two-dimensional view. You find the ELS pattern, and like a crossword puzzle, you find the associated words horizontally, vertically, or diagonally. But always two-dimensionally."

"Yes, and?"

"That method—looking at it two-dimensionally—has provided us with only a certain level of disclosure."

"The past," answered Neil confidently.

"Exactly. But what if we look at the Torah in a three-dimensional way? I believe that a whole new revelation will appear. In other words, if you place the Torah into a three-dimensional pattern, the revelation of the two-dimension stays intact. But now, rather than having just length and width, you have depth. The whole thing started to make sense to me. There was poetry about it too. All the time, I had been searching for meaning on the surface—the surface being another way of saying two dimensions. I needed to go deeper in my search. The third dimension, which I needed to look at, signified depth. Neil, the third dimension will reveal what we are looking for."

"The future? The holy grail?"

"Yes. If we can find the right three-dimensional model, we will find our answers. Now you know what I know."

Neil looked stunned. The professor picked up one of the symbols on the table, his eyes gleaming.

"All of these symbols have a third dimension. Somewhere, somewhere, there is a symbol whose pattern will lead us to where we want to be—to a depth in our search."

"But what if we never find it?"

The professor's eyes instantly changed from excitement to sadness. He paused a few seconds before he answered.

"For me, maybe the redemption is in the journey itself. And regardless of whether we ever find the right combination to unlock the future, it will have been worth the effort. And if you were to ask my father whether this journey will be worth it, I believe he would answer yes—yes, it was worth it."

Lisa walked into the room with a basket of sandwiches. At the same time, Biltmore appeared out of nowhere from the opposite side of the room.

"We are almost out of food. I need to go to the store," said Lisa, Biltmore now standing beside her.

"Absolutely not. It's too dangerous. We will send Biltmore."

"No, Father. I will be careful. If Biltmore buys all of that food, people might get suspicious."

"Maybe I should go. No one knows who I am," said Neil.

"Dad, trust me. I will be careful. I know exactly what we need and can get in and out of there quickly. Neil needs to continue working."

The professor rarely won these arguments. "Lisa, you are probably right. Let Biltmore drive you in his truck."

The professor reached into his pocket for some cash. He had remembered to withdraw money a few days earlier. The use of a credit card was clearly out of the question. He was dealing with people who had power at very high levels.

"Be careful, Lisa," said the professor.

"I will." Lisa took a quick glance at Neil as she walked out of the room. It was the same flirtatious look she had disarmed him with so many times before.

The two finished their sandwiches. The professor wondered by now whether they had buried his father. He knew he could never replace the hole in his life. Although they had not discussed it, he knew that his father had seen the change in his life.

"How long should they be gone?" Neil asked.

"It is twenty minutes each way. I'd say an hour or so."

*****

Neil kept staring at his watch. Whether he realized it or not, his feelings for Lisa were stronger now than ever. He did not know where this adventure he had started two days ago would lead, but he did know one thing. Wherever it led, he hoped upon hope that it would include Lisa the whole way. He screwed up once; he was not going to make that mistake again.

"Professor, it has been over an hour and a half."

"I know. She's in good hands. But I am a little worried too."

Neil tried to work, but he could not concentrate. Everywhere he looked, he saw Lisa's face.

It seemed like an eternity before they heard the door open from the back of the large room. It was Lisa, alone and out of breath.

"Are you okay, Lisa?" asked Neil, his face reflecting the worry.

"Yes, I'm okay. They have their people in town. Biltmore noticed them while we were in the market."

Their people. That sounds ominous.

"Did they see you?" asked the professor.

"That's hard to say. Biltmore convinced the owner to let us leave by the back door where Biltmore had parked the truck. We went the opposite direction from the cabin to one of his cousins. He dropped me off there. His cousin drove me back here."

"Where did Biltmore go?"

"He said he was going to ride back through town and try to get them to follow him out to the lake area. There, he felt he could lose them in the flats on the south side of the lake."

"How many were there?" asked Neil.

"That was the odd thing about it. Biltmore said that he saw a black SUV parked in front of the market with two men inside. But he said that a white van was also parked there. He knows these parts and every car or truck in the whole county. Biltmore knows who lives here and who is visiting. He said neither the black SUV nor the white van was from the area. The odd thing, he said, was that they didn't seem to be working together."

"That is odd," replied the professor. "When did Biltmore think he could safely return?"

"He was going to try to lose them in the flats by the lake. He said if that didn't work, he would abandon his car and lose them in the foothills where a truck or SUV can't go."

"Does he have a gun?" asked Neil.

"A rifle. But I don't think he will need it. He grew up in this area. He knows more caves and caverns than anyone. They will never find him."

"I hope you are right, Dad."

Neil spoke. "Boy, you got everybody looking for you. They must think you have found something special, Professor."

Then Neil looked at Lisa. "I am glad you are okay."

Chapter 15

Have You Found Them Yet?

The El Al flight from Israel to Raleigh Durham International Airport through New York finally landed. It had been a long flight, and Steve Gold realized how tired he was as he walked toward the car rental signs.

He was glad the meeting with Larry Haggerty had been scheduled for tomorrow morning. It would give him time to get organized and to get some much-needed rest. The next few days were going to be very important in his life.

He sorted through the options in his head like he had so many times before. The rabbi was right to terminate the partnership. There was no way the Israelis could continue with the Americans, particularly after that last tragic episode with the professor's father. Plus, the members of the rabbi's group in Israel were now convinced that the Americans did not have what it took to advance the discovery.

The rabbi was right about another thing. The Israelis did not have what it takes to progress the codes to the next level either. There was only one person who had a chance to advance the code research, and that was Professor Lange.

There was also no question in Steve's mind that there was gold at the end of that proverbial rainbow, and he knew where—better yet, upon whom—that rainbow ended, and he had no doubt it was the professor. One thing was for sure: Steve never apologized for being a capitalist. Now he just needed to find a way to capitalize on the professor's advancements.

*****

"It's Haggerty on the phone. He seems agitated."

The young man in his early thirties took the cell phone from the passenger.

"Yes, Mr. Haggerty."

"Well, have you found them yet?"

"We saw the girl with a large mountain man in town. We watched them go into a local market. We waited outside, but they must have gone out a different direction. We saw the truck again, but only the mountain man was inside."

"And?"

"We followed the truck onto an unpaved road, but he turned off his lights. It was dark, and there was no way he could see where he was going. After a few minutes, we found the truck beside a lake. We searched the truck, but there was no one around. We shot the tires so he couldn't leave. There was only one way in and one way out. He can't be far from here. We will wait him out."

"Forget it. He's gone by now," said Haggerty.

"Mr. Haggerty, I need to know something. Are we the only ones working on this?"

"Yes. Why do you ask?"

"Last night, there was a white van in town. It was dark, and we couldn't tell for sure, but we think there was one man inside. He followed us for a while."

Haggerty prided himself on being in control of every detail, but this time, he wasn't sure himself. *Was there competition for this material I don't know about?* He was pretty sure it wasn't the rabbi's group. They didn't have the heart for the chase. He knew it wasn't the Defense Department. He had assurances that they would not get involved unless he specifically asked them. *Who else could it be? Maybe another country has entered the sweepstakes.*

"You're seeing things. You have one job and one job only. No one else is involved." Haggerty paused for a second. "Do not disappoint me. Find the professor."

The young man would not question Mr. Haggerty, but he had his doubts that they were alone in this mission.

Chapter 16

Kind Words

The next morning came, and there was no word from Biltmore. The professor knew that he was more than capable of taking care of himself, but he still worried. Over the years, Biltmore had become more than a friend; he was family.

He remembered the first time he met Biltmore. They were both kids. Biltmore was a few years younger than the professor. Even at an early age, Biltmore's physical features dominated the professor's first impression. They were the kind legends are made of. He was tall and thick with huge hands and huge feet. The professor learned that Biltmore's Christmas present every year was a new pair of shoes his mother ordered from a special catalog. He recalled once asking Biltmore how tall he was. Biltmore didn't know because it never mattered to him. The professor guessed it was close to seven feet, if not more. A different place, a different time, and a different set of circumstances, Biltmore could have been an NBA center.

The professor admired many qualities about Biltmore. He was a gentleman, a characteristic that belied his physical size. Confrontation was never a part of Biltmore's world; for one thing, his size discouraged such confrontations.

Although he rarely spoke, Biltmore was by no means slow intellectually. Even though he had very little formal education, he enjoyed reading. The professor would always bring a few books along for Biltmore during his trips to the cabin.

Biltmore relied on his keen intuition, which was usually right. He did not know what the professor was working on, nor did he ask, but he knew it had to be a good thing and worthy of his protection.

It was the conversation the professor had with Biltmore right after he moved into the cabin for the first time that he will never forget.

"Professor, you are working on somethin' mighty important."

"Yes, Biltmore. It is important."

"Important to you or important to your dad?"

The professor seemed stunned at the insightfulness of the question. "Why do you ask, Biltmore?"

"Your daddy is very proud of you."

"Well, I think he is, but why do you say that?"

Biltmore told his story. "Many years ago, when you were real young, probably before you was a teenager, your dad would bring you to the mountains to go fishin'. You probably don't remember, but my pop was your guide. He would take you and your dad to the parts of the lake where the bass were biting. After a while, you stopped comin' with him. Your dad said you were doing other things, and fishin' really didn't, well, you weren't interested in it anymore.

"Then one winter, my pop died. Your dad didn't know that my pops died. So when he came back the next spring, he asked for my pops like he always done before. The owner of the bait shop told him my dad had died last winter. He asked where I was—that he wanted me to be his guide. From then on, I was your dad's guide. He always treated me real nice.

"Well, a few years later, my mom got real sick. You know she really liked your dad. She used to always talk about when he would come to her small church for revival services. Well, as she was dying, right in her last days, she asked me if your dad might come visit her. I called your dad, and he came right away. You know he held mama's hand right up until she died. He kept telling her she was going to a better place where she wouldn't be sick no more, and she would be back with my pop. Every time he would say that, a smile would come across mama's face.

"Your dad did mama's funeral. He really said some important things about mama and everything, but I think he was talking more to me and my cousins. He said how, you know, livin' right was an honor to our mama. He said that children become adults, and they can make their own decisions. But when they honor their mama, they honor God. It all made sense to me."

"Those are very kind words, Biltmore."

"And the thing is, we didn't know your wife was sick too."

"That was a tough time for both of us."

"Well, we kind of lost contact with your dad for a little while until one day he came to see me. He said that you was working on somethin' real important. He said that it might be kinda dangerous for you and that you might need a place to work where no one knew where you was. He didn't say much more but that he would like it if I would help you."

"My father never said anything about this. He never told me where I should go. I decided to come here myself."

"Your dad said that you would come back to the only place where you thought you could hide and that I was to take care of you. When you came to town that day, well, I almost didn't recognize you. You have changed a lot in all those years. Well, I guess we all changed a lot. Anyway, it was no accident that I took you to the old whiskey mill and cabin."

Remembering that story brought a rush of feelings to the professor. He would never know all the ways his father had shown his love for him. He knew he could never repay him.

The professor's mind jumped back to two nights ago when he returned to the cabin with Neil and Lisa. He couldn't decide whether he should tell Biltmore what had happened to his father. He finally decided that if Biltmore was family, he should know everything. The professor had never seen Biltmore show any emotion, but the news of his father's death caused the huge man to cry like a baby.

Chapter 17

Plaintext

The professor reassured everyone, including himself, that Biltmore would be okay. Biltmore knew more about this terrain—every nook and cranny, every cave and back road—than anyone alive. He was born here and, to the best of the professor's knowledge, had never traveled more than a hundred miles away from these parts his whole life.

The three of them settled back to the table, each to their computers.

"Professor, you are looking for a sign—if I can be so bold—a sign from God, and this sign, or symbol, is going to direct you to the unrevealed message of the codes, or as you say, the holy grail. Correct?"

"Incorrect. The sign is only going to lead us to a three-dimensional model or pattern—better yet, a clue. From there, it would be up to us to build a model using the three-dimensional object."

"And from there, we finally get to the unrevealed message of the codes." Before the professor could answer Neil's rhetorical comment, he continued, "And where are you looking for these signs?"

"To be honest, Neil, I have been searching for a clue. I keep feeling like I am to receive some 'sign,' and when I do, I believe I will know it."

Neil stood up, walked around the table, and then sat back down. He wasn't even aware of this unusual mannerism. At this point, Neil was mentally locked in. "When you were explaining the codes to me, you said something about how the words revealed by the codes correlated directly with the Hebrew text itself."

"That is correct."

"What did you mean by that?"

"There is the plaintext, and there is a hidden text. The written text, the Hebrew Torah, is referred to as the plaintext, and the events revealed by the codes are referred to as the hidden text."

Neil could see the excitement return in the professor's eyes. "Let me explain it this way. The encoded words, even though they may refer to a historical person, have some relationship or connection to the section of the Torah where they are revealed."

"The hidden text relates to the plaintext."

"Yes, Neil. Let me show you an example."

The professor walked to one of the computers and typed in a few words. "In Genesis 1:29, the plaintext says, *'Behold, I have given you every seed-bearing plant on the face of the earth.'* The hidden text reveals all seven edible species of seed-bearing fruit found in Israel. They were found encoded in just this passage that alludes to them, and at ELS, smaller than anywhere else, those words could be found in the Torah. The Torah refers to seed-bearing fruits, and the codes identify what those fruits were. Amazing, huh, Neil."

"Therefore, Professor, if we are looking for a 'sign,' maybe we should look in the Hebrew Torah, the plaintext, for all references to *signs*." Neil was smiling confidently.

Before the professor could bark instructions, Lisa had already typed into her computer. "According to my search, the word *sign* occurs sixty-seven times," said Lisa, now smiling herself.

"Let's start from the beginning. It appears that it first occurs in Genesis, sometime after the flood, when God sends a rainbow," replied the professor.

The professor went to a computer on another table. He quickly typed in some words. "Okay, I've found it. Genesis 9:8." He typed in the first reference to a *sign*. A program had already been set up to search for the identified word—in this case, *sign*. Horizontally, vertically, and diagonally. It only took a few seconds. *No match.*

Undeterred, the professor typed in the next reference to a *sign*. *No match*.

"Professor, you have already gone down this path. You even have a program prepared to analyze references to signs. Is that correct?"

"I have gone through as many references to signs as I could locate in the Torah."

"Then why did you let us think we were on to something if you already knew it was a dead-end?"

Ignoring Neil's question, the professor asked, "Lisa, can you think of another text that refers to signs?"

Lisa went to another computer. She opened the program that had been installed with the King James Version of the Bible. There in the concordance section, she found every place where signs had been used in the Old Testament. She copied the references. "Here, there are a few dozen more places we can try."

Patiently for the next several hours, Neil went through each reference to a *sign*. There were no matches.

"I thought the idea that we had independently come up with was a good one, Neil. Unfortunately, not good enough."

Neil stood up again and walked pensively in a circle before sitting down. At this point, he was undeterred. "Professor, you often refer to this as the search for the holy grail. That is your term for the ultimate prize. And that ultimate prize is that the codes will be able to reveal the future to us. Right?"

"Yes, that is correct."

"This is the prize, greater than any earthly prize. It satisfies the ultimate test—at least for some—of whether the scriptures were really given to us by God and not by man. If He can tell us what happens in the future, then we know it is divine, not human. When that occurs in the Bible, it is referred to as prophecy. Isn't prophecy no more than telling us what the future holds?"

"Yes. Where are you heading with this?"

"What if we look at the sections of the Old Testament that deal with prophecies?"

"I can identify all of the prophecies given about the future of man, nations, peoples, and cultures," said Lisa.

"That's where we need to be looking, Professor. It makes sense that if the plaintext deals with the future of Israel six thousand years ago, the hidden text might reveal the future six thousand years later. I am convinced that's where our answer will be."

"I think that is a worthy lead," said the professor.

"And am I to assume—"

"No, Neil. This time, I have not already tested this theory. Thanks to you. We are in uncharted territory."

For the first time in many days, Neil felt a part of the team.

Chapter 18

The Meeting

It would be the first time Steve Gold had visited the American facility since he brokered the deal between the Israeli group and the American Corporation. In the beginning, the partnership had all the makings of a win-win situation.

It was true that the rabbi had discovered the codes. But at first, even the rabbi thought the partnership with the American Corporation was an opportunity to not only benefit from their latest technology but more importantly to also gain scientific credibility for his initial discovery.

For the American Corporation, it was an opportunity to advance the research, possibly discovering something that would give them an incredible ground-floor opportunity.

And for Steve Gold, it was a way to capitalize on the discovery in a, let's say, financial way.

In the beginning, it was a deal made in heaven. But what appeared to be made in heaven seemed today like it was destined for hell.

Steve was not looking forward to this meeting. He knew one thing about the Americans; Larry Haggerty did not like rejection even when it seemed inevitable.

It was raining slightly, and Steve wanted to make sure he gave himself plenty of time, even though the hotel was less than fifteen minutes away. As he exited the hotel parking lot, he noticed a white van parked in a shopping center lot across from the hotel. Normally, he would not have noticed the van, but it was Saturday morning, and it was too early for customers. He glanced back as he exited the hotel parking lot. There appeared to be no one in the van. *Maybe I am paranoid*, he thought.

Steve entered the driveway to the Creedmoor Corporate Headquarters. A portly older man signaled him to stop at the guard gate.

"Mr. Haggerty is expecting me."

"Yes, sir, Mr. Gold. Please go through. Parking is in the rear. Enter the door on the dock. Someone will meet you there."

Before Steve could reach the door of the main building, a technician with a cutoff white jacket met him.

"Mr. Gold?"

"Yes."

"Mr. Haggerty is waiting for you."

The technician escorted Steve down a hall to a large conference room. A large wooden table dominated the room. Thirty chairs lined all sides of the table. A series of mirrors lined one of the walls. Other than the mirrors, there was no art or pictures on the wall. In fact, the color of the walls and the decor made the room feel eerily dark.

Waiting at the end of the table was Mr. Haggerty. He did not stand up when Steve entered the room. He just pointed to a seat at the table.

"I trust your trip was a pleasant one, Mr. Gold?"

"Yes, but I wish it was under more pleasant circumstances."

"Oh?" responded Haggerty. "You sound like you have bad news for me."

"Larry, Mr. Haggerty, the rabbi asks that I give you his message personally."

"And his message is?"

"When the rabbi first discovered the codes, needless to say, he was extremely excited. He saw it as an opportunity to convince a secular world that the Torah was divinely given, and somehow this discovery could, even in a small way, be used to ensure Israel's future independence. When I first learned of the hidden codes, I, too, was mesmerized. My mind raced to all the possibilities it could offer to the world.

"I argued with the rabbi that in order for his research to be taken seriously, it had to be scientifically and mathematically verified by someone the scientific world would respect. He realized that need and instructed me to have his work independently verified by Professor Lange.

"I lied to the rabbi, something I am not particularly proud of. I told him that the professor had his own agenda—that he had already advanced the research to a whole different level.

"At first, they didn't buy my story and requested a meeting with the professor. As luck would have it, the meeting did not go particularly well. By the end of the meeting, the rabbi suspected the very thing that I had lied to him about—that the professor had, in fact, advanced the research to a whole different level."

"Why are you bothering me with these details?"

"So that you will understand why the rabbi agreed to cooperate on this research with you and your company."

"Don't you think that is old news?"

"Yes, but I think it is important for you to understand where we have been before I tell you where we want to go."

"Go ahead if you must, but you are wasting my time."

Haggerty's body language told Steve that there was not much to be gained by this monologue. But he had a message to give, and he was going to give it. "Those close to the rabbi thought what had been his discovery, his baby, his dream, his legacy, had been stolen by an American professor, and that American professor would reap all the rewards that rightfully belonged to the rabbi. All of the benefits the research might one day offer were going to be taken by someone else. He and the Israeli people would be left with nothing. Needless to say, they got nervous."

"We have all of the resources the rabbi could ever want and more than the professor could ever hope to have."

"Yes, perhaps you are right. However, now the rabbi has reconsidered. He never bargained for bloodshed."

"I don't know what you are talking about, Mr. Gold."

"The professor's father was killed. The rabbi believes it was done by one of your operatives."

"The professor's father was killed by a burglar," answered Haggerty. "That was the police's report as well as reported in the newspaper."

"You can take that position, Mr. Haggerty, but you know that is not true. And the police—I assume you have ways—maybe the police report and the newspaper said what you wanted them to say. After all—"

"Mr. Gold, get to why you saw a need to meet with me."

Steve was starting to feel nervous and uncomfortable. Haggerty's eyes did not move and never blinked as he stared at Steve. They had an uncomfortable way of making Steve feel like he was in front of both the judge and the executioner. Steve's instincts were to finish what he had to say and get out of there.

"Even if what you say is true about the old man's death, the rabbi is convinced that what you are looking for."

"And that is?"

"You know that the excitement about the codes was their ability to predict the future."

"And."

"And the rabbi now does not believe that is possible."

"So, may I ask again, what is your message for me?"

"The rabbi has specifically requested that I deliver the message that he no longer wants to be associated with your research. He wants to distance himself from this association."

"And this comes from the rabbi, or were there other parties involved?"

"It is the rabbi's decision, if that is what you are asking."

"And the prime minister is in agreement with this position?"

Steve knew that Haggerty would ask that question, and regretfully, Steve had to lie again. "To be honest, the prime minister takes a more secular approach to these things. He has no interest in pursuing this further, you know, as between the two countries."

THE REDEMPTION CODES

"I am sorry to hear that. We are making progress with our research. I believe the citizens of Israel would want to be here when we make the breakthrough."

"The rabbi believes that if you were making progress with this research, you would not have taken such drastic measures to obtain information from the professor's father."

"The professor may have the intellect but not the means to run the programs necessary to find out this information," responded Haggerty.

Steve could tell that Haggerty was getting very frustrated. "It is not for me to agree or disagree with you on this matter. I am here specifically to give you the formal position of the rabbi. They are officially removing themselves completely from your research. You can choose to be upset at this position, but I am only the messenger."

"Mr. Gold. Please tell the rabbi that we regrettably accept his position."

There was no regret at all with Larry Haggerty. This was the best information he could receive. Once he had received the rabbi's initial discovery, his group of skilled mathematicians would take it from there. Any advance of their original discovery would not have to be shared with the rabbi or the Israeli government. And if there is additional collateral damage, he does not have to worry about some sanctimonious third party. Haggerty was not at all concerned that the rabbi might make additional discoveries before his people did. Now Professor Lange, that was a whole different matter altogether.

"Mr. Gold. I am curious about one thing. I thought you and I had an understanding. We are alike in many ways. Now you realize that you will no longer share in any financial windfall that comes from our research. I regret your position in this matter. You could have been a very wealthy man."

Haggerty starred at Steve to see what reaction he would get from this comment. Steve nodded as if to acknowledge Haggerty's position. Although he attempted not to show it, Steve was not the least bit concerned about Haggerty's veiled threats. The American Corporation was never going to make any significant discoveries. Steve had his eye on the prize and where that prize was going to come from, and if he was right, he would not have to share it with Haggerty.

Haggerty stood up but made no effort to extend his hand. "I will tell my contacts with the administration that the rabbi, along with the consent of the Israeli government, has withdrawn their involvement. Steve, if you convince them to reconsider, please let me know."

Steve hurried back to the rental car. He had places to go and, now, a real plan.

Chapter 19

Black SUV

The north wind further chilled the already cold mountain air. The sun would soon set behind the foothills that spanned along the western side of the mountain range. Fresh from the chase, Biltmore walked back through the woods to an empty cabin on the outskirts of town. He had heard the shots and, from his vantage point, knew the tires on his truck had been blown out.

If Biltmore's instincts were correct, and they usually were, the men in the black SUV would not be going away until they got what they came for. He just didn't know exactly what that was. The one thing he did know: He had to protect the professor and his family—at any cost. That was a promise he had made to the professor's father.

Biltmore was standing on the sagging porch of the small, empty cabin when the professor walked up. Biltmore appeared startled. "Professor, how did you know where I was?"

"I remember my father telling me once that if you can't find Biltmore, check the empty house on the hill overlooking the lake." *Biltmore goes to the old house on the hill when he needs to figure things out.* "I just knew that with people killing my father and chasing you, you probably had a lot of figuring out to do."

"You got that right. I got a lot of figuring out to do."

The professor turned back to look out over the ridge to the lake several hundred feet below. The lake where he had fond memories of fishing with his father on many a spring and summer day.

"I can see why you come up here. It is beautiful."

"And peaceful. This is where I came after my pops died, and this is the place I came after my mama died."

The professor smiled. For someone so physically intimidating, the large man had a heart of gold and a quiet and sensitive spirit.

"This is where I wanted to bury my dad and my mama. But the people in the town said I couldn't do that."

"Because you don't own the property?"

"No. We own the property. There was some other reason, and the rest of the kin didn't think it was a good idea anyway. So I just let it go."

The professor reached up and placed his hand on Biltmore's shoulders.

"Biltmore, we need to talk."

"Is it about the secret project you are working on?"

"Yes. It's only fair that you know what's at stake here and how dangerous it could be."

"You don't have to explain nothin' to me, Professor. I made a promise to your dad."

Neither Biltmore nor the professor saw the black SUV turn the corner on the ridge above the old house until it was too late. The gunman on the passenger side had the professor clearly in his sights. Biltmore, hearing the skidding of the tires, reacted just in time to push the professor down onto the wooden porch of the old house. Left standing, Biltmore caught the bullet flush in the chest. His large body landed on the porch with a hard thud.

The black SUV continued on the road toward the old house, aware that they had missed the intended target. The professor rolled off the side of the porch onto the ground below. He did not want to leave Biltmore, but when he took one look back at the fallen man, it was clear that Biltmore was not moving and probably dead. He had no choice now but to run.

The professor could hear the sound of the black SUV sliding to a stop on the steep gravel road in front of the house. Trying to escape and knowing that he was their target, the professor ran up the small mound covered with brush behind the house in the direction of the road that leads to town. He knew that he could never make it as far as town before they would catch him.

He paused for a second, paralyzed by the lack of options. Standing on the road, he could see that the two men had gotten out of the SUV and were heading in his direction. He ran as fast as he could, trapped by steep rock formations on each side of the road.

By now, the two men had reached the road. If they could hit Biltmore from a distance in a moving SUV, he was probably already in their sights.

He ran anyway, so frantic and disoriented that he hardly noticed the white van that passed him heading toward the two men. That is until he heard their screams. The two men had been so focused on the chase that they ignored the van until it was too late. The van hit both of the men head-on, throwing their bodies high into the air.

Once in hot pursuit, now their twisted, bloody bodies lay prone and still. The white van, damaged from the incident, continued down the road in the direction away from the professor.

The professor hesitated for only a moment. He desperately wanted to know all the answers: who wanted to kill him, who saved him, and why did they? Should he go back to Biltmore? Instead, his instincts told him to run, and he ran and ran as fast as his fifty-two-year-old body would let him.

*****

Lisa was pouring through several books of the Old Testament when the professor entered from a small, hidden passageway near the rear of the large room. His ashen face and trembling hands spoke to the danger he had been in. He walked to a table, where he collapsed onto a chair.

"Dad, are you okay? You left without telling us where you were going."

It took the professor a few seconds to gain enough composure to speak.

"Biltmore!"

"Yes?"

"Biltmore is dead."

"Oh my god!" exclaimed Lisa.

"He was shot by the men in the black SUV—the same black SUV you saw in the parking lot and the same one who chased him last night. I went to find him when he didn't come back today. I found him at the abandoned house on the ridge overlooking the lake, just outside of town."

"Biltmore was dead when you found him?" Neil asked.

"No. He was hiding there until he thought it was safe enough to return here. We were talking on the porch. I didn't see the SUV coming, but Biltmore did, in time to take a bullet that was intended for me. Biltmore saved my life."

Lisa went to get the professor some water as the shock from the whole series of events was staring to take its toll.

"Biltmore saved my life. He was the finest—the gentlest. I am not worthy of the sacrifice he made for me." The professor dropped his head into his hands and wept for his friend, the gentle giant.

The three sat in silence for a long time before the professor collected his thoughts enough to tell them the rest of the events. "When Biltmore was shot, I started running. I got back to the road that leads into town, but it would have only been a matter of time before they would have killed me too. If they could hit Biltmore from a moving car, I was nothing more than a sitting duck. Then from nowhere, a white van ran over the two men chasing me."

"And you don't think it was just an accident?" asked Neil.

"Oh, no, it was no accident," said the professor. "The white van drove around me in the middle of the road to hit the two men on the side of the road. It was as if the man in the white van was there to protect me."

"And you think that the people who killed your father are the same ones who killed Biltmore and who tried to kill you?" said Neil.

"That is obvious. But who is the man in the white van?"

"Maybe he is related to Biltmore's family," said Neil.

"No. Biltmore would have told me that at the market. He said that neither the black SUV nor the white van were from this area. He also didn't think the black SUV was connected with the man in the white van," recalled Lisa.

"Going forward, we have to assume that the man in the white van wants the same thing as the men in the black SUV, and he, too, is willing to kill for it."

"Maybe he represents a group in competition with the men in the black SUV," said Lisa.

"But that doesn't make sense," replied the professor. "The rabbi and the American Corporation agreed to work on this project together. Who else is out there who wants this so badly?"

"Perhaps it is a disgruntled employee who saw the value of the information and took it upon himself to get it. That would explain how he knew where to find you," said Neil.

"Maybe, but if he wanted to get to me, that was his perfect chance. I was all alone on the road, far from town. He could have made a move at that moment, and no one would have known. No, I think there is more to it."

The professor couldn't get the image of Biltmore lying on the porch out of his head. "Now two people whom I loved are dead. Both of them were innocent victims. Both of them died to protect me. Both of them made the ultimate sacrifice. Who wants this information so badly they will kill for it?

"I must notify Biltmore's cousin of what happened," said the professor.

"Professor. How are you going to explain Biltmore's death without disclosing what we are working on? He died a brave man. Someday, we may truly appreciate the value of his commitment to a cause he was not even aware of. But for now, you have to let it go. We cannot involve anyone else. We cannot risk any more lives."

Neil was right. He would have to let this one go for now, just like he let the death of his father go.

*****

The man in the black SUV answered his cell phone.

"Have you found the professor?" asked the caller.

"Yes. He and his daughter, along with one of his ex-students, are held up in a cabin just outside of town."

"Do you know where the cabin is located?"

"Not exactly. But it can't be too far from town."

"And Haggerty's men?"

"They are dead."

"What?"

"I had to kill both of them."

"My god! You killed them?"

"I had no choice. I did not want to kill them, but they were about to kill the professor."

"You shot them?"

"No. It's a long story. I'll explain later.

"So you saw him, the professor?"

"Yes, he ran away while all of this was happening."

"Why didn't you stop him?"

"That's not the plan. I believe that he is close to making the discovery that we all seek so desperately for our country. If I approach him before the discovery is made, he will close down and be of no value to us."

"So what is your plan?"

"I believe he will leave as soon as he makes *the* discovery. I need to find where he is located. Then I will make my move in the next day or so."

"What should I say to the prime minister?"

"You are a smart economist, Mr. Goldstein. You will figure it out. I will call you when I've got the information."

The phone clicked dead.

Chapter 20

He Saved My Life

Neil and Lisa had retired for the night. The professor desired more than anything to sleep, if for no other reason than to temporarily escape the constant reminder of loved ones being killed. *And for what? What could be so important that they would sacrifice their lives?* Unfortunately, his mind would not let him forget the reason why they were dead—to protect him. He did not deserve the anguish caused by those whose ambition exceeded their value of life. But he also knew he didn't deserve the ultimate sacrifice offered by two people he loved so much.

The combination of the work and the emotion of the day's events was taking a toll. For the first time since he heard about the codes, he questioned whether it was all worth it. Only time would tell. He remembered his father's words: *There is a reason why you are involved, son.* Right now, he had his doubts.

The professor walked to the table where Lisa and Neil had finished their research for the day. He sat down and began to review their work.

How long he had been asleep, his face resting on his folded arms on the table, he did not know. He knew it was not long enough to provide any true rest, and it certainly wasn't comfortable. He got up from the chair and headed for the couch next to the fireplace when he heard the side door rattle. At first, the professor thought it was the wind. Then he remembered that particular door went to another room that would have protected it from the wind. The door rattled again. This time, he grabbed his rifle, propped up next to the fireplace, and darted to the corner of the room behind where the door would open.

He wondered if he could ever use the rifle that he now clutched in his hands. It certainly wasn't in his nature. If he couldn't kill an animal, what made him think he could kill a human? One year ago, he would have said definitely not, but his world had been turned upside down in just a few months. New times and conditions demanded drastic measures.

The door rattled again. This time, it clicked and opened.

The intruder did not give the professor the time or reason to be alarmed.

"Professor? Hello, Professor. Are you here? This is Jimmy. I am Biltmore's cousin."

The professor appeared from behind the door. "Yes, I am Professor Lange."

Standing in front of the professor was a diminutive figure, probably no taller than five feet four inches and thinner than any man he had ever seen. His long hair was tied in a ponytail and bushy sideburns practically hid his small and weathered face. Somewhere in that genetic pool, Jimmy and Biltmore had departed in dramatically different directions.

"Biltmore told me I would find you here."

"But Biltmore is."

"Dead. I know."

"You found him?"

"Oh, no. I was there when it happened."

"What do you mean you were there?"

"I was inside the cabin when you was talking to Biltmore. I saw everything. When I heard the gunshot and saw Biltmore laying there, it was like my whole world crashed down. But I remember what he told me. He told me that if anything happened to him, to make sure I took care of you.

"Well, when you ran up the hill toward the road, I stayed in the cabin. At first, I was scared, but then I remembered what I had promised Biltmore. I waited for the two men to get out of their car, and I followed them up the hill. I had my rifle pointed at them from behind when I saw the white van coming. Then I pointed the rifle at the van, but it went right by you. When I heard the screams from those two men and saw them fly in the air, well, I knew they were dead.

"I waited a few minutes to see if the guy in the van was going to turn around and come after you. Instead, he drove away. He went down the road, stopped, and turned around. By that time, you had run away. The man in the white van came back, stopped the van, and got out. He wrapped the men in blankets and put them in the back of the van. He got back into the van and drove it to the ledge overlooking the lake. He jumped out of the van right before it went over the ledge. He walked back to the black SUV and drove it away."

"Did he see you or Biltmore?"

"No. I don't think he even knew what happened at the cabin. Say, Professor, does he work for you? That man in the white van?"

"Jimmy, I don't know who killed Biltmore, and I don't know the man in the white van. I just know that it's me they are after."

"Well, by the time the man came back, it was getting pretty dark. I just knew I had to take care of Biltmore."

"Do you think there was any chance that Biltmore might have made it if we could have gotten him to the hospital?"

"No. As far as I could tell, the bullet hit him right in the heart. By the time I got back to the cabin, he was not breathing at all."

"Biltmore's body, did you take it?"

"Yes, sir. I'll bury him right next to his mama. We don't have many relatives left, so the ceremony will be kind of simple."

"Don't you need to tell the sheriff?"

"Well, I think that would be a little tricky, Professor. He would want to know everything. It didn't sound like you probably wanted to do that, you know, talk about this—whatever you are working on."

"You are right, Jimmy. That might really complicate matters. With the people we are dealing with, I don't even know who we can trust."

"I hear you."

"I am so sorry, Jimmy."

"You don't have to say anything. Biltmore really liked you a lot. I think he would have done anything for you."

"He did. He saved my life."

"I think he knew that was going to happen. Biltmore was not real book smart, but he could figure things out. And he usually knew when things were important. He told me that you was workin' on something mighty important. He could trust me like that. He said it was important and that there were people who might try to hurt you. The last thing he said before you showed up was to make sure that if anything happened to him, I was to take care of you."

"That means a lot to me. But too many have sacrificed their lives for this already. I can't let you be another."

"I don't have family left, well, except for my mama and one cousin. And you know, I made a promise to Biltmore. A promise is a promise."

"Jimmy, I'll think about it. But for now, I'd like you to just be careful."

"I'll try my darndest."

Jimmy turned to leave the way he had come in.

"Jimmy?"

"Yes, sir?"

"Have you seen the black SUV again?"

"Yes, I saw it leaving town tonight."

*****

It was early morning when the professor finally fell asleep on the couch. He hadn't been asleep long when he was awakened by the clicking sound of computer keys. Neil and Lisa attempted to work quietly, but the professor's sleep was a shallow one.

"Dad, let me get you some coffee."

"That would be nice," said the professor, trying to push the effects of the last few days from his mind. "I had a visitor last night after you guys left."

"You had a what?" asked Neil. "You mean there was a visitor who did not try to kill us?"

"Jimmy, Biltmore's cousin. It is the most amazing story. Well, actually, both tragic and amazing. As it turns out, he was inside the cabin when Biltmore was shot. He saw the whole thing."

"And you didn't know he was there?" asked Lisa as she handed him the coffee.

"No. Biltmore had just given Jimmy his gun and told him to be on the lookout. Apparently, he walked inside the cabin right as I was walking up."

"This must be hard on him. Biltmore was about the only family he had left," said Lisa.

"He said we are his family now. He really wants to help and says that he made a promise to Biltmore that if anything happened to him, he would look after us. I told him that I didn't need anyone else in harm's way."

Neil could not believe what he was hearing but was learning every day to expect the unexpected.

"Do you think he got a good look at the guy who ran down your attackers?" asked Neil.

"Yes, he thinks he did."

"I hope we never need to know," said Lisa.

"My guess is that we haven't seen the last of Jimmy."

"Or the guy in the white van."

"It's a long story, but there is no longer a white van. The guy in the white van traded it for the black SUV."

"Okay, I hope we never see the guy in the black SUV," said Neil.

The professor drank some coffee. He felt a little faint, realizing he was getting weak from not eating. He needed some food even if he was not hungry, knowing he would need all the strength he could muster in the next few days. But food would have to wait for now. It was only a matter of time before someone else would come after him, and there was still work to be done. Next time, he might not be so lucky.

"So have we made any progress with the research?" asked the professor.

Lisa responded yes, while simultaneously Neil responded no.

"It depends on whether the glass is half full or half empty," said Neil.

"We support the validity of the codes to expose historical events by purely looking at them from a two-dimensional format. The ELS exposes related events at low P values," said Neil. "And it is safe to say that nothing beyond historical events can be discovered from the two-dimensional model."

The professor drew a circle with his hands, a gesture he used in the classroom with his students to encourage them to be more creative in solving problems—to think outside the box. "So where do we go from here?"

"I think we look at the writings from a three-dimensional model," replied Neil, recognizing in midsentence how silly his rhetorical statement sounded.

"You have an uncanny sense for the obvious, Neil," said the professor, wanting to smile but not able to. "But which three-dimensional model do we use? That is the question, isn't it? That is the sixty-four-thousand-dollar question."

And what is going to allow me to escape this dangerous game before I am killed? thought Neil.

"Yes, Dad, that is where we are stuck. That is where we have been stuck now for the last twenty-four hours."

"Do you remember yesterday that you were convinced that if we focused on those prophetic statements that occurred in the plaintext—"

"Prophetic statements in the Torah that were later fulfilled," interrupted Neil.

"Yes. That would be where we might find a correlating future event."

"Like if a war was discovered in the plaintext, the hidden text might reveal a future war for our generation."

"Yes, Neil. Exactly."

"Okay. I did say that."

"And?"

"Well, Lisa has identified hundreds of those references to prophecies."

"And nothing has turned up?"

"Nothing that would lead us to identifying a three-dimensional model if that is where you are heading. My instincts told me that we are on the right track, looking for the plaintext reference to prophecies. That is where we were going to find the three-dimensional model that would lead us to the holy grail. It just made sense that the concept of a prophecy would lead us to a model that would eventually show the future. It was just too logical. I was absolutely convinced we were on the right track," said Neil.

"I don't want to be pessimistic, Dad, but if we can't identify the three-dimensional, we are not much further along than we were when we started."

"Yes. That sticky *how* part. We are still back to identifying the three-dimensional model. That's it!" shouted the professor.

"What's it?"

"We have made this search for a three-dimensional model more complicated than it needs to be. We are looking for a three-dimensional object that can serve as a model to extract the information, correct?"

"Yes," replied Neil and Lisa almost simultaneously.

"Then we need to search for every three-dimensional object used in the Torah and see where it leads us. I am convinced there is a three-dimensional object out there that is going to lead us to which three-dimensional model to use."

*****

Lisa meticulously identified every three-dimensional object used in the Torah.

The process was always the same. After the three-dimensional object was identified, Neil would isolate the three-dimensional object in *plaintext*. Then using the two-dimensional model, he would look for a *sign* from clustering related words around that three-dimensional object.

Neil was not even sure what the *sign* was and if he would even know it if he saw it. The professor, on the other hand, was absolutely sure he would know it when he saw it.

Hours had passed, and a little more discouragement came with each passing hour.

"I have gone through hundreds of three-dimensional objects already, Dad."

"No luck so far?"

"Unfortunately, not yet," replied Lisa.

This continued for several more hours. The stress was showing on their faces as one by one the references did not reveal a match.

"How about this one, the Ark of the Covenant? That's a three-dimensional object, all right."

"Yes, the Ark of the Covenant is a three-dimensional object," said the professor.

Without much enthusiasm, Neil created the grid with the *plaintext* reference to the Ark of the Covenant like he had done with so many words before.

"Okay, Vanna White Computer, show me the letter, or, in this case, show me some clustered words."

"Now you must be getting punchy, Neil, talking to the computer," said Lisa.

Neil ignored the mild ribbing. "The computer has slowed down for some reason. Okay, now it's showing me. Well, this is odd."

The professor turned towards Neil's screen. "That is an odd reference." The professor read the highlighted section of the screen. "Ezekiel's wheels."

The professor repeated it again and again to himself. "You started with a three-dimensional object, an ark, and it referenced another three-dimensional object, 'Ezekiel's wheels.' What is the ELS?"

"The words are spaced pretty tightly. Low P factor. In fact, the lowest we have seen so far."

"This might have some promise. See if there are any more associated words in the cluster."

The computer ran for a few minutes before additional words were revealed.

"Well, there is *seek*, *future*, and *carefully*. They each run horizontally and at fairly low spacing. And let's see. Okay, there is another one. The words *Jeremiah* and *price* run diagonally, intersecting the other words. That, too, has a remarkably low space sequence."

"I think you are on to something," said the professor, his face reflecting an air of anticipation.

"It sounds like the instructions are to 'seek the future carefully,'" said Lisa.

"That's what we are doing, *seeking* the *future carefully*. We are seeking to discover the future, and we are doing that carefully. Right, professor?" said Neil.

"You're right, particularly the careful part."

"But what about the reference to *Jeremiah* and *price*?" asked Neil.

"Well, Jeremiah was an Old Testament prophet, much like Ezekiel," replied Lisa. "Maybe it is directing us to the book of Jeremiah."

"Good. Try to find any reference to Jeremiah and price," responded the professor.

Lisa went to another computer. There, she pulled up the book of Jeremiah in the original Hebrew. She searched for the word *price*. There were no matches. "I cannot find any match for *price*. Perhaps there is a synonym for *price*."

For the next few minutes, Lisa searched the thesaurus and other references for any word that might lead to a match.

While Lisa was looking for a match, the professor appeared to walk aimlessly back and forth in the room. He would periodically stroke his chin. This had been a habit of the professor when he was working on a complicated mathematical problem.

Finally, Lisa returned to the table where Neil was working. "I could not find a match. Does anyone have an idea where else to look?"

"Maybe it's not just a reference to the Old Testament prophet," said the professor.

"Then, who could it be?" asked Lisa.

The professor's face grew somber. "Everyone called your grandfather Jerry, but his real name was Jeremiah. He told me his father always called him Jeremiah. Lisa, I think this is a reference to your grandfather and his sacrifice for us. *Jeremiah* and *price* are a reference to grandfather's death."

A mixture of pain and joy filled the room. They were on to something very dramatic, and they could feel it. But they were reminded again of the sacrifices it took to get to this point.

The professor knew that they had just experienced one of those wow moments in life that were meant to be savored. Unfortunately, there was one thing that they did not have, and that was time.

"Now we need to figure out what 'Ezekiel's wheels' means," said the professor.

Lisa went back to the computer with the King James Version and typed in the reference. "Here it is. Ezekiel 1:15."

> As I looked at the living creatures, I saw a wheel on the ground beside each creature with its four faces. This was the appearance and structure of the wheels. They sparkled like chrysolite, and all four looked alike. Each appeared to be made like a wheel intersecting a wheel. As they moved, they would go in any one of the four directions the creatures faced. he wheels did not turn about as the creatures went. Their rims were high and awesome, and all four rims were full of eyes all around.

"What do you make of that, Professor?" asked Neil.

"Well, I think that the three-dimensional object we have been searching for has something to do with a wheel."

"Yes, that's it!" shouted Neil.

"Neil, before you start working on a model, let's think through this. Are we looking for a wheel?"

"A wheel really doesn't give us the number of combinations that I think we need. It is no more than what we already have, a two-dimensional drawing. The only difference is that this two-dimensional drawing is on a curve or, more specifically, a circle. If you cut the circle and roll it out, you'll really just go back to another two-dimensional object."

"I think you are right, Neil. Remember the reference: 'Ezekiel's *wheels*,' not Ezekiel's *wheel*. Plural. *Wheels*. I think the three-dimensional object we have been searching for is right there in the passage. It's a wheel intersecting a wheel."

"At ninety degrees so it can go in any direction."

"Yes, see the poetic meaning. It can go backward," said the professor.

"Like in time…past events."

"And it can go forward."

"As in the future."

There was a long silence. If the professor was right, they were on their way to seeing the mysteries of the world—the future, the holy grail.

The excitement could hardly be contained. Each of them hugged one another. Neil wanted to shout for joy. He was on the doorstep of a discovery that could change the world forever. He wanted to sit back and enjoy the moment, but he knew there was not much time. Finally, he spoke. "How do you see this model working?"

The professor took a piece of paper and drew a grid of horizontal and vertical lines. Then he took the paper and rolled it into a cylinder so that the writing was on the outside. He taped the ends of the paper and set it on the table. He picked up another piece of paper and drew a grid just like the first paper. He cut a hole in one of the cylinders and stuck the other cylinder through the hole so that they were at a ninety-degree angle. Now there was writing going in all four directions: north to south, east to west.

"My bet is that we will find related words on each of the papers similar to the two-dimensional discoveries we have made before," said the professor.

"But where the papers intersect…"

"Bingo, Neil. I believe that is where we find what we have been searching for."

Neil jumped up as if he had been shot from a canon. "I have to get busy building this model on the computer. This is going to take some time."

"In the meantime, I will find the reference about America that I had discovered before. As I recall, the references highlighted everything from her wars to her glory: revolution, the Civil War, and man on the moon. There were so many I can't remember them all."

"Why the reference to America?" asked Neil.

"We need something to test your model on. The future of America will be our first test."

And with that, they each returned to their respective computer. They knew it was only a matter of time before there would be more visitors.

CHAPTER 21

Failure Continues

The team assembled by Larry Haggerty was supposed to be the brightest mathematicians and code breakers in the United States. A collection of men and women from academia, NASA, and the Pentagon made up this all-star group.

Haggerty's orientation speech to the members ten months ago was part prep rally, part marching orders. His dark eyes did not appear to blink as he addressed the group.

"Hidden in the Torah is a code. It was placed there several thousand years ago by what many say divine inspiration. It is my opinion that it was not placed there by a god but by a civilization outside of ours. A civilization far more advanced than our own from a galaxy far away from our own. I believe it was hidden by this civilization of extraterrestrials to be discovered by a new group of extraterrestrials that are either already on our earth or on their way back to our earth. I do not know if this civilization comes as friends or enemies to the earth. We cannot take that chance. We must find this code. It is not about fame or wealth. No, scientists, it is about survival.

"What will these codes do for our world? When found, it will point us to the solution for all the maladies that now burden our civilization. The cure for cancer. The antibody for aging. Control of the weather. There will no longer be the threat of global warming. There will be no more war. This will usher in a new age of peace and enlightenment.

"Both the United States and I have bet a lot of money on the successful outcome of this project. You were asked to be a part of this because you are the best the world has to offer." And in a Knute Rockne–style conclusion, he finished with these words. "Now let's go out there and break this code."

On paper, the strategy seemed fairly straightforward. There were thirty-four groups, and each group was assigned a book of the Old Testament. The elite groups were assigned the books that made up the Torah. A second group made up of very bright individuals, just not as bright as the first, was assigned the remaining books of the Old Testament.

Each group worked autonomously with the others. Not only was each group in a separate office, but they were also discouraged from discussing what they had found or comparing notes in general. Haggerty insisted this was to foster more creativity. To many members, it came across as pure, unadulterated competition. A rumor had spread that the group who made the discovery was assured millions of dollars in bonuses. Haggerty was not only aware of the rumor but might have even been its instigator.

It was Monday, and as usual, the groups had worked nonstop through the weekend. There had been no vacation since the project had started, and the head of the operation, a military man by the name of Sherman Stevenson, was worried that morale had started to deteriorate.

Sherman was perfect for this assignment. He had the skill of being a team leader and the experience of working on all the most recent code-breaking operations performed by the military since the Cold War. Now in his fifties, he was as energetic as he had ever been and in as good a shape as he was in his twenties.

However, he did not look forward to Mondays. Monday was the day of the weekly update to Mr. Haggerty.

The meeting with Haggerty was always held in the large conference room. As was most often the case, the meeting was just him and Haggerty. On occasions, if he thought that a particular group might be nearing a breakthrough, he would invite the head of that group to give an update.

Today, it was just him and Haggerty. Haggerty always appeared a little creepy to Sherman, and his presentations never seemed to go as he had rehearsed. For one thing, Sherman could not get past those glaring, never-blinking dark eyes.

Sherman finished his weekly briefing and left Haggerty's office. As had been more often the case recently, he reported only small advances in the research. Nothing strategic. Nothing earthshaking. At best, additional historical events at ELS spacing were no better than when they first started.

Haggerty was getting more impatient every day. He had made commitments, and he was getting behind schedule. What had been presented as a miraculous discovery with phenomenal potential was unraveling right before his eyes. And he did not like it one bit.

There was a reason that Haggerty had gotten where he had in life. He was a man of action, not contemplation—a man more concerned about results than how many friends he made along the way. Sherman suspected that Haggerty had no real friends.

Haggerty grabbed his phone and dialed the number. There was no answer. He dialed the second number. Again, no answer. He looked at the Global Positioning screen that tracked each car and SUV in his fleet. The black SUV was moving. *Perhaps they had entered a dead zone where there was no cellular service.* He would give it a few minutes and try again.

Haggerty tried several times over the next hour, but his men in the black SUV did not respond. Haggerty went through all the contingency plans for making contact. Every attempt was unsuccessful. *The mission has been compromised. My men have been killed and the SUV stolen*; that he now knew for certain. By whom, he was not so certain. *Who else has the guts for this high stake's drama? Certainly, not the Israelis. Who else could be involved?* Then he remembered that his men said something about a white van.

It was obvious that he couldn't trust anyone else to do the job that had to be done. He would do it himself. *The professor had to be stopped. Now. It was time to initiate plan B.*

Chapter 22

Shaken to the Core

Neil's efforts were nothing less than miraculous. A few hours later, and the model was programmed into the computer. For the first time since that infamous call from Lisa, Neil felt like he had made a real contribution. Along this short journey, he had matured; whether he liked all the pain that came with the hard lessons of the journey was another matter. Maybe the professor was right; maybe he could redeem his future by using his gift for a noble cause.

The professor found the references he was looking for within a few minutes after he had started. He used the remaining time to eat, get some much-needed rest, and find an answer to a question that had been bothering him for a while. He would share the answer to that question with the others at a later time.

Lisa stayed to help Neil. There wasn't much from a technical point she could do at this point. Her emotional support was what he needed now.

The professor returned as Neil was putting the final touches on the program.

"How is it coming?" asked the professor.

"I am finished, ready for a test. That will show me what bugs I have left to get rid of."

The professor retrieved the references about the United States he had found earlier in the day. He gave Neil the *plaintext* reference. Neil loaded it into the new program.

"By the way, Professor, where did you find these references to the United States?"

"I was looking at some references of Israel in battle, and there appeared related references to battles that the United States had been involved with."

"Interesting."

It only took the computer a few seconds, and the two-dimensional crossword grid was displayed.

"These are the associated words you discovered before: Revolutionary War, Civil War, World War I, World War II, Desert Storm."

"Yes, those are the same ones I discovered before from the two-dimensional model."

"Okay, let's see how this new baby runs." Neil typed a series of commands and pressed enter.

This time, it took the computer longer to generate a response.

"You will see a lot of gibberish on the screen. Ignore that. The clustered words will be highlighted so that they can be easily seen."

Neil was staring at the computer screen as it was processing the information. He was not sure how long it would take, but he could feel a mixture of anticipation and anxiety building. He imagined this must be the way a new father feels about the birth of a child.

It seemed like forever before the computer stopped processing. Neil stared at the screen in total disbelief. The professor knew something was wrong.

"What do you see, Neil?"

"Nothing. I see nothing."

"No clustered words?"

"Only the words from the two-dimensional. Nothing from the three-dimensional model. Professor, I was as sure as I have ever been that I programmed this model correctly. I don't understand how absolutely nothing showed up."

"Don't be hard on yourself. I have confidence that you prepared the model as I described. Maybe I misunderstood how the wheels intersected."

"Lisa, read the Bible reference again."

Lisa pivoted her chair around and read the reference that was still on her screen. "As I looked at the living creatures, I saw a wheel on the ground beside each creature with its four faces. This was the appearance and structure of the wheels. They sparkled like chrysolite, and all four looked alike. Each appeared to be made like a wheel intersecting a wheel. As they moved, they would go in any one of the four directions the creatures faced. The wheels did not turn about as the creatures went. Their rims were high and awesome, and all four rims were full of eyes all around."

"Do not be discouraged, Neil. We are on the right track. Let's think what we are missing. We know we were given *Ezekiel's wheels*. The reference clearly said they were at ninety degrees. That is the only way they could go in every direction. And there were four rims. Am I missing anything?"

Lisa continued to stare at the passage that was displayed on her screen. Finally, she spoke. "We started with a wheel intersecting a wheel. Obviously, that was wrong because it only accounted for one of the four creatures. The passage said that each creature had a wheel intersecting a wheel."

"What?" replied the professor and Neil almost simultaneously.

"We are missing that *each* creature had four rims. Here it is."

"As I looked at the living creatures, I saw a wheel on the ground beside each creature."

"Yes, Lisa is correct. There are four rims for each creature. It's there in black-and-white, and we missed it," said the professor.

"So four creatures, each with a wheel intersecting a wheel," said Neil.

The professor took a sheet from the table and drew a picture. He turned the paper over and drew another picture. "So we know that there are four creatures, each with a wheel intersecting a wheel. But are they two side by side, like a square, or four in one long line, like a tandem? That is the question, Neil," said the professor as he showed both drawings.

"Neil, you create a model with the four wheels intersecting four wheels in a tandem. I will create a model with two wheels intersecting two wheels in a square configuration."

"Okay, but why do I get the feeling that you know something I don't."

"I have no idea what you are talking about."

"Okay, Professor. I'll go along with your plan. But you have had me chase rabbits before."

It took several hours for Neil and the professor to complete their respective models. The professor finished his model much quicker than Neil but continued to stare at the monitor as if he was still actively working. Neil was not confident but agreed to test his model first. After loading the data, the computer started processing the program.

Rather than stare at Neil's screen, Lisa and the professor decided to move away from the computer. It took only a few minutes for the response. Lisa and the professor did not need to see the computer screen; they could see it in Neil's expression.

"Unfortunately, either the model was wrong, or I made an error in programming."

Lisa went to where Neil was sitting and kissed him on the forehead. "Rather than reworking yours, let me try my program, and then we can decide if we need to rework yours."

Dejectedly, Neil agreed.

The professor started the program he had already loaded. Like Neil's, it only took a few minutes. Unfortunately, like Neil's, it, too, yielded no positive results.

Neil and Lisa looked at the professor, who did not appear discouraged but was rather in deep thought.

"I am going to try another configuration," said the professor. "I will stack two wheels on top of two wheels."

The program was loaded, and Neil had a good feeling that the professor was right about this one. *This might be the one.* But once again, the program yielded no positive results.

"I had a feeling you were on to something with this model. What do we do now?" asked Neil.

The professor paced back and forth in the room for several minutes. "I think we overcomplicated the model. Let's go back to the original model of a wheel intersecting another wheel."

"But we've already tried that, Professor, and it did not reveal any positive results."

"We add another dimension," responded the professor confidently.

"Come again?"

"We add another dimension to the model."

"Professor, I was number one in your class, but please explain what you mean."

"The problem with the model is that it is static. It needs another dimension, and the only other dimension available to us is…time."

"I still don't follow you."

"We could vary the revolutions per minute for each wheel, and that would create an almost infinite number of permutations. But I think it might be simpler than that. I suggest we leave one of the wheels static and rotate the other wheel."

After some collaboration between Neil and the professor, it was agreed that each one would create a model. The professor agreed to leave the wheel facing east and west static and move the north and south wheels. Neil would leave the north and south wheels static and move the east and west wheels. If the model worked, clustered words would appear on the screen as the wheel rotated.

As if it were a miracle, it only took a few seconds before words started to appear on the professor's screen. To everyone's amazement, the words appeared as short phrases, not just clustered words.

"It worked!" shouted the professor. The professor continued to stare at the words and short phrases highlighted on the screen as Lisa and Neil were jumping around and hugging.

After a short celebration, Neil could see that something was wrong. The professor was not celebrating with the others. Neil went to the professor's screen. It took Neil only a few seconds to comprehend what the words and phrases were saying. He stopped reading. His face grew pale. All of a sudden, he felt sick. He turned from the highlighted words on the screen.

"My god," was all Neil could say.

"What is it?" asked Lisa as she rotated the professor's screen around. It took only a few seconds before she, too, was able to focus on the highlighted words.

Each of them slumped in their chair. The professor closed his eyes, hoping that he could somehow unsee what he had already seen. Lisa was visibly shaken. There were no words to adequately describe the deep, raw emotion they felt at that moment. In less than a minute, the mood went from celebration to devastation.

Neil looked at the screen again, hoping that what he had seen before was some cruel joke.

After a few minutes of silence, the professor stood up. He realized that the time called for him to be a friend and father rather than a fellow collaborator.

"I don't think any human is equipped mentally, spiritually, or any other way for what we just saw. God has graciously allowed us to see into His divine appointment book. I was not prepared for what we saw about the future of America."

Neither Lisa nor Neil responded, as if the shock sucked all the life out of them.

"My father was so convinced that this day would come that I occasionally allowed myself to imagine what it would feel like if I could see into the future. Would I be ecstatic? Would I be giddy with happiness? I never saw myself feeling this way. So inadequate. The awesomeness of this might be more than we are emotionally able to handle."

"So what do we do, Professor?"

"This is only the beginning of the mysteries. I must ask, do we stop, or do we dare proceed?"

"We stop, Dad. We destroy the model, and we never speak of this day again. Maybe with time, these memories will dim. Do you agree with me, Neil? Dad, you agree with me, don't you? I have to get some fresh air."

"Professor, I will never be able to forget the words that I saw and the images those words created. Yes, I do wish they were different—that the outcome was more positive, but it is what it is. I know that

I do not have the life experiences that you have, but I vote to see this to the end."

The professor was about to speak when Lisa came back through the door. "Dad, you and Grandpa are the wisest men I have ever known. I heard Neil's opinion. Whatever you say, I will agree too."

To their surprise, the professor did not immediately respond but rather went back to the screen and, for several minutes, read the screen in silence. After a while, he walked back to the table and sat down.

"When my father so confidently said that I would be the one to make this discovery, he said there was a reason that I was involved. He made me promise that we would never use the information for personal gain. But interestingly, he never said what I should do with the information. He just said that we would know what to do when that time came. Deep down, I believe I am to do something with this discovery. And I do not believe it is to totally deny it ever happened. The decision to what you are going to do is up to you. For me, I have decided to continue on."

Chapter 23

Shimon Arrives

The bell inside the gas station responded as the black SUV ran over the cord that stretched across the driveway. The gas station owner made a mental note that when he got around to it, he needed to remove that bell, as the irritating sound had long ago served its purpose. With sophisticated self-serve gas pumps and the loss of business to that new gas station on the highway, he just didn't need to be awakened from his naps for every Tom, Dick, and Harry that passed this way.

The owner didn't recognize the man in the black SUV. He was relatively short with jet-black hair and a full black beard. *Must be a tourist, maybe a salesman. Just passing through, I guess, or probably just lost.*

The man appeared to be uncomfortable as he approached the gas station owner.

"What can I do for you, mister?"

"I am looking for someone."

"Say, you are the same man who was in here a couple of days ago in a white van."

"No, you got the wrong person."

"Don't think so. I am pretty good with faces. Anyway."

"Do you know where I could find a man by the name of Professor Lange? He is in his fifties, and his daughter, early twenties. There may be another gentleman with them, also twenties."

"No, I can't say that I do. During the tourist season, there are quite a few people who pass this way." It certainly wasn't tourist season, but the owner of the gas station would never volunteer something so personal. That just wasn't how it was done in this part of the world. Plus, the man's mannerism made the gas station skeptical of his motivations.

The man looked around nervously as he reached into his pocket, pulled out a .45, and pointed it at the owner. "You must understand where I am coming from. It is a matter of life and death that I reach the professor. And for you, it may be a matter of life or death if you don't help me."

The owner of the gas station jerked to attention and was visibly shaken by the sight of the gun pointed at him.

"I'll tell you all that I know, but please, don't hurt me. I have a wife and kids."

The man lowered the pistol and placed it back into his coat.

"He is probably in the abandoned cabin about a mile and a half out of town. Story is it is a cabin with a lot of rooms. Some cut right into the mountain. I think that I heard somewhere that somebody was usin' the cabin. It might be the guy you are looking for."

"One and a half miles up this road," repeated the man. "For your sake, you better be telling me the truth."

"Yes, sir. It is the only place between here and five miles that has a gravel road. You can't miss it."

The man walked back toward the black SUV. After a few steps, he turned around.

"By the way, don't bother calling the police. They're looking for this man too."

The owner was still shaking as the man in the black SUV pulled out of the station. He picked up the phone hanging on the wall. There were no police in these parts to call even if he had wanted to.

"Hello, Jimmy, is that you?"

*****

The black SUV pulled off the two-lane country road and turned onto the gravel road. It was exactly one and a half miles, just as the gas station owner said.

Ahead, there was a short but steep drop-off from the main road to the gravel road before the gravel road resumed its steady incline up the mountain. It was dusk, and the man could hardly see ahead of him. The lights from the SUV provided little help.

He certainly did not see the gulley that snaked across the gravel road until it was too late. He tried to brake, which caused the black SUV to slide across the loose gravel mixed with wet clay. The man turned the steering wheel sharply to the right, but he continued to slide, this time sideways down the gravel road. The black SUV did not stop until it wedged itself at the bottom of the gulley. To compound the problem, the recent rainstorm had filled the ditch with water, which was flowing at a rapid pace.

The man grabbed his coat, tapping his pocket to make sure the gun was still inside. He tried to open the door but was fighting the angle of the door against the side of the gulley and the pressure of the flowing water. There was more water than he expected. He looked across at the passenger side, but the same conditions existed there too.

Realizing that he was fighting a lost cause, he rolled down the window. He was a small man, so fitting through the window was not going to be a problem. First was his head, and then his shoulders came through. He sat on the opening of the window with his legs still inside, trying to figure out how he could avoid getting wet. He did not realize that the gulley he had driven into ended twenty yards ahead with a large drop-off down the mountain.

The SUV started to slide. As it slid, the man could feel it picking up speed. The man quickly pulled himself from the window opening and climbed onto the roof. The SUV was now sliding faster and faster.

Not knowing where he was heading, his instincts told him to do something and to do it quickly. The man jumped from the roof to the bank of the gulley just in time. The black SUV did not stop its slide until it came to rest against several trees more than a hundred feet down the side of the mountain.

The sound of the crash reverberated through the opening in the mountain peaks. The man hesitated on the bank of the gulley, attempting to collect his thoughts. His heart was racing at the thought that he would have been killed if he hadn't jumped when he did.

It was a good thing he remembered his coat. The night air was cold against his pants, which had gotten wet after he slid back into the water when he jumped. The gun was safely in one of his coat pockets, his phone in the other. He couldn't think of anything left in the SUV that he needed. At least, he hoped not. It would be treacherous to scale down the mountain to where the black SUV now rested.

He began the walk up the steep incline of the mountainside. It was dark now, with only the light of the full moon to guide him. There did not appear to be a light coming from the direction of the cabin, or at least where he assumed the cabin was located.

How long he had been walking, he did not know. He could not see his watch, which, like him, was not designed for darkness and adventure. Finally, he thought he heard the sound of a door closing, but still, he did not see the light. He continued in the direction he assumed was correct, each step deliberately planting into the slope of the mountain.

He finally reached a small clearing where the land leveled off. The wooded area he had been climbing through ended, and he could see in all directions. Ahead, there appeared smoke coming from two different chimneys.

He sat down for a moment on a boulder to catch his breath and to survey the area. Although there was little light emanating from the cabin, it appeared in the moonlight that the front door was directly ahead of him.

The man at the gas station was right about the cabin too. It appeared to grow right out of the side of the mountain. There did not appear to be another way to access the cabin other than the front door.

He did not bother to reach into his coat for his gun as he walked toward the door. He would not need it. There would be no resistance from the professor.

Approaching the front door, he could see small windows which ran vertically on each side of the door. Curtains obscured any possible view into the room. He hesitated for a moment, listening for any sound coming from inside. There were no voices or movements, and the only sound he heard was the periodic crackling of the fireplace. He turned the knob, and to his surprise, the door was not locked.

He opened the door slowly. Once inside, he canvassed the single room. The cabin was not that big for there to be no sound. Maybe I have the wrong cabin. There were no signs that this was the right one. No family portraits. *Could they have left already? No, the fireplace is going strong.*

He walked through the main room in the direction of the one large bedroom. Entering the bedroom, he saw the large metal door next to the bathroom. It was open, and a light emanated from behind it. The light from the bedroom gave him some perspective as he entered the hallway. The floor did not appear to be finished, almost like he was walking on small rocks. He slowly walked in the direction of a pinhole-size light shining ahead.

The darkness obscured the diminutive figure of a man crouching under a boulder to his left. He did not see the movement occurring behind him until it was too late. The force of the swing caused the large, wooden object to break as it hit his head, and splinters of the wood penetrated his scalp.

Jimmy proudly looked down on the motionless man. He knew he had not killed him, but the man was going to be in some pain for a while. The important thing is that he had protected the professor just as he promised Biltmore—this time, thanks to the tip given by the gas station owner.

Jimmy reached into the coat pocket and removed the man's gun. He thought about carrying the man back to the cabin but decided against it. He was proud of himself and wanted to show the professor what he had done. He reached down and locked his arms under the man's armpits and dragged him in the direction of the large room.

The three were so preoccupied with their work that they did not notice Jimmy enter the room. Jimmy propped the man against a wall opposite the fireplace.

Finally, the professor noticed the man. "My god, Jimmy! What happened?"

"I got a tip that this man was on his way to the cabin. He already threatened the gas station owner with a gun, so I knew he probably meant you harm."

By now, Lisa and Neil had come to where the man was sitting. His eyes were closed, and a small drop of blood trickled down the side of his face. The man appeared to be in his early to midthirties, with a relatively dark complexion and Middle Eastern facial characteristics. A yarmulke covered his head.

"Did you kill him?" Neil asked.

"No. He's not feelin' too good, but he's not dead."

Lisa grabbed a towel and soaked it with cold water from a nearby sink. Bending down, she wiped the man's face. His eyes were glazed over.

"Concussion," said Lisa. "He'll be out for a little while."

"How did he get here?" the professor asked.

"He came off of the main road. Parked there and walked up the side of the mountain. His SUV lost its grip near a ditch and rolled down the incline until a tree stopped it," said Jimmy.

"SUV. What color? Let me guess."

"Black."

"Could it be the same SUV the man was driving who killed Biltmore?"

"Yes, sir. The same one," replied Jimmy.

"Do you think it's the man who killed the two who were chasing me? You said that after he drove the white van over the cliff, he went back and took the black SUV."

"We are going to find out soon," said Lisa. "He is starting to wake up."

The man's eyes opened. He blinked and looked around as if he had been asleep for a century. Though groggy, the man finally spoke. "Professor, we meet again."

The professor looked puzzled. "I'm sorry, but I don't remember meeting you before."

"I was with the group who met with you in New York. My name is Shimon Breuer. It is understandable you do not remember me. My father, Rabbi Breuer, did most of the talking that day."

The professor remembered that the rabbi had introduced him to his son. He recalled that the young man did not say much during the meeting.

"I don't understand. You had a gun, so you must have come to harm us. The rabbi, your father, did not strike me as someone who would promote violence."

Shimon tried to stand up. He quickly became dizzy and sat back down. "I did not come to do you any harm. I will tell you everything, Professor. But may I have some water and pills? I have a terrible headache." He reached back to touch his head. It had already swollen to the size of a lemon. "And some ice for the swelling?"

Lisa headed to the cabin while Shimon slowly moved to the couch by the fireplace.

"Shimon, this is Neil Coles, one of my gifted ex-students. Lisa is my daughter. And you met Jimmy already."

Shimon nodded in Neil's direction before turning to Jimmy. "Yes, unfortunately, I have met Jimmy. He is gifted in his own right."

Jimmy smiled with pride.

"Now, I must assume that you are here to either harm us or to obtain information that you think we have. Or both," said the professor.

Lisa returned to the room. Shimon hesitated only long enough to pop the medicine and drank a little water. Lisa applied the ice to his swollen head.

"Professor, I am here to warn you that you are in serious danger. The same people who killed your father want you dead. They killed your father looking for information they mistakenly thought that he had. They will kill you. These are dangerous people."

"You are not telling us anything that we do not already know. Why would we have escaped the city to this small cabin with its modest accessories if we were not aware of that danger? If that is all you have come to tell me, I must assume that you, too, have come to harm us."

Shimon adjusted the position of the ice against his head.

"I realize that there must be good faith on my part if you are going to believe me. Did they not try to kill you two days ago at the cabin overlooking the lake?"

"How do you know this?"

"I was in the white van. I passed you on the road."

"You were the white van who hit the two men?"

"Yes. Surely, you realize that if I had not been there, they would have killed you."

The professor glanced at Jimmy, who was listening to Shimon's story.

"And if I meant you harm, I could have that day."

Again, the professor nodded. This was not the time to tell Shimon that Jimmy was also there. He had enough of Jimmy for the time being.

"After I saw that they were dead, I loaded them in the white van and drove it over the ledge. I took the black SUV because I knew it was equipped with a GPS sensor. If I continued to drive it for a few days, maybe that would delay them sending someone else. That would give me enough time to find you."

"When you say 'them,' who are you referring to?"

"The same people who killed your father."

"The American. Larry Haggerty?"

"Yes."

The professor wanted to believe everything Shimon said. If there was one thing the professor desperately needed, it was an ally. Up to this point, he felt like it was him, Neil, and Lisa against the world.

"I still do not know what purpose killing me serves their purposes."

"Professor. There is a story circulated that you had uncovered a way to predict the future from the codes."

"What!" exclaimed the professor.

"Wait, the story gets better. Not only had you advanced the code research, but you had contacted agents in foreign countries, enemies of the United States and Israel, to sell the code formula. Why do you think there are two countries also looking for you?"

"That is crazy. Even if I had discovered what they are saying, I am a loyal American. I would never even consider betraying my country."

"I know that, and my father knows that. But don't you think there are forces in play here that will do anything to undermine your efforts?"

The professor shook his head in disbelief. He could not remove the thought that there were people who believed he was a traitor.

"And this idea of determining the future from the codes is a preposterous notion," said the professor.

"You say one thing, but your actions tell another story. Are you hiding in a cabin in the mountains surrounded by computers just to prove the codes expose historical events? I think not. You had already satisfied yourself that they are capable of doing that."

The professor could not argue against what appeared so obvious. "I don't know what value this would have to other countries, anyway. Don't you think that if these so-called future events were unfavorable to a particular country, they would exercise their 'free will' to change whatever it is so that the unfavorable outcome is changed?"

"You tell me, Professor. We have had prophecies written in the Old Testament about Israel that my people were keenly aware of. Did they change their ways? No. And is your New Testament not filled with prophecies about the end of time? And have we, as a civilization, said we will do whatever it takes to avoid these outcomes? Again, I would say no. Yet our arrogance as a people says that no one, not even God, will tell us what to do or how to live. And then what happens? We inexorably travel down that very slippery slope foretold many years ago."

The professor knew Shimon was right.

Shimon continued, "I know you have uncovered the deep-hidden meaning of the codes. And if you tell me you have not, I will tell you that it is just a matter of time before you do."

"And what gives you the confidence that we will make this discovery that you speak of?"

"You have all the important components: enough computer capacity and unrivaled scientific and mathematic minds at work."

"Both of which the American Corporation has, arguably more so."

"Yes, the American has all of those things. But they lack two important ingredients."

The professor was intrigued.

"The American Corporation lacks the creativity to apply the knowledge they have. They are lost when it comes to even knowing where to start, much less how, or should I say where, to apply that computer power."

"And the second ingredient?"

"Recently, you picked up the one ingredient the American Corporation will never have—faith."

"Need I remind you that I am a scientist? Faith is what my father had. I rely on proof, evidence."

"Are faith and science incompatible? I don't think so, and neither do you. If you did at one time, I don't believe you do now. I think it would surprise you how much faith you actually have."

"Even if you are correct, I am not sure that I understand how that fits into this whole process."

"Sir, in time, you will know exactly what I mean."

The professor recognized that was a better discussion for another time. "I still don't make the connection of why you risked your life to tell me these things."

Shimon took the ice pack off his head. He could feel his head throbbing as blood was desperately trying to reach the swollen area.

"It was my father who, after our meeting in New York, was convinced that if the codes could reveal more, you were the only one to find them. He saw something in you that none of us saw. Unfortunately, he made the mistake of telling the American Corporation that same thing. They recognized that once you did not join them, you became their competition.

"The American Corporation treated you like a competitor and took the classic path corporations take. First, they tried to acquire you, you know, one corporation buying another corporation. That didn't work with you. You were not for sale. If they could not buy you, they would attempt to marginalize you. They attempted by spreading rumors about your motivations and your relations with foreign countries. If all failed, they would ultimately attempt to destroy you."

"And by destroy, you mean—"

"Professor, their term for destruction is your term for murder."

"And by destroying me, they ensure that if they don't find the hidden meanings of the codes, no one will."

"Exactly, Professor. And make no mistake about it. They will attempt to destroy you."

"What is in it for you?"

"We have seen enough bloodshed already. My father and the other Israeli scientists regret that we made a pack with the American Corporation. Mr. Gold convinced my father that the discovery could help ensure the future sovereignty of Israel. When we heard that they had killed your father, that was the final straw. We wanted out."

"And you have told the American Corporation?"

"Our position has been communicated to their principal, Mr. Larry Haggerty."

The professor was not surprised by this information. He suspected as much. "The rabbi could wash his hands of this whole situation at any time. I still don't understand why you came here and risk your life?"

Shimon's face became very serious. "Professor, we got involved in this project because we saw—very selfishly, I must add—how the codes could do things for our religion, our culture, and our country. At first, we wanted the Americans to find the ultimate messages of the codes in the worst way. Now, now we pray that they remain hidden for eternity."

"What has caused this change of heart?"

"What good can come from a program that is motivated by death, greed, and personal advancements?"

The professor suspected there was more to this piety, but he would have to wait for that answer.

"So for different reasons than the American Corporation, you need to make sure that we don't succeed also."

"Actually, I am here to request that you discontinue your search for the hidden meanings of the codes."

The professor looked at Lisa and then Neil before he spoke. "Shimon, you have given us much to think about. And I am sure you are still in pain. Please use one of the couches in the cabin to rest for now. Jimmy can assist you in any way that you need. We will talk more about this later."

Shimon was in no position to argue with the professor. He got up slowly, holding his head still. Just a slight movement made the pain unbearable. "I suppose that is a good idea for now."

Shimon started to walk in the direction of the cabin. Lisa walked ahead, shining a flashlight. Jimmy started to follow before the professor grabbed Jimmy's arm and signaled for him to stay behind. The professor waited a few seconds to make sure that Shimon could not hear his instructions.

"Jimmy, I appreciate what you have done for us. Biltmore would be very proud of you. But I need you to do something more. Shimon came here tonight to destroy our operations. Would he have killed us? That I don't know. I don't think so, but I cannot be sure. What I do know is that he would have destroyed all of our equipment and programs so that we could not finish our work."

"Yes, sir," replied Jimmy.

"I need you to watch this man's every move when he is not with us. Did he have a gun?"

Jimmy reached into his pocket, pulled out the gun, and proudly showed it to the professor.

"Good. How about a cell phone?"

Jimmy looked a little puzzled. "I don't know, sir."

The professor reached into his pocket and pulled out his cell phone. "When he sleeps tonight, look through his things. If you find a phone like this, please bring it to me."

"Yes, sir." Jimmy walked toward the cabin.

"Thanks again, Jimmy."
Jimmy smiled proudly as he walked away.

*****

Somewhere in Lisa's past, maybe as a Girl Scout or maybe later in premed, when the thought of being a doctor was still strong, she had learned not to let someone with a head injury fall asleep immediately. She would mother Shimon, making sure he stayed awake for at least another hour. Jimmy remained at a distance, periodically touching the gun in his pocket to make sure it was still there.

The pain in Shimon's head finally subsided enough for him to eat. A little food and the culmination of the last few days of the hunt finally took their toll. Shimon fell asleep on the couch. Lisa returned to the large room while Jimmy remained on watch.

The professor and Neil were seated at a table when Lisa walked in. She updated them on Shimon's status.

"We are going to have to make a decision soon," said the professor.

"A decision?" Lisa asked.

"Actually, we need to make two decisions. We need to decide where to go. It will not be safe here in twenty-four hours. Between the American Corporation and Shimon, this place is going to be swarming with people."

"What is the other decision?" Neil asked.

The professor hesitated before he spoke as if to weigh every word. "Now that we have discovered the model, the holy grail, we must decide what to do with this information."

"But, Professor, we have not finished our work. There is more to be learned. We have just scratched the surface," replied Neil, his arms outstretched for effect.

The professor was going to respond when Jimmy walked into the room. "Professor, I brought the phone like you asked."

He handed the phone to the professor. "Unless you need me, I'll go back to the cabin in case he wakes up."

"Thank you, Jimmy,"

The professor immediately searched for the last calls received by Shimon. Call no. 1: "Two one two, that's a New York area code. It was received at six thirty tonight. That would have been right before Jimmy brought him in. A call from Israel at 8:30 p.m. That had to be a few hours or so after Biltmore was shot.

The professor tapped on the number from New York. It rang once before it was answered.

"Shimon. I was waiting for conformation before I left. What's going on? Do you have the professor?"

The professor immediately terminated the call.

Within seconds, the phone rang. The caller ID identified it as Steve Gold. He was calling from the same number the professor had dialed. The professor turned the phone off and threw it into the fireplace.

Neil asked, "Who was that?"

"His name is Steve Gold. He is affiliated with the Israeli group. He was the guy who attempted to recruit me to work for the American."

"And this Gold guy, I sense you have your doubts about him."

"Yes, Neil. In many ways, he is no different from Haggerty."

"And Shimon?"

"Shimon, I am not so sure. When he wakes up, he will have a lot of explaining. Once we get those answers, we will leave."

"But you said we needed to decide where we are going," said Lisa.

"I have decided where we are going," replied the professor.

"Where?" both Neil and Lisa asked almost in unison.

"Israel."

*****

There was no light shining through the windows when Shimon woke up. He did not know how long he had been asleep, but he assumed it was early morning. His head was still aching, but the pain was now tolerable. The spot where Jimmy applied the wooden object was still sore and swollen. He sat on the edge of the couch before standing up to make sure that he did not succumb to vertigo.

Looking around, he was surprised there was no one else in the room. The cold morning mountain air permeated the cabin. No one had kept the fire going in the fireplace through the night, which he assumed meant that he had been left unattended.

Shimon reached for his coat, which he had hung on a chair next to the couch. Putting it on, he instinctively tapped the right pocket. His wallet was there. He tapped the left pocket. It was not there. *The professor has taken my phone.* He desperately needed to make a call, and no phone was visible in the cabin.

He rubbed his eyes as he walked to the bathroom next to the hall leading to the large room. He had to figure out how to get control of this situation. Too much was at stake, and there was little time left.

The drawer of the table next to the bathroom was slightly cracked. He quickly glanced around. Seeing no one, he opened the drawer. To his amazement, inside the drawer was his gun. He grabbed it. *It is loaded, just as I left it.* He stuffed it deep inside his coat pocket. *That Jimmy guy really screwed up this one.*

He splashed some cold water on his face and headed for the large room. *I am in control again. No mistakes this time.*

The three were working at their computers when Shimon entered the room. They casually looked up from their work.

"Shimon, how are you feeling now?" the professor asked.

Lisa went to pour a cup of coffee for Shimon as he sat down on the couch.

"I feel a little better." He looked around the room. Jimmy was nowhere to be seen. *Yes, I am in control.*

"How is your work progressing, Professor?"

"We are almost finished with our work here. We have done what we needed to do and have found what we were looking for," responded the professor nonchalantly.

"Oh," replied Shimon, trying as hard as he could to camouflage his excitement. "So you have found the hidden messages of the codes?"

"Oh, no," said the professor. "Your father found the hidden messages of the codes. We just took what he found to a different, let's say, a deeper level."

"You have seen into the future, Professor?"

"As I said, we have found another level that perhaps your father had not yet found."

"Or the American Corporation."

"I do not know what they may have found."

"Let me ask again, Professor. Have you seen into the future?"

"We have seen what the codes have let us see."

"And the future, Professor? Is it a bright future?"

"I suppose that depends on whose future you are talking about. For some, it is very bright. For others, there is no future, at least on earth."

"I don't understand. For some, ah, people, the future is bad? What do the codes say about those people?"

The professor sat back in his chair. "Shimon, I have said enough."

Before Shimon made his move, he needed to know the most important thing. "Professor. I respect that you chose not to tell me some things. I am certainly in no position to demand that you do. Can you tell me just one thing? I promise not to inquire any more deeply."

"And that is?"

"I must assume that you have discovered the way to advance my father's discovery. Yes?" Shimon's eyes were riveted on the professor for any facial expression that might give away his answer.

"We have found that at the level the rabbi discovered the codes, they tell us certain things, certain historical information. They do not show us the future. To see the future, you have to go to another, let's just say, another dimension."

"And you have found that dimension, Professor?"

"Our model employs two new dimensions, yes. Perhaps everything we need to know about the future will be in those dimensions. Perhaps more dimensions will show us even more detail. Only time and further testing will allow us to know for sure."

Shimon had heard enough. The professor had to be stopped. He staggered from the couch to the wall next to the fireplace. There were no openings behind him, and he could see both the hallway door and the door to the side of the mountain. He reached down into his pocket and pulled out the gun.

"I am sorry, Professor, but I can't allow you to keep this information. It is too sacred. We must have it."

Shimon pointed the gun in the general direction to where the three were standing.

"We? Do you mean your father or you? I can tell him what he needs to know. Violence is not the answer."

"This is not for my father. Don't you understand? His reason for this information is totally different from my reason. He has no concept of the financial rewards of this information, nor does he care. He just wants to know the future of his homeland, Israel. I have no interest in that."

"Are you telling me that you work on behalf of Haggerty?"

"More like a partnership, but that is going to change soon. Your knowledge is my power, Professor."

"When did you have this change of heart? You were working against Haggerty's group just two days ago," said the professor.

"Oh, you mean the incident near the cabin on top of the hill? It was not as it appeared. You see, they didn't shoot the big mountain man. I did. I was parked up the hill. When they got near the cabin, I shot him—from behind. It was actually a very good shot. You almost got in the way, Professor."

"Why did you kill Biltmore?" asked the professor, not at all convinced that Shimon was telling the truth or that his motivations were as he described.

"As long as he was around, I was worried that I could not get to you. Once he was eliminated, well, you were an easy target."

"And the two men on the road?"

"I thought that Haggerty needed to understand what was at stake here and who was in charge. He needed to take me seriously. You see, from the time you met with my father, I knew you had what it took to find this information. I could not take a chance that Haggerty's men would screw it up."

"And my father?"

"That was Haggerty's work. Regretful and unnecessary. No, I did not get involved until my father pulled the plug on the project. You should know the truth. It was the murder of your father that pushed my father to say enough. He did not have the heart to continue. But you must understand what I am saying. My father discovered the codes. It was his knowledge exclusively. It was my birthright. Not yours, not Haggerty's."

"Shimon, we are not working on the codes so that we can benefit personally from any discoveries."

"Professor, don't take me for a fool. Why would you go through the hardship and heartache you have gone through if you didn't want to benefit from it personally? This could make you rich and famous."

"Shimon, you may not understand this, but I have already benefited from the discovery."

"That statement is preposterous. How could you have already benefitted from your findings? What do you mean by that?" Shimon's hand was shaking even more.

Jimmy, crouching behind the door, heard the details of Biltmore's death. Jimmy was not a violent man, but it took every ounce of his willpower not to kill the man. He took a deep breath before he opened the door.

As he opened the door, a rush of adrenaline filled Jimmy's small body. His relentless charge toward Shimon was punctuated by the sound of the gunshot. He didn't drop until his body slammed into Shimon's body. The gun went flying.

Shimon tried to catch himself, twisting around, reaching for the wall, his arms outstretched. His feet couldn't keep his balance and flew out from under him, leaving him totally defenseless as he fell to the floor.

Spinning and with nothing to protect his fall, Shimon could not see the iron poke that had been unexplainably wedged upside down against the side of the fireplace. The prongs of the poke cut right under his shoulder near his heart out through his back. He lay motionless.

Lisa gasped as the professor ran toward Jimmy. He was conscious as he rolled over onto his back. There was no evidence of a gunshot anywhere. Jimmy sat up, looking in Shimon's direction.

"I didn't mean to kill him."

"I thought he shot you. Are you okay?" asked the professor.

"I'm okay."

"I could have sworn that he had dead aim on you," said Neil.

"I think that he did. Well, he practically had it stuck right into my stomach."

"But I don't understand," said the professor.

"He didn't have bullets."

"Huh. I heard the gunshot," said the professor.

"I took them out last night while he was asleep."

"You did what?"

"When I first hit him in the hall, I took his gun. Last night, I took out the bullets and replaced them with blanks. Then I hid it in a place where I figured he would find it. I figured that if he used it against you, then that would tell you what kind of person he was. Professor, I promised you and Biltmore that I would protect you."

The professor turned back to where Shimon was lying to see if he could render any aid. It was obviously too late for that. He quickly turned his head away from the gruesome scene, as did the others. None of them could stand to look at the contorted body that now lay still beside the fireplace.

They turned their attention back to Jimmy, who had stood up and was dusting himself off.

"So you heard the part about Biltmore?"

"Yes, sir."

"I'm sorry," said the professor.

"It didn't change anything. Biltmore ain't coming back. But the man wasn't telling the truth. He was not the man who killed Biltmore."

"Jimmy, you are wise in many ways. We will never be able to thank you enough."

"That's right, Jimmy. Thank you," echoed Neil. Lisa nodded as she touched him in his hand.

Jimmy walked to where Shimon was lying and locked his arms underneath Shimon's. "I will lay him in the cave until we can give him a proper burial. We can't tell the authorities."

"You are right about that, Jimmy. Unfortunately, there is no one we can trust now," said the professor.

Chapter 24

Duplicity

As instructed, Steve Gold waited for the phone call. It finally came at 7:00 a.m., which was early afternoon in Jerusalem. Steve had requested the call be placed to his cell phone.

Rabbi Breuer sounded distraught. "Steve, you gave the American the message regarding our position on the partnership going forward?"

"Yes, without equivocation, Rabbi."

"And how was the message received?"

"Actually, with a degree of indifference, Rabbi. At this point, they believe we offer them nothing more of value."

"I assume they have not made any significant advances in the research."

"I think that is a safe assessment, Rabbi."

"And they are not going to make any significant advances. They lack what it takes."

"Then we can feel comfortable that we have washed our hands completely with this association."

"It is the professor they want more than anything right now."

"Yes, Rabbi, you are correct about that."

"Steve, I must tell you some most distressing news. We have reason to believe that my son will try to make contact with the professor. He abruptly left for the States at the same time as you."

"Yes?"

"Our information is that he has rented a white van."

There was a white van in the parking lot across from the hotel when he left for his meeting with Larry Haggerty.

"You must find my son and stop him. Do you understand?"

Stop him. What does he mean by that? "Do you know where Shimon is?" At this stage, Steve could act with the best of them.

"We understand that the professor is using a cabin in the mountains of North Carolina, just north and west of Charlotte. We believe Shimon is there or will be soon. Are you in Raleigh?"

That is why I wanted him to call me on the cell phone. "Ah, yes, I am in my hotel."

"Head in that direction. Someone will call you back with specific instructions."

This is going to get interesting, thought Steve as he hung up the phone. He opened the curtains to the window of his hotel room overlooking the valley below. It had been over twelve hours since Steve last spoke with Shimon. Then there was another call from Shimon that never connected, which Steve thought was strange.

The plan that Shimon and Steve contrived was now in place. Both were convinced the professor had discovered the model that would unlock the predictability of the codes. Shimon would make his move on the professor first. After he got the material, he would call Steve and agree on where to meet.

Steve could not shake the lingering doubts of whether he and Shimon were on the same page. It was clear what his intentions were, but it was out of character for Shimon to have this sudden interest in the research.

And the matter of the phone call Steve was to receive after Shimon got the material. It never came. Had Shimon encountered some problems? Had he met with more resistance from the professor than he expected? Had he taken the material for himself? Shimon could not have possibly figured out Steve's motives. *And if he did, he certainly did not know my plan. I have not shared my plans with anyone. No, I guess I am being paranoid for no reason.*

Steve let his mind wonder as he put his clothes into the suitcase. Growing up together, he and Shimon had been best friends for as long as he could remember. They would go away to summer camps and vacations with their families and even agreed to go to the same university.

Shimon's relationship with his father and his faith were a model of perfection. Shimon never rebelled against his father's wishes or fought the "old world" traditions. In that regard, he and Shimon were complete opposites. Maybe that is why they got along so well for so many years.

Steve, on the other hand, struggled to throw off all the trappings of tradition and faith. My goodness, it's the twenty-first century, the age of innovation, of change—the age to question, not accept, the beliefs of parents.

For Shimon, there was value in the belief held by his ancestors for generation after generation. For Steve, value was always measured with a dollar sign.

Those differences made these recent events seem even stranger. Did Shimon really want to profit from this research, or were there other reasons? Profiting would have certainly been out of character, but he knew he would find out soon.

There was a battle waging between them and their ideologies, whether they acknowledged it or not. Which side won would have a profound impact on the way the events of the next few days would unfold. To the degree it did, neither one could ever have imagined.

Steve couldn't wait any longer for Shimon's call. He had the directions and would soon be heading to the cabin. The directions were clear and straightforward. He only wished that everything else about this matter was as clear and straightforward.

Chapter 25

The Chase Begins

Neil and Lisa packed all the charts and three-dimensional figures, and Jimmy stacked them in the same cave where he had placed Shimon. He promised the professor he would bury them beside Biltmore's body. The computers were resting at the bottom of the lake, thanks to the efforts of Jimmy and his bass boat. The professor kept the important material, including three zip drives, in his briefcase, which he carried with him at all times.

The professor had the foresight to purchase the airline tickets several weeks ago, something that did not go unnoticed by Neil. Among many other things along the way, it was a mystery to Neil that the professor could have possibly had the confidence that their research would have progressed this far.

The three started their mile-long trek to a destination where Jimmy would be waiting with a truck to carry them to the airport.

"I need to know something. How did you know to get three tickets?" asked Neil.

"I convinced my father that I could get you involved in this project," said Lisa, smiling.

"Tricked me is more like it."

"Guilty."

"But how did you know I would have my passport with me?"

"That wasn't hard," replied the professor. "You have been known to take junkets to this casino and that casino all over the world and sometimes at a moment's notice."

"How would you know that?"

"Lisa keeps me informed."

Neil started to question how Lisa would know such a thing when his eyes met Lisa's. Among all her enduring qualities, it was her eyes that had always captivated Neil. If it is true that the eyes are the window to the soul, then her eyes are the window to a pure and beautiful soul. They were the one thing that could almost immobilize Neil. When he looked into her eyes, it was nature's own lie detector. If he tried to lie, she could tell immediately.

"I know it was dark when I came to the cabin the first time, but I don't remember this path," said Neil.

"There are several ways to get to the cabin and several ways to get out. The first time, we came the back way through the woods to ensure maximum cover. The highway is closer to going another way, but we don't dare go that way. It is too easily seen. This way will take us to the opposite side of the lake, where we should be able to leave unnoticed," said the professor.

"Unnoticed by whom?" asked Neil.

"We know that Shimon's presence here did not go unnoticed by the American Corporation. Once they realized they lost contact with their operatives, they had to make their move. My guess is that before the end of today, this place will be crawling with interested parties, all of whom want to do us harm."

"And will you tell us why we are going to Israel?" asked Neil, breathing heavily from the last incline. "Better yet. Will you tell us how you knew we would be going to Israel when you bought the tickets?"

"I will tell you what I know when we are safely on the plane."

"How about Jimmy?" asked Lisa.

"I don't think it is safe for Jimmy to stay here, but I could not convince him to leave. This is his home, not to mention that he does not own a passport. I gave him some money to spend a few nights in Charlotte until the commotion died down. After everyone realizes that we have left for good and are not coming back, then it will be safe for Jimmy to return home. When he returns, he will bury Biltmore along with our research."

All three of them were breathing heavily as they reached the top of the mountain overlooking the lake. They sat down on some boulders. From this vantage point, they could see the lake below. The professor paused long enough to look around and appreciate the natural beauty of this place.

He would miss this place even though it represented a contradiction in his life. On the one hand, it had been the place where he experienced heartache and more intrigue than he cared to endure. It also was the place where he discovered not just the power of the codes but also the power of sacrifice.

Enough nostalgia. I need to focus on the task at hand.

"Professor. I thought Jimmy was picking us up. There are no roads up here," said Neil.

"He is not picking us up here. We have to get to the other side of the lake."

"But how do we get to the other side of the lake? That has to be a two- or three-mile walk," questioned Lisa.

"Follow me."

With that, the professor started down some steps that appeared to be chiseled into the side of the mountain. The steps were only wide enough for them to walk single file.

About two-thirds of the way down, the path switched back, almost as if it was going underneath the mountain. Continuing down, the steps stopped at a lagoon that had been formed under the mountain. Waiting for the threesome, tied to a rock, was Jimmy's bass boat.

Though he had never seen this feature of the mountain before, the professor could understand its function. Those in the business of making illegal whiskey had to have ways of escape from the authorities.

The professor looked at his watch. It was almost 5:00 p.m., and Jimmy was to pick them up at 5:15 p.m. They climbed into the boat, and the professor started the engine. They would have to hurry to keep the strict schedule the professor had set.

It only took a few minutes to transverse the lake. It was a bright, sunny, late fall day, and the air was refreshing. The lake was a beautiful blue color and as smooth as glass. Memories of those days fishing with his father briefly interrupted the adrenalin he felt from the chase.

The rendezvous point was a section of heavy brush on the opposite side of the lake where they could hide until Jimmy arrived.

The instructions given to Jimmy were clear. If anyone followed him, he was to continue driving past the rendezvous point. He would go through the routine again in thirty minutes.

*****

Steve's rental car struggled as it tried to climb the steep incline of the mountain. It was clearly not a car suited for this terrain. He pulled off the side of the road to look at the directions again. The view across the mountains was spectacular, but the drop-off was a clear reminder of his fear of heights. He knew he was close to the cabin. Shimon's directions had been spot-on.

As he looked around, he couldn't help but notice where a patch of thick brush was leaning almost all the way to the ground. If it was from a wayward car, there were no tire tracks to indicate that the car had tried to stop.

Steve turned off the engine and pulled the parking brake. His curiosity had gotten the better of him as he walked to the edge of the crevice and peered below. It looked like a car was lying wedged between two trees several hundred feet below. He strained to get a better view. Upon his first view, it looked more like an SUV. *Oh my god. It's a black SUV. Shimon said he was driving a black SUV.*

Steve fought the temptation to scale down the steep incline. It had taken him much longer to find the cabin than planned, and there were only a few hours of sunlight left, and he had an important destination to make. *A black SUV. Could that be Shimon's black SUV? Is he inside? That would explain why he did not call me. If that really is him, that will make this whole facade of cooperation a moot point, at least.* He had a feeling that the SUV might contain the answer to his question, but that answer would have to wait for now. He was late and had a plan to carry out.

The directions indicated his destination was only a few more yards up the road. The pavement gave way to gravel and wet, red clay that the small rental car was not equipped to maneuver. He wouldn't even try. He would walk from here.

His thirty-something-year-old body was out of shape, and it reminded him of that on every step as he scaled the steep incline. Fortunately, there was still enough light to see a cabin ahead.

Out of breath, Steve paused just outside the cabin. There was no sound whatsoever coming from the cabin, and the fire in the fireplace appeared to be almost entirely burned out. He looked for another opening or door, but there was none in sight. He turned the handle. It opened, and he went inside.

He walked through the bedroom to a hallway that was partially lit by a light coming from the opposite direction. He continued down the hallway to a metal door that opened to a large, well-lit, and empty room.

They have already left, he thought. Looking around, it didn't appear there were any more rooms they could be in. *They are gone.*

He turned to walk back in the direction of the cabin when he heard a noise coming in that direction. He started to call out but decided against it. Instead, his instincts told him to hide.

He scampered back to an opening near a side door. There was just enough room between two rocks, which the room wrapped around to accommodate an adult of his size. The sound got louder as the figure approached the room.

Steve knew himself well enough to know that he was not mentally or physically equipped for this level of suspense and intrigue. He tried to take shallow breaths as the figure entered the room. He strained to get a view between the crevices of the rocks. Finally, the figure came into sight. Steve gasped, surely loud enough, he thought, that the man could hear it. *My god! It's Larry Haggerty.*

Haggerty took deliberate steps, taking his time to canvas the room. A gun was prominently held in his right hand.

"Damn," Haggerty said out loud. He made a gesture like he wanted to kick something, but there was nothing to kick except the wall. Haggerty walked to the fireplace, where he knelt down and held his hand above the coals that were still simmering. As he did, he placed the gun on the floor. Steve momentarily thought of trying to surprise Haggerty but quickly dismissed the idea.

"One hour, two at the most," he said to himself out loud.

Before he stood up, he bent even lower to the floor. There was a circle of dried blood on the bricks in front of the fireplace. He could see that the stains continued in the direction of an outside door. Haggerty followed the path, which brought him perilously close to where Steve was hiding. Steve held his breath. *They cleaned up the area pretty well*, thought Haggerty.

Haggerty didn't care to be bothered with details of what might have happened. He had one and only one mission, and that was to find the professor. Unless it was the professor's blood, it didn't matter to him. He had seen enough as he headed back to the cabin at a quick pace. *They could not have gone far in just a short period of time.*

Steve waited in the cabin long enough to be certain that Haggerty had left. He had no way to defend himself, and he was not going to take any chances that Haggerty was still hanging around.

It was during this wait that Steve got the break that he was looking for. While standing at the spot where the blood was dried, he noticed that there was some paper in the fireplace that hadn't yet caught fire. He grabbed them using his shoe to extinguish the portion of the paper that was still smoldering.

The fire had damaged the paper's edges, but the main part of the contents was still intact. It was a copy of the professor's travel itinerary.

The professor is heading for Israel. Steve pulled out his phone. He needed to make an important call. No, that would have to wait. He needed to get to the airport.

*****

The bass boat nestled into a patch of bulrushes where the professor tied to a wooden dock that was totally obscured by the dense vegetation. The professor looked at his watch. It was 5:15 p.m., and Jimmy was nowhere in sight: 5:30 p.m., and still no Jimmy. Finally, at 5:45 p.m., the professor saw the truck approaching through an opening in the pine trees.

"Okay, everybody. He appears to be alone. Let's get ready to move," said the professor as he collected his briefcase.

The three jumped into the cab of the truck. "Sorry, I am late, Professor. You had a couple of visitors at the cabin. They just left, so we have a jump on them."

"A couple of visitors? I assume one was Larry Haggerty," said the professor, as if he was talking to himself. Jimmy would not know who Larry Haggerty was.

"They weren't together, Professor. One of them was already in the cabin when the next man came in. The first one hid. The second one, he had a gun. He looked very upset."

"I wonder who the other person could be?" asked Neil.

"I'd say the man with the gun was in his forties. The young man was, oh, about thirty, early thirties."

"I take it that they did not find Shimon?"

"No. I laid him in one of the caves behind some rocks."

Jimmy made his way through the low brush of the field and was now on a rock road. There were holes everywhere, and the truck was bouncing around. Lisa, for one, would be happy when they were back on the pavement again. Three more turns, and they reached a small bridge, just large enough for the truck to pass. Jimmy slowed down as he navigated the last few yards. The paved road finally opened in front of them as Jimmy raced to gain speed.

"Don't attract attention by going over the speed limit, Jimmy. I wouldn't be surprised if the highway patrol was involved in this whole matter."

It took an hour to reach the Charlotte International Airport, just in time to complete the necessary interrogations before boarding EL AL Airlines to Israel. The professor produced an invitation from the Department of Mathematics at Hebrew University to provide the

EL AL screener. The process was smoother than he expected. Before he knew it, they were in flight—destination, Tel Aviv, Israel.

The professor looked forward to the flight. It would give him a chance to collect the thoughts that had been swirling around in his head for the past few days. He had an idea where this adventure was taking him, but he knew there were many more surprises ahead.

Chapter 26

Escape To Israel

Steve Gold did not have time to return the rental car. He parked in the "no-parking" zone beside the drop-off area of the terminal and rushed to the ticket counter. He would use diplomatic immunity for that petty criminal act, but he had no choice. An airplane ticket would be waiting for him inside, and a parking ticket would be waiting for him when he returned home.

He could take no chance that the professor might recognize him. His first-class ticket allowed him the luxury of boarding after the professor had taken his seat in the main section of the plane. An early disembark would also preserve his secrecy.

*****

Larry Haggerty's connections ran deep throughout government agencies and even to local law enforcement, and he was not timid about using this power. On this occasion, the highway patrol was able to identify the red truck leaving the small mountain town and the direction it was heading. That information was enough to convince Haggarty that the professor was heading to Charlotte. At speeds in excess of one hundred miles per hour, it did not take him long to catch up to the red truck. He followed the truck at a safe distance all the way to the Charlotte International Airport. *Where is the professor heading?* The answer to part of that question became evident as the red truck headed to the Concourse C drop-off area for international flights. *The professor is leaving the country.* There was no way he could stop the professor from boarding the plane without causing a major scene. He would have to rely on the surveillance of his people in whatever country he was heading to keep track of the professor's whereabouts.

Mystery solved. It appeared from the gate where the truck stopped that the professor and his group were heading to Israel. If his final destination was Israel, Haggerty had ways of monitoring his every move.

Right now, he needed to gather as much information as possible. It was clear that the professor was not bringing his computers, so the driver of the truck or, if he was lucky, the truck's contents might just provide all the information he needed.

Haggerty tapped the gun in the pocket of his coat. *The kid is no match for my persuasive capabilities. I will get what I need, and I may not even have to follow the professor to Israel.*

He stayed back as, one by one, the professor, Neil, and Lisa exchanged their goodbyes with Jimmy. Haggerty was totally void of sentiment or emotion. When he saw Jimmy wipe his eyes, it did not register with him at all.

Jimmy pulled the truck out of the drop-off area and gained speed as he headed in the direction of the interstate. Once at full speed, Jimmy darted across all three highway lanes, avoiding traffic. If his instincts were right, the black SUV that followed him most of the way to Charlotte and parked at the terminal as the professor was leaving would be right behind him. Jimmy had not told the professor about the black SUV. He figured the group had enough already to worry about. And after all, they were now safely inside the airport.

Immediately, he saw the blinking lights behind him. He remembered what the professor said. *We cannot trust anyone. There are those in high places who want this information.* He crossed back to the inside lane and slammed the gas pedal to the floor, but the little red truck was no match for the patrol car. His only hope was to turn at the first available exit and possibly lose them in traffic. But as fate would have it, Jimmy picked a little used exit that led to an older section of town.

To make matters worse, Jimmy got stuck behind a caravan of food trucks heading for their spot in the downtown commercial district.

The patrol car was gaining on him, and another patrol car had joined the chase. Jimmy knew he could not outrun the patrol cars. *He had to protect the professor.*

Jimmy hit the brakes, fishtailing the back of the truck so that it was now heading in the opposite direction. The patrol car did not anticipate Jimmy's maneuver and couldn't stop in time, almost hitting the truck head-on. Jimmy was almost back to the interstate when a black SUV appeared on the street ahead. It was weaving back and forth across the two-lane street.

Chapter 27

The Missionary

Neil tried to wait patiently until the professor had eaten and rested awhile, but the anxiety of not knowing what might happen next forced him to break his silence.

"Professor, I have two questions that I need for you to answer."

"Let me guess. You want to know why we are going to Israel."

"Yes. That is one."

"And the other?"

"How you knew, three weeks ago, that we would be finished with our research on the very day we left for Israel."

"I'll do my best to answer them. We are in this together, and you need to know what motivates my decisions."

The professor raised the serving tray so that he could turn toward Neil.

"Why are we going to Israel, you ask? It goes back to my meeting with the rabbi in New York. I was very impressed with his credentials and even more of him as a person. I never felt that he or the group he represented wanted to capitalize on the research for personal gain. I sensed that turning the code research into a moneymaking business was very uncomfortable for the rabbi and his group. However, he had been convinced by members of his group that advancing the research would be in the best interest of Israel, particularly as it related to security matters. Unfortunately, his love for his country caused him to compromise his beliefs along the way.

"When I promised my father that we would not personally benefit from these discoveries, I committed to myself that if we made certain discoveries, the holy grail, that I would share some of the discoveries with the rabbi, at least the part about Israel's future."

"Israel's future? I thought we only looked into America's future."

"After we found the reference about America's future, I applied the model to Israel. I worked on it while you and Lisa were packing the material. I was already certain where the *plaintext* reference was. I just needed to apply the model we created."

"And the outcome?"

"In many ways, the outcome is bright for Israel. In fact, as a country that is surrounded by neighbors that hate her, I would say dramatically so."

"Do you wish to share it with me?"

"I think I would like to wait until I meet the rabbi. It will be my gift to him."

Neil decided not to pursue this point with the professor. He was certain that he could not change his mind anyway. "Professor, for someone who, when we started, said we weren't even close to finding the model, we had a lot of confidence that we could finish the research before it was time to leave for Israel."

"I don't think we had much of a choice. You assume that I thought we would be finished when we did. We were going to move after a few days, regardless of our progress. It would not have been safe to stay at the cabin any longer. If we had not found the model, we would have moved to another location. You saw how quickly they found where we were."

"So it was luck that it turned out the way it did."

"I tend to think we had a committed team. And it never hurts for providence to be on your side."

"Providence?"

"Yes. God allowed us to see what only the prophets had ever seen."

Something continued to nag at Neil. For the next two hours, he did not say a word. Even Lisa's attempts at conversation were to no avail. The stewardess offered food, but Neil had no appetite. There was something that he sensed the professor was not telling him. If he was going to put his life on the line, he deserved to know everything. Finally, he could wait no longer.

"Professor, we need to talk."

"Yes, Neil, you appear to be bothered by something, not that we all haven't been on edge the last few days."

"I think there is more to why we are going to Israel than you have told me."

The professor looked at Neil and then at Lisa. He knew they deserved to know everything that he knew. His fatherly instincts were to insulate—to protect them from as much as possible. *After all, they are young. They have seen enough. I know how much this discovery has affected me. I can only imagine what they are thinking. They have seen what no human has ever seen. They have seen the future.*

"Yes, you deserve to know more than I have told you."

Lisa instantly looked up from the book she had been reading.

"When Lisa found the reference to the Ark of the Covenant, you remember that it started a sequence of events which led us, well, it led us to the holy grail. We found the three-dimensional figure, which allowed us to create the model that unlocks the future."

"Yes, and?"

"There was something about that process that seemed incomplete to me."

"Incomplete? I don't understand," asked Neil.

"Didn't it ever appear to you that the ark was more than just a means that led us to discover the model? Maybe there was something about the ark we should know. While you were working on the final model, I researched all *plaintext* references to the ark I could find."

Neil and Lisa stared intently at the professor.

"Why do I feel you are about to tell us something earthshaking," said Neil.

"*Earthshaking* is an appropriate adjective. During this search, I found in one of the *plaintext* references two hidden instructions: *hide until the Appointed Time* and *hide at the Appointed Place.*"

"Hide until the Appointed Time. Hide at the Appointed Place. What does that mean, Dad?"

"I don't know. But I know someone who does."

"The rabbi?" answered Neil.

"Yes."

"What makes you think he will know what that means?" Neil asked.

"It goes back again to the meeting in New York. Our meeting had ended, and the rabbi said he would walk me to the door. As I was saying goodbye, he said something to me, which, at the time, I didn't think anything about. In a muted tone so that no one around us could hear, he said, *'I will see you again at the Appointed Time.'*"

"He said he would see you at the *Appointed Time*, which is the same words you found in the codes. How could he have known that?" Neil asked.

"At first, I thought maybe that was a Jewish way of saying goodbye. But when I found it in the hidden text, I realized he had found the same words."

"What do you think this means?" asked Neil.

"I think the rabbi knows the *Appointed Time*, and hopefully, he can tell us the *Appointed Place*."

"So you think that the rabbi is expecting us?" asked Lisa.

"Yes, I do."

"But do you even know where to find him?"

"Yes."

"But do you think we can trust him?" asked Neil.

"That is what we have to find out."

Neil decided to get up and stretch his legs. He could not shake the uneasiness that he felt. He was not convinced that the timing of the discovery and the prescheduled trip was as coincidental as the professor said. Nor was he convinced that the professor had been straight about how far the discovery had advanced before he and Lisa got involved. He was satisfied in knowing that whatever the professor's motivation was along the way, it was in his and Lisa's best interest. He would have to wait like everyone else to get his questions answered.

*****

THE REDEMPTION CODES

The EL AL plane landed at the Ben Gurion International Airport. Steve gathered his carry-on bag and quickly exited the plane. Safely out of sight of the remaining passengers, Steve waited for the professor to exit. He was sure he would recognize the professor even though it had been awhile since he last saw him.

Steve didn't have to wait long. The professor exited the plane, his briefcase under his arm, Neil and Lisa beside him. Steve wanted to make his move, knowing that what he was looking for was probably in the professor's briefcase. But this was too risky an area to make a scene. Instead, he followed them to the cab stand.

The professor settled into the back seat of the cab between Neil and Lisa. The Palestinian cab driver half-turned to acknowledge his passengers.

"Dan Tel Aviv Hotel," said the professor.

The professor only had an address, which he assumed would not be necessary since the Dan Tel Aviv Hotel was considered one of the finest hotels in Tel Aviv.

The cab trip took less than twenty-five minutes from the airport. The professor, finding out the fare in American dollars, handed the driver the cash.

"No change?"

"No change."

On the walk from the cab to the front door of the hotel, the professor tried to look calm. He had already given instructions to Neil and Lisa. "Just follow me. No conversation."

"Why no conversation?" asked Neil.

"I don't want them to pick up our accent."

"They don't like southerners?" quipped Neil.

The professor did not respond even though he wanted to smile.

They walked through the lobby of the hotel. The professor nodded at one of the gentlemen behind the desk as if he had been there a hundred times. He continued through the lobby to the elevator, which took them to the parking garage. There, he found a dark blue Volvo parked exactly in the location described. He opened the door of the Volvo and reached under the floor mat on the passenger side. A single key was there, just as he had expected.

"Jump in," said the professor as the key turned the ignition.

"I thought we had reservations here?" asked Lisa.

"Technically, we do. I couldn't take the chance that someone would track us."

"So we are not staying here?" asked Lisa.

"No."

"How about the car?" questioned Neil.

"It is owned by a missionary. Friend of my father."

"Missionary…in Israel?" asked Neil incredulously.

"Yes. It sounds kind of strange, doesn't it?"

"If we aren't staying here, where are we staying?" asked Lisa.

"Jerusalem."

*****

According to the GPS, the forty-one-mile drive from the hotel up to Jerusalem should take about an hour. Fortunately, the plane arrived by midafternoon, so it was still daylight during the drive.

"Are we staying with the missionary?" asked Lisa.

"Yes, I believe that will be the safest place for us until we can figure out what to do. Unless they were able to follow us, no one will know we are there."

"Until you make contact with the rabbi," said Neil.

"Which I am not quite ready to do."

"Why?" asked Lisa.

"My instincts tell me that I can trust him."

"But?"

"I would like a little more assurance before we meet."

"And where are you going to get that assurance?" asked Neil.

"That I don't know exactly. I asked the missionary if he could do some checking for me."

"By the way, Professor, what is his name, the missionary?" asked Neil.

"His name is Peter. His wife's name is Mary. Peter and Mary Simmons."

"Certainly, biblical names."

The professor took a hard left and two blocks later took another left. "If I am not mistaken, I just passed the street I was supposed to turn right on." He turned into an alley and backed back onto the street. After traveling one block, he turned left. "Yes, this is his street. Now I need to find the right house."

"I think you mean the right apartment," said Neil.

"You are correct about that. I thought they were individual houses. Actually, there are at least four units in each one," said the professor.

"Try eight," replied Neil.

"They must be really small inside," said Lisa.

"Hello. The professor said he is a missionary. Of course, he isn't going to live in palatial surroundings," said Neil.

"How are we all going to fit there?" asked Lisa.

"We'll have to do the best we can. It is not safe in a hotel for now. Okay, here it is, 6766 Bally Lane."

The professor pulled the Volvo to the curb in front of the apartment. By the time the professor could get out of the car, he was face-to-face with a short, stocky, bald man with bushy eyebrows and a large grin.

"Let me look at you," the man said, bear-hugging the professor. "How long do you think it has been?"

"Mr. Simmons, it is so nice to see you again."

"Thirty years. Has it been thirty years?"

"It has been a long time."

"I think you were just going off to college. Wow, time sure flies."

"Mr. Simmons, I would like for you to meet my daughter, Lisa."

The missionary hugged Lisa before she could even manage a word.

"And this is one of my ex-students, Neil Coles."

Neil immediately stuck out his hand in a gesture of preemptive self-defense.

"Let me help you with your bags."

"That won't be necessary. All that we were able to carry were a couple of handbags. You have already been too kind to let us use your home for the night."

"For the son of Pastor Lange, that is the least I could do."

The apartment was even smaller on the inside than they had pictured. There was a small living room that doubled as a dining room. The kitchen was big enough for one person to work. There was one bedroom and a small bathroom. A small deck stuck out from the rear of the apartment, where a grill took up most of the space. The remaining space was taken up by two bicycles.

"Speaking of Pastor Lange, you didn't mention how he was doing when you called. You said you would fill me in on the details when you arrived."

The professor sat on the end of the couch, making room for Lisa and Neil.

"Look at my manners. My wife would kick me. Please sit down. I know the apartment is not much, but it is plenty big enough for Mary and me."

"Thank you for your hospitality and the use of your car. I know it was a hardship, leaving it in Tel Aviv."

"That is the least that I could do for Jerry's son. Now, your father. I know he has been sick."

"Mr. Simmons, I wanted to tell you in person. I am sorry to report that I have some really bad news."

"Oh, not your father?"

"Yes, my father died a week ago."

"Oh, no. I am so sorry. The stroke…yes, I know he was suffering with it."

The professor did not respond as the missionary stared into his eyes.

"What a good man your father was. He always took care of Mary and me. I wouldn't still be here if it wasn't for all of those times he helped me raise money. He gave me money he said he raised, which I think actually came from his own pocket. I am going to miss him."

"Thank you for those kind comments. I know he loved you and appreciated the work that you do."

"He has been a friend to Mary and me during good times and when times weren't so good."

"By the way, where is your wife?"

"She had to go back to the States. We ran out of money. Unfortunately, I am going back next month."

"Sorry to hear that unless that is what you want."

"Oh, no. I wanted to work here until I died. It was the lack of money. Plus, the Israeli government has threatened not to renew our visas."

"Your work here, has it gone well?"

The missionary smiled. "This is a tough area to gauge success. I hear missionaries in other parts of the world where they have hundreds of converts a year. Here, you can't judge your success that way. We are lucky if we can get someone to attend two of our meetings in a row."

"But you don't seem discouraged."

"No, I am not. I know many of the Jews in Israel have blinders to the truth. But there will come a day when they might remember something that I said. That is up to them and God to decide. I, at least, planted the seed."

The missionary stood up and walked to the kitchen. "I am not much of a host. Let me get you some food. I know you must be hungry. Do you like hummus?"

Neil looked at Lisa. Before they could say anything, the professor responded. "We would love some."

Chapter 28

Economic Disaster

The black SUV pulled next to what was left of the mangled red truck wrapped around a large oak tree. Larry Haggerty got out and walked to the driver's side of the truck. The windows were broken, and the limp body, still tethered by the seat belts, showed no signs of movement. It was obvious to him that the driver was dead. As Haggerty was surveying the inside of the truck, he could see the approaching blue lights of the patrol car. Not appearing to be in a hurry to assess the damage or render any aid, the patrolman got out of his car and walked to where Haggerty was standing.

"Mr. Haggerty?"

"Yes."

"I received word from my captain not to detain you. I suggest that you leave as soon as possible. The ambulance is on the way."

"Officer, I have reason to believe that this person has stolen some material, and it might be in the truck. Do you mind if I look quickly?"

"I suggest that you leave immediately. If witnesses appear, it may be difficult to cover up your involvement. We will search the inside and let you know what we find." With that, the patrolman returned to his car.

Haggerty looked through the broken window again before returning to the SUV. He would have to explore other options to get the professor's material.

*****

The hummus actually tasted better than he had expected, or maybe Neil had not realized how hungry he was. This he knew for sure; in the past few days, he lost most of the extra weight he had gained the past year.

"Mr. Simmons," started the professor.

"Please call me Peter."

"Okay, Peter. I know that I didn't give you much to go on, but did you have any luck getting information on Rabbi Breuer?"

The missionary appeared very excited. "I was very successful or maybe just lucky. Well, lucky is not a term we Christians like to refer to. Anyway, it turns out that one of the young men who has been attending our meetings was an ex-student of the rabbi. And now he is one of the rabbi's teacher assistants."

"Oh, very good."

"I thought you would like that."

"And he was willing to talk about the rabbi?"

"He was quite willing to tell me all about the rabbi. He was curious why I wanted to know."

"What did you tell him?"

"I told him that an American friend might be doing some business with the university and was curious what I knew about the famous Rabbi Breuer. Is that an accurate answer?"

"That's a clever answer."

"I didn't want to say too much for fear he might become suspicious and not agree to cooperate. It is difficult enough for an Israeli citizen to be involved with someone who might be suspicious of proselytizing."

"Mr., ah, Peter, I am sorry that I can't be more forthright about my business now. At the appropriate time, I will share everything with you."

"That will not be necessary. I know what is going on. Well, I should qualify that statement. I knew what was going on up until the day your father was murdered."

The professor's face instantly reflected the shock of hearing those words: *your father was murdered*. "What? You knew that my father had been killed?"

"Well, I put two and two together. I knew there were people chasing you and that your father was going to make an effort to divert them. When you told me he had died, I assumed that was the cause."

"I am sorry that I was not honest with you. I didn't know."

"If I could take it."

"Well, no. I know you were close. And for his life to end that way…"

"Your father's life has always been one of sacrifice—whether for family or friends. God will reward him in heaven."

The professor nodded. "So you know what I have been working on?"

"My goodness, yes. Your father and I spoke regularly. Who do you think brought the code research to your father in the first place?"

"That was you?"

"That's right. I read about the discovery soon after the rabbi first disclosed it to the press. I immediately thought of your father. For years, I sent him everything about the code research I could get my hands on."

"So you are aware of what I have been involved with recently?"

"Your father kept me informed of your progress all along. He called me after you returned from your visit with the rabbi in New York and the visit of the gentleman who tried to convince you to work for the consortium."

"Did he tell you about the conversation we had after I first tested the codes?"

"Yes. It was one of the happiest days of his life. He thought for the first time in years that you and he had found some common ground."

"So when I called inquiring about the rabbi, you knew why I was interested?"

"I knew it had something to do with the code research, but that is all."

The professor smiled like a new father. "Peter, I must tell you something very important and also very confidential."

"And what is that?"

"We have advanced the code research beyond anything the rabbi could ever even imagine."

"Yes?"

"Unfortunately, our discoveries are sought by an American and others who want to use the information for personal gain."

"And you promised your father that if you were successful in what you refer to as advancing the code research, those discoveries would never be used for that purpose?"

"Yes, Peter, that was the promise I made to my father."

"And those who want this information are obviously willing to kill for it."

"Unfortunately, yes."

There was a twinkle in the missionary's eyes as he inched to the edge of the couch. "These advances that you have made, am I to assume that you were able to see into the future?"

It was now clear to the professor that the missionary knew everything about what the professor had been working on for the past year.

"Yes, Peter. I must humbly say your assumption is correct. Thanks to the work of Neil and Lisa."

"Your father had a lot of confidence in you, probably more than you will ever know. He said it was just a matter of time before you discovered that the codes could reveal the future."

"He had more confidence in me than I had in myself."

"He also said that you would do the right thing when you made the discovery."

"My father was a good role model for doing the right thing. Now I need to figure out what the right thing is."

"And that is where the rabbi enters the picture, I presume?"

"Yes, I believe the rabbi is the key to determining what I am to do with the research. But I need to know for sure whether I can trust him. The methods and models we have discovered cannot ever get in the hands of the wrong people."

"It was a good thing that I knew what I did—the backstory. It allowed me to inquire more specifically."

"I am sorry if you think that I did not trust you. I just need to be very careful."

"I understand completely. You are entrusted with an awesome responsibility."

"Sometimes, I think more than I am capable of handling."

"Maybe I can help in a small way."

"You have already helped. Now tell me more about the rabbi."

"There were several things the assistant said about the rabbi, which I found interesting. You must understand that the rabbi is a very powerful man in Israel. He heads a secret group that advises the prime minister on major issues dealing with Israel. My student-friend has seen written agendas of these meetings, and they are very forward-thinking."

"Written agendas? Don't you think it is a little careless to put things down in writing that might be this sensitive?"

"Once, he overheard the rabbi chastising one of the members of the group who had apparently not returned an agenda after a meeting. The rabbi had the member personally bring it to his office. After each meeting, the rabbi shreds the agendas. I am told he is quite a stickler about his privacy, not to mention the privacy dealing with matters of the country."

"Did your contact give any details about what they discussed in these meetings?"

"The meetings almost always deal with the future of Israel. He said the group is obsessed with the idea of the future of Israel if the United States ever withdrew its support. One meeting was entirely devoted with world conditions if there wasn't a United States anymore."

The professor looked at Neil and Lisa to see if they reacted.

"Let's face it, other than the United States, Israel does not have many friends in the world. If you take away the United States' support, Israel is a sitting duck to her enemies," added the missionary.

"Why have they been preoccupied with that idea? Do they know something that we don't know?" asked the professor.

"That I can't answer, and nor could my friend. I have a theory, which I will tell you later."

"What else did you find?"

"He said the last few meetings have been about the code research."

"Did he see the agenda for those meetings?"

"No, but he overheard their discussion. The rabbi's office at the university is right down the hall from the meetings. My friend works in the rabbi's office when these meetings are being held. He said that even though the meetings are secret, they are not quiet. When they argue, he can hear every word they say. Apparently, the discussions on the code research have been very loud.

"During these meetings, there have been two guests. One of them is the rabbi's son. He did not know who the other person was."

"The rabbi's son?"

"Yes, I think his name is Shimon. He and the rabbi are very close."

The sight of Shimon's twisted body impaled by an iron poker flashed through the professor's head. He was not looking forward to giving that news to the rabbi, and the less said about that incident now, the better. "What do you think is the significance of their attendance in those meetings?"

"I am not sure about the son. I know he is far more, shall I say, orthodox than the rabbi, not to mention being obsessively Zionistic. He is an avid critic of many of the politicians who have supported appeasement for the sake of peace. He is in the news periodically. I believe he gets a platform because of his father."

"And the other gentleman?"

"All I know is that he has close contacts with the prime minister."

"Interesting, very interesting. We kind of got away from my original question," said the professor.

"Can you trust the rabbi?"

"Yes."

"I asked my friend to tell me about the personal side of the rabbi. He described a man who is kind and gentle. A man I believe that your father would have liked and admired. A man who visits his wife's grave every week, who is never too busy to have lunch with his son once a week."

"Surely, as an employee, he had something negative to say about him. No one is perfect."

"If he did, he did not tell me."

"I must admit that I felt that way about him when we met. Even if he didn't want to gain financially from this research, I just can't seem to get past the fact that his loyalty to his country is so great that he would want the research for that reason. I can't take the chance that this research will ever be used for any reason. At least until it is the right time."

The missionary's face shone, and his cheeks became red. "This information you found, it must be profound for you to feel the way you do."

"Peter, no human is worthy to see what we were privileged to see."

The portly missionary had an expression of awe. "What can you tell me?"

"I will only say this to you. Stay steady. The end is in sight. Your work is not in vain."

"That is enough for me to hear. You can't tell by the way I look as an old man, but you know I was a runner in college, a long-distance runner. I was good at the start, not too good in the middle, but when I saw the finish line something, I guess adrenalin just shot through me to get to the end. That's what I hear you telling me, Professor. The finish line is in sight."

"As my father would say, 'Amen.'"

The missionary stood up and walked to a small bookshelf in the corner of the room. There were books piled everywhere on and around the bookshelf. He reached for a folder that lay across the top of several books. Inside the folder were several newspaper articles. The missionary grabbed the one on top.

"Do you remember the last time your father visited me?"

"Yes, it was, shortly after my wife died, when I took a leave of absence from the university."

"I think you will get a kick out of this."

The missionary unfolded the article from the *Jerusalem Post* and handed it to the professor. "It's a picture of your father. Do you recognize the gentleman next to him?"

The professor's face reflected his surprise. "Rabbi Breuer. My father is pictured with the rabbi. What was that all about?"

"Your father contacted the rabbi. When the rabbi heard he was the father of the famous mathematician, Professor Lange, he gladly agreed to meet. I think there was an implied kinship, you know, you being fellow mathematicians. According to your father, the rabbi is a big fan of yours."

"What was the occasion for the picture in the paper?"

"Back then, it was not unusual for the rabbi to have his picture in the paper quite regularly."

"I can imagine, but why with my father?"

"The caption was cut off, but it described your father as a respected clergyman from the United States. Frankly, I do not believe that the rabbi would have made time for a clergyman. But he would make time for Professor Lange's father."

"Do you know if they had a chance to talk?"

"According to your father, they hit it off. They spent an entire afternoon together, discussing various things. Needless to say, your father was interested in hearing about the code research."

"That is about the time I got involved with the codes," said the professor.

"Your father had an uncanny sense for knowing when things were going to happen and being prepared for them. My guess is that he knew you were going to get involved with the code research before you did."

The professor could not argue that point. "What else did they talk about?"

"Somehow, the discussion got around to Bible prophecy. Your father was somewhat of an expert on the subject, though he would never make that claim himself."

"I know he wrote a couple of books on the subject."

"Five. He wrote five books on Bible prophecy. Did you ever read them?"

"I am embarrassed to say that I have not."

The missionary went to the bookshelf, pulled out a book, and handed it to the professor. This is the one that captivated the rabbi. *America's Role in Biblical Prophecy* by Jeremiah Lange.

"Oh, yeah."

"The Rabbi wanted to know what your father thought about the future of America."

"What did my father tell him?"

"He told the rabbi there were forces in play in America that, if left unchecked, could cause the country to implode—a cultural tug-of-war between those who had no regard for our religious heritage and the church for the right to America's soul. But that was not what got the rabbi's attention."

"No?"

"He told the rabbi there would be one defining moment that would send America into a tailspin. There would be a worldwide event of such proportions that would cause the financial markets to collapse. Family fortunes would be wiped out practically overnight. One bad economic disaster spawned another and another until the momentum of the catastrophe could not be stopped."

The professor almost could not contain himself. He looked at Lisa and Neil, who both appeared shocked at what the missionary said. They had found what was described in the codes. *Economic disaster.*

"Then he told the rabbi something that apparently made the rabbi very sad. I remember the words your father used. He said America would lose its three—he called them—idols: comfort, possessions, and financial security—quickly and decisively. He described an America that went from a nation of luxury to one of panic and desperation—almost overnight."

THE REDEMPTION CODES

The professor's mind began to race. There were too many similarities to what he had found in the codes. Even though he wanted to tell the missionary everything, he had to be careful what he disclosed about the discovery.

"Peter, I need to ask you something."

"Yes?"

"You don't think that because my father was so definitive with his prognostication that the rabbi suspected that maybe I had...never mind. Never mind. That was a stupid question."

"That is not a stupid question at all. I could see where someone might get the idea that those were not your father's ideas but came from the codes. He gave a copy of his book to the rabbi. It was copyrighted a year after the rabbi's initial codes discovery."

"And this event that my father said to the rabbi, which got his attention...that precipitated economic disaster, what was my father referring to?"

"Professor, I'll let you see for yourself." He flipped through the book's pages he had taken from the shelf until he found what he was looking for. He handed the open book to the professor.

The professor started reading the chapter "The Disappearance of the Church." After a few minutes, the professor laid down the book. "This is what he shared with the rabbi?"

"Yes. Now you know why it got the rabbi's attention."

The professor shook his head as he was trying to make sense of the parallels between what his father interpreted from his faith and the study of the Bible and what they had seen in the codes. For sure, this odyssey, in many ways, was as much about learning the ways of his father as it was about discovering the hidden meaning of the codes.

The professor did not speak for several seconds before he finally broke the silence. "Well, we really got off the topic, didn't we?"

"But you learned something more about your father that you didn't know."

"Yes, why bother getting worked up about the codes? I should have just listened to my father or at least read his books."

"There you go."

"So, Peter, how do you suggest that I proceed?"

"I think you meet with the rabbi. I believe you will know what to do after that."

"I appreciate your advice. You confirmed what I thought was best."

"There is one more thing you need to know about the rabbi," said the missionary.

"What is that?"

"The rabbi is dying of cancer."

*****

It was still dark outside when the professor woke up. He initially thought that it was the result of the time change, but more likely, the anticipation of the meeting with the rabbi caused him to toss and turn all night. Finally, after realizing that any notion of sleep was futile, he got out of bed and quietly walked to the living room. Maybe he would look at the books his father had written and compare them with the discoveries he made with the codes. He suspected his father's words were closer to the discoveries than he thought possible.

He did not notice the missionary sitting in his chair reading and was startled at his voice.

"Professor, some coffee?"

"Oh, yes, please. Were you unable to sleep too?"

"No more or less than usual. I have been bothered by many things recently."

The missionary got up slowly. "My legs do not respond as quickly as my mind. Cream or sugar?"

"No, black."

Handing him a cup, he said, "I make it strong. I hope you like it that way."

"Yes. I think that would serve me well today."

The two sat silently for a few moments before the professor finally spoke. "What are you reading, Peter?"

"Psalms."

"Yes, a beautiful book."

"Professor, you wouldn't think that this book speaks about Israel's yet-to-be-fulfilled future, would you?"

"Yes, even I know that is not generally considered one of the prophetic books of the Bible," replied the professor, hoping that this conversation would not lead to where he thought it would.

"Would you like to know why I am reading Psalm 83?"

"Sure, I guess. I do not find it strange that a missionary would be reading the Bible. After all, that's what you do."

"But there is a specific reason I am reading Psalms 83."

The professor could sense that the missionary was not going to end this conversation until he asked the critical question.

"So what is the significance of Psalms 83?"

"Psalms 83 deals with a war with Israel."

"I am not surprised. It seems like the Old Testament is replete with wars that Israel fought."

"No, this is not a war that Israel has fought. This is a war that Israel has yet to fight."

"I see."

"Professor, I see that your facade of apparent indifference is not working for you. I see it in your eyes. I know that you know much, much more than you are telling me. I also understand that your discovery is sacred, and your desire to destroy this information before it gets into the wrong hands is to be commended. However, as a resident of this wonderful country and one who has given his life for its people, I need to know. This request I beg of you."

"Yes, Peter, I am aware of this war. Israel is attacked by Egypt, Jordan, and her other neighbors."

"Yes, yes, I see that in the scripture." The missionary moved to the edge of his seat. "But is it soon?"

The professor took a sip of the coffee before he answered. He knew that if his father were alive, he would want him to answer honestly.

"Yes, it is soon. But do not be dismayed. Israel wins the war, and as a result of this victory, her homeland, Israel's territory, is pushed out to the borders originally promised to Abraham."

"And America? What role does America play in this war?"

"I am afraid that America does not come to Israel's defense. Israel fights this war alone."

"I suppose that I should not be surprised, at least the part about America's position. Recently, there have been factions in the United States who want to distance themselves from Israel. I read about it from political elites, college campuses, not to mention many of the mainline Protestant churches."

The professor sat quietly. He respected that the missionary had given his life to this country. He would give an honest answer but no more information than necessary.

"Maybe America's loss of the church, you know, the Rapture. Do you think that had anything to do with America's indifference?"

"That is a difficult one to answer. I guess the fact that the United States is not involved in this war could lead one to that conclusion."

"Guess? I suppose you could not possibly have found the date of the disappearance."

"No, that was not found. We found many profound events, but the date of the church's disappearance—the Harpazo—it was not found."

"Yes, I understand. That was not for you or anyone to find. Only God knows that date. Just think of it. I have been living in Israel for thirty years, and if I live a little while longer, I will have a firsthand witness to the most amazing time in the history of the world."

"Peter, I don't think you can even imagine what is about to happen. I certainly was not equipped for what I saw."

"Professor, you have been kind to answer my one question. You made a promise to your father that if you saw into the future, it would not be used for any personal gain. I respect your father's wish. You have said enough. Thank you."

The professor managed a shy smile. "Peter, I appreciate that you understand and respect the promise that I made to my father not to share this information. Also, let me assure you that we were not able to find dates of any of the future events."

"Thank you, Professor."

THE REDEMPTION CODES

"Let me finish by saying this. We believe we are close to the end—very close."

The missionary was about to speak when Lisa and Neil walked into the room.

*****

After all of the effort to follow them from the airport, he somehow lost the professor at the Dan Tel Aviv Hotel. According to the security office of the prime minister, the hotel verified that they had not yet checked in. Steve punched in the contact from his cell phone. The rabbi answered the call.

"Don't worry," said the rabbi. "If they are in Israel, they will show up somewhere. This is not a large country. I am not worried that we will find them, Steve, and neither should you." With that, he hung up.

No sooner had the rabbi hung up his cell phone when the phone in his office rang.

"Yes, Professor, it is so good to hear from you again."

The call from the professor to the rabbi had been brief. They agreed to meet that afternoon at the lobby of the King David Hotel. The professor decided not to tell the rabbi about his son. That would have to wait for a later time, if ever.

Chapter 29

King David Hotel

Walking through the luxurious lobby of the King David Hotel, the professor could see why it was considered the finest hotel in Israel. The plaque near the front door indicated it was built in 1930. Its splendor represented a bygone era; today, it was still a beacon in the middle of a city tortured by both its checkered past and its uncertain future.

As he strolled through the hotel gardens, the professor could see the Old City of Jerusalem in the distance with its walls and domes. He was early for his meeting and did not expect to see the rabbi for at least forty-five minutes. That was okay; it would give him time to collect his thoughts and decide how to best approach the rabbi with the discoveries.

At Neil's insistence, the decision was made not to bring the files that contained the model's program. The professor's summary would have to do for now. If it turned out that the rabbi could not be trusted, no one would ever find the information. It was locked safely under the floor in the home of his missionary friend. For now, the rabbi would have to trust the professor's explanation. At the *appropriate time*, if and when that ever occurred, the professor would produce the program used to unlock the future.

Lisa and Neil agreed that it was better that they not attend this meeting. Instead, they sat at a table just off the lobby in eyesight of where the professor and the rabbi would be meeting. If anything went wrong, they were to exit through a side door and follow a contingency plan that the professor had carefully laid out the night before.

The professor had no doubt that he would recognize the rabbi. Even though they had met on only one occasion, there was something about his facial features that made him distinctive. If he still wasn't sure, the professor remembered that the rabbi had a distinct limp when he walked.

It was 3:00 p.m. sharp when the rabbi, who agreed to come alone, limped through the front door of the hotel. The rabbi and the professor embraced. It was a spontaneous expression from two people who truly respected each other.

"It is so good to see you again, Professor."

"The feeling is mutual, Rabbi."

"I trust that your flight was satisfactory and that your stay has been as you had hoped."

"So far, yes. Let's hope that the remaining portion of the trip is fruitful."

"Fruitful? That sounds a little like a business trip to me, Professor."

"Well, you might say that I do have some business to conduct."

The rabbi motioned to a pair of chairs next to a fountain. He appeared to be in a great amount of pain as he struggled to walk, and even with the aid of a walking stick, he fell hard into the chair. "I am sorry, Professor, but my condition is not compatible with standing, particularly if there is a suitable chair nearby." The rabbi shifted around in the chair, attempting to get comfortable. The pain etched into his face appeared like a permanent feature. The professor wondered how long he had to live.

"Do you wish to have anything to drink or eat?"

"No. The prospect of meeting with you and delivering my message has sapped any appetite I might have."

"If you change your mind, please let me know."

A man suddenly appeared from around the corner, carrying a small tray. He carefully set the tray down by the rabbi and left without saying a word.

"Forgive me, but I must partake of a cup of tea and a cookie. It is my daily indulgence, as well as an afternoon ritual."

The professor noticed a slight tremble in the rabbi's hand as he spooned the cube of sugar into his cup. He appeared to have aged a great deal since their last encounter in New York.

"Before we discuss whatever is on your mind, Professor, let me say, on behalf of my group of consultants and from the prime minister, that we are very sorry to hear about the death of your father."

The professor nodded. "Thank you for those kind words."

"Yes, it is unfortunate that there were those who carried the desire for this information to such drastic measures. Your father, he was a good man. You can be proud."

"I am proud."

"When you get to my age, you often wonder about your legacy. You know, what people might think or say when you are gone. So I must ask you, what makes you the proudest of your father?"

The professor thought for only a split second before responding. "That he never wavered from the truth, at least the truth as he saw it, and believed it."

"And he shared our excitement of the codes. Yes?"

"Maybe not for the same reasons as we share. I believe that he saw a simpler value to the codes."

"In what way, may I ask?"

"Rabbi, the code research for my father was never more than a means."

"A means?"

"My father saw the research as a way for me, and others like me, to get excited about rediscovering God."

"Very interesting. My son, Shimon, has said the same thing. Maybe with a little Zionist twist."

The mention of the rabbi's son caused the professor to momentarily look away.

"And this search, this rediscovery you speak of, did you find God?"

"Yes, or maybe more accurately, He found me. In either regard, I am convinced, more than ever, that there is a God, eternal, preexistent to man, not a God, as my colleagues are fond of saying, created by man. One Who knew the course of events before time itself."

"And you needed the codes to show you that?"

"I did not have the faith of my father, Rabbi. I am a mathematician, a scientist. I needed proof. Hard-core proof."

"And you found this proof you speak of?"

"I found proof, but it came at a great price, Rabbi. Many have suffered unnecessarily along the way."

"That is very unfortunate, very unfortunate, indeed. But why, may I ask, have you decided to come to my country to tell me this?"

"Rabbi, I have not come to tell you this. I came to ask for your help."

"Yes? How can I possibly help you? I would think it would be the other way. If you have made certain discoveries, as many people have claimed that you have, you certainly don't need my help. You have made discoveries, have you not?"

"Yes. But I think you already knew that."

"Then how can I help you, Professor?"

"Aren't you the least bit interested in my discoveries?"

"I am. I assumed that if you wanted me to know, you would tell me at the *Appointed Time*."

"I can't expect your help unless I at least tell you the magnitude of the discoveries."

"You have my undivided attention, Professor."

The professor shifted to the edge of his chair and leaned in the direction of the rabbi. "Your original discovery of the codes existed at Equal Letter Sequences, ELS, on a two-dimensional model—words across, words up and down—in what I would call a crossword pattern. It was an amazing discovery and one that you should be very proud."

"Thank you."

"That model showed us historical events, information that we already knew, albeit events that occurred thousands of years after they had been imbedded."

"Go on."

"And in my period of unbelief, I verified statistically the value of your research that these imbedded words did not occur there by chance."

"I am assuming there is a *but* here."

"Yes, but as phenomenal a discovery as it was, it had its limitations. It could not tell us information about events that were yet to happen. Of course, I am not telling you anything you don't already know."

"Yes, I am very familiar with the limitations of the research. And if I wasn't, I get reminded of it by both my colleagues and critics frequently."

"Your discovery was made on a two-dimensional level. To get more than historical data, we knew we had to look at a model that consisted of more dimensions, maybe three, maybe four. Someday, maybe even five dimensions. Our discovery was made in the fourth dimension."

The rabbi leaned forward, smiling. "And? You are keeping me in suspense, Professor."

The professor paused, and with a muted tone, as if to speak reverently, he spoke those words the rabbi had been waiting for years to hear. "We saw what we have reason to believe are future events, Rabbi."

The Rabbi's once-smiling face appeared pale. He started to speak but stopped to gather his thoughts. He often dreamed of this day. Finally, after what seemed like several minutes, he spoke. "You saw the future?"

"Yes. We saw the future of people, nations, and cultures. We saw triumph, and we saw tragedy."

Israel, my beloved homeland. "The future of nations and cultures?"

"Rabbi, I know of your love and concern for Israel. Let me ease your mind. The model shows that Israel survives until the Messiah returns."

"Professor, you don't know how happy this makes me feel." Tears formed in his eyes. It only took a few seconds before the statement replayed in his mind. "But you said until the Messiah returns."

"That is what I said. The code *Messiah returns* occurs in a section near the end of time."

"In all due respect, *returns* implies that He was here before."

"I understand that we have a difference of opinion theologically on this matter. But the references were clear, Rabbi."

"I see." The Rabbi's mind was now racing in many directions. "Please tell me more about my country."

Sensing that the rabbi would have no patience for anything other than the bottom line, the professor started right in. "Israel will soon be in another war with her neighbors—your neighbors—who share a common border. Your country is attacked by Egypt, Jordan, the Saudis, Syria, and Lebanon, as well as Hamas, Hezbollah, and the Palestinians."

"I suppose that should not surprise anyone. After all, these are the countries and people who openly desire to push us into the Mediterranean Sea. But what precipitates this war with our neighbors?"

"You are forced, in a preempted attack, to use weapons to destroy Iran's nuclear reactor. As a result of the fallout from the explosions, large sections of Iran become inhabitable. And as a response to this act by Israel, your neighbors coalesce quickly and attack you. It is not shown whether the neighbors just sought retribution for your actions against Iran or whether they thought to attack you before you attacked them."

"And this war you speak of, are we—"

"Israel is successful, but there is a lot of collateral damage."

"Collateral damage to my country?"

"Some, but mostly to your enemies. Damascus is wiped off the face of the earth. One day, Damascus is a city. The next day, it is a heap of rocks."

The rabbi leaned back in the chair and tried to collect all the thoughts running through his head. After a moment, he continued the questioning. "Egypt's involvement. That is a bit of a surprise. We have a treaty with Egypt."

"Although many in Egypt try to prevent Egypt from getting involved, her leaders break its treaty with Israel and join the coalition that invades your country. Your military forces practically destroyed Egypt. It starts a spiral of hardship that the country is never able to overcome. There will be a total economic collapse. Egypt ends up looking more like a third-world country."

The rabbi sat in silence. The professor chose not to break the silence. He knew this was profound information, and the rabbi needed time to process the magnitude of what he just said.

Finally, the rabbi spoke. "This war that you speak of, does this war finally give us the peace we so long for?"

"For a short time after this war, you live in total peace. And in a bit of irony, many countries seek to befriend Israel at this time."

"Befriend Israel? What do you mean?"

"Many countries—how should I say this—they have an interest in Israel."

"And what is the cause of this international interest?"

"The success of your military efforts gives you certain benefits."

"Benefits. I don't understand."

"Spoils. Bounty. The resources of the countries that attacked you are now yours."

"Oil?"

"Yes, oil and natural gas."

"Oh, my, Professor. Tell me more."

"In addition to the oil reserves from the countries that attack you, you will get back all of the land that was promised by God to Abraham. In a short period of time, tiny Israel will go from a small country to a major superpower."

"Peace. How we long to live in peace. I could die now, knowing that the future of my country is secure."

The professor did not say a word as the rabbi glowed in the moment. Finally, as if he awoke from a beautiful dream, his face turned serious again. "I have a feeling that the story does not end here, does it?"

"No, unfortunately, it does not. With the accumulation of wealth and resources, you are attacked again. This time, it is from a coalition of countries made up of Russia, along with many countries south of Russia that made up the old USSR, Turkey, Iran, Ethiopia, Sudan, Somalia, Libya, Algeria, Morocco, and Tunisia."

"Did you mean to include Iran? I thought Iran was destroyed in the previous war?"

"Israel did destroy a portion of Iran, but there remained a section of the country that was habitable even after the nuclear fallout. The remaining portion of the country was able to amass an army to assist the other invading countries."

"And the outcome is…"

"The outcome is the same. This coalition is defeated in a dramatic fashion. But there is a difference."

"A difference?"

"In the war with Jordan, Egypt, and your other neighbors, Israel wins because of a superior military force. In the war with Russia, well, that victory is the result of a divine intervention."

"Divine intervention?"

"Your military cannot take any credit. Russia and her allies are destroyed as a result of confusion caused by a series of earthquakes. In fact, your enemy becomes so confused that it actually turns and kills itself. Friendly fire, you might say."

"So our military might win the war against Egypt and Jordan, but we win the following war with Russia as a result of divine intervention. That is what you are saying, yes?"

"That is not what I am saying. That is what the codes revealed."

"Professor, in either of these wars, you did not mention the United States. I assume that was an oversight on your part. Surely, the United States would be fighting beside us."

"No, it is not an oversight. I could not find a reference to the United States in either war. Perhaps there is a logical reason why the United States is not involved." The professor stopped in midsentence. "I have said enough for now, Rabbi."

"I beg your patience, Professor, please, if the codes gave you faith that you did not have before, will your discovery not give me, my country, and, for that matter, all humanity more faith?"

"Rabbi, I will answer this as my father might have answered. Your discovery of the hidden codes was well publicized, yes? Did that discovery increase the faith? No. Did we not have the Torah and later the Bible and still many people don't believe?"

The rabbi nodded. He knew the professor was right. "But might there be some, like you, where the hidden meaning of the codes might make a difference? Surely, America would benefit from this information. At least spiritually."

The professor hesitated. He did not see value in sharing more information with the rabbi. However, he knew this journey was far from over, and sharing this information might be the only way to ensure the rabbi's help. "I saw America's future too."

"Oh, America. Surely, her future is bright. Yes?"

The professor grew silent. Words would not come as he slowly shook his head.

"Tell me, Professor. Is something wrong?"

"America, at least the America I know—I am sorry to say—has a very difficult future ahead. While she will exist as a country, her once-held claim as the world's only superpower is drastically diminished."

The rabbi recoiled in his chair. "Oh my!" he exclaimed. "America is the greatest country on earth. Surely you made a mistake in that regard. Perhaps you misinterpreted the words."

"I hesitated to share this information. But from the day we first met, you impressed me as someone I could trust."

The rabbi did not respond, as if the magnitude of what he just heard rendered him speechless. "I am certainly in no position to demand that you tell me. But I should remind you that America and Israel have been friends for a long time. What has been good for America has been good for Israel. And what has been bad for America has been bad for Israel."

"What you say has historically been correct. There will soon come a time when our fortunes go in opposite directions."

"And you know when this will happen? The codes showed you that date?"

"Oh, no, the codes never revealed specific dates, and I can assure you that we searched long and hard to find any references to dates."

"Then how do you know the time?"

"I don't know exactly. I do know, from certain—let's say, extrapolations—the approximate time."

"Extrapolations?"

"More specifically, we created markers when an event in the United States appeared to correlate to an event in Israel and vice versa. If we could approximate the time, or at least the sequence of events in one country, we could use that time and sequence to estimate the timing for an event in the other country."

The rabbi appeared to be in a great deal of pain. The professor was not sure whether it was his illness or just his natural reaction to the information. "Although I am a proud citizen of Israel, I love the United States. Forgive me, but this is difficult to comprehend."

The professor nodded but did not respond.

"What causes this sudden misfortune, Professor?"

"We believe the downward spiral started shortly after the United Sates brokered a two-state solution with the Palestinians. The ink had not even dried on the agreement when certain events started."

"Events?"

"Well, there were a series of natural disasters followed by several major attacks that killed millions of people on the east and west coasts."

"Nuclear?"

"Yes, I am afraid so."

The rabbi was visibly shaken.

The professor continued, "That spun the world economy into a tailspin—a depression much worse than we had ever experienced. In America, that led to a classic case of civil unrest. There were riots in the streets, which the politicians were unable to stop for several months. You must understand, as a people, we have never experienced scarcity or hardship. At least not of this magnitude."

"Anarchy in America?"

"I told you. This might surprise you."

"And? Tell me America rebounds from this."

The professor hesitated. "This is going to sound wacky to you, but I will tell you anyway. You can choose to believe me or not. That is your choice."

"It isn't a matter of believing you, Professor. I knew all along that there was power in the codes. Are you are really asking me if I believe in the codes?"

"You may question the codes after I tell you this," responded the professor.

"That I will never do."

"Okay. Here it goes. You have heard of the Rapture of the church?"

"Yes. The sudden disappearance of Christians when the…actually, whether you know of this or not, your father schooled me on this notion several years ago."

"It is not a notion. It happens."

"What do you mean it happens?"

"It happens just as my father wrote about. Millions of people vanish all over the world."

"And in America?"

"Many adult Americans disappear at once as well as the babies and young children."

"And you saw this in the codes?"

"Yes. I saw two references. Sudden appearance. Sudden disappearance."

"Sudden appearance?"

"I assume that references the *sudden appearance* of the Messiah."

The rabbi appeared to ignore the professor's response. "And sudden disappearance?"

"That, we believe, is a reference to the Rapture. We saw it identified as *Harpazo*."

"So these disappearances immobilize a country as great as America?"

"It wasn't just the impact of the number who suddenly disappeared. There were many included in that group who held leadership positions: presidents of companies, doctors, nurses, teachers, police officers, firemen, and even a few college professors. Not to mention airline pilots with planes in the skies, doctors during surgery, firefighters fighting fires. Gone. In a flash."

"And the impact?"

"The country could never recover from that impact, psychologically, economically, and, of course, spiritually. The European Union and the United Nations tried to fill the economic and power vacuum, but no one could fill the emotional and spiritual loss."

"Oh my!"

"Think of it on a human scale—parents missing their children, teenagers missing their parents, babies gone right from their mother's lap, one spouse missing another. Just the agony for those left behind practically immobilized the country all by itself. Although those who vanished was a smaller percentage of the population than you might think, the spiritual effect was the most devastating of all."

"The spiritual effect?"

"Yes, those who disappeared represented a kind of genuine goodness which had always served as a restraint on certain, ah, evil forces. Whether it was their prayers, love, good deeds, whatever, it served to balance or restrain the evil that always existed. You remove that restraint. You can imagine that vacuum is filled with evil."

"The codes were clear on this?"

"Yes, they were very clear. We found several keywords that painted a sad future. The one which gave me chills: *unrestrained evil.*"

"And the date, you said it was not revealed."

"No. Unlike other events where we could extrapolate an approximate time based on certain other events, this event had no time markers at all."

"In her weakened state, is America invaded by another country?"

"No. The words we found in the codes were *withered like a vine cut above its roots*. With a portion of the country still suffering from the nuclear fallout, even with a wounded military, invading the United States was too much for another country to risk."

The rabbi appeared distraught.

"Are you okay, Rabbi?"

"Yes, I will be fine. I am embarrassed that we ever sought to gain anything by the codes. The American Corporation, Haggerty—it was all a mistake. I am reminded, as I was before, when I first discovered the codes, that this is sacred information. Not to be used for gain but only for redemption."

"Speaking of redemption. You have a chance to redeem yourself, Rabbi."

"What do you mean?"

"You can help me hide the program so that no one can find it, at least not until it is time."

"Why not just destroy it?" asked the rabbi.

The professor leaned closer to the rabbi. "There was one message that I didn't tell you about."

"Yes?"

"We were instructed by the codes to hide them until the *Appointed Time* and to hide them at the *Appointed Place*," said the professor, his eyes searching the rabbi for a response.

"So you must do as you were instructed."

"There was one more instruction, Rabbi."

"Yes?"

"You would be the one to tell us the *Appointed Place*."

"I was mentioned in the codes?" asked the rabbi humbly.

"Not by name, of course. But with enough detail that your involvement was predetermined. But I think you already knew that, didn't you, Rabbi?"

"I knew there would come another that would show me what I was not able to find myself. Sometimes, I questioned whether it was my lack of faith. Other times, I thought maybe we did not have the technology. But now I know."

"Know what?" asked the professor.

"I know that another was to show me what had been hidden. And I am to hide that which had been discovered by another in a place that others cannot find. God has a sense of humor, Professor."

"So, will you help me?"

"Professor, I don't have a choice."

*****

Haggerty was impressed at the detail of the intelligence he received from the American ambassador. Just twenty-four hours after Jimmy's untimely accident, Haggerty was landing at the Ben Gurion

International Airport. The American ambassador was waiting for him as he exited from the terminal.

"Mr. Haggerty?"

"Yes, I'm Haggerty."

"Welcome to Israel. I was told to meet you here and to pass on some additional intelligence."

Haggerty was not prone to small talk, even when it was a dignitary or someone as important as an ambassador. "What have you found?"

"Our intelligence indicates that the professor met with the rabbi this afternoon at the King David Hotel. The meeting lasted for about an hour."

"Was there any transfer?"

"By transfer, I assume you mean material given to the rabbi?"

"Yes, that is exactly what I mean."

"Not that we could tell."

"You had your men in strategic positions, I hope."

"Yes. You have nothing to worry about. We are in control."

"And Mr. Gold?"

"He was not at the meeting. Do you wish for one of our men to surveil him?"

"No, not at this time. I will take care of Mr. Gold myself. Where is the professor now?"

"He left with the rabbi. We believe he might be staying at the rabbi's home."

"Now if you could take me to my hotel, I would like to freshen up from the flight."

"As you wish," replied the ambassador. "I have been told to provide you with whatever resources you need."

CHAPTER 30

Correlations

The rabbi slowly and painfully stood up. "If I am going to help you, I need to know more. Maybe we can talk over dinner." The rabbi was never late for a meal. That was a habit that took on almost sacred proportions, and today was no exception.

The professor waved in the direction of where Neil and Lisa were sitting. On cue, Neil and Lisa appeared from behind a potted palm tree where they had been drinking coffee and trying to interpret the body language between the rabbi and the professor.

"Rabbi, I would like for you to meet my daughter, Lisa. And this is one of my ex-students, Neil Coles."

They exchanged greetings.

"Rabbi, they have been with me throughout this whole discovery. I would like for them to join us for dinner."

"It would be my pleasure, Professor. I wish my son could be here to join us. He is quite a young man who has his priorities in the right place."

The rabbi stared at the professor as if a reply was necessary. "I understand your sentiments exactly, Rabbi."

The Rabbi turned and started to walk. The professor's eyes made contact with Lisa and Neil. They understood that no comment was required, at least for now.

The walk to the Michael Andrew restaurant in the Zionist Confederation House on Botta Street took only about ten minutes.

They exchanged superficial comments about the weather and politics as they walked. The rabbi's limp seemed even more pronounced than when they had met several months ago. Had the professor not known the rabbi's age, he would have guessed that he was many years older than he was. The rabbi appeared frail as the cancer was obviously working its evil intent.

Entering the restaurant, they were immediately escorted to a table inside a small courtyard at the rear of the restaurant. It was obvious from the comments made by the manager that he was aware the rabbi was coming.

"As you can see, I frequent this restaurant quite often. When the weather is pleasant, I like to sit in the back where there is some privacy. I recommend the sea bass. That is one of their specialties."

"I'll go with your recommendation," said the professor, not even bothering to open the menu.

Neil and Lisa studied the menu. Lisa chose the eggplant ravioli, which the rabbi commended her for. Neil reluctantly conceded to the sea bass as well.

"The food is excellent, but the service is a little slow. We will have plenty of time to talk before the food arrives." The rabbi's demeanor suddenly became very somber. No longer was he the tourist guide.

"Professor, in order for me to help you find the *Appointed Place*, I would like to know more."

"Fair enough. Well, where do I start?"

"Start from where my discoveries left off," said the rabbi.

For the professor, it felt like a classroom, and for a few minutes, the rabbi was his student. As the rabbi requested, he started from the original discoveries made by the rabbi. Meticulously, he went through the process right up to their most recent discovery. He withheld the technical details of the four-dimensional model the group discovered to unlock the future. As the professor spent more and more time with the rabbi, he felt comfortable that he could trust him, but until their work had been completed, he still had to be careful.

"Let me see if I understand you correctly. You first identified something in the original Hebrew text, the *plaintext*, which had similar characteristics to a future event. For example, a war in the *plain-*

text might provide us with the area where the codes would reveal a historical war or, as in the case of your discoveries, a future war."

"Correct."

"Then you applied your model to that portion of the Hebrew text. The two-dimensional model, as you like to refer to it, revealed historical information in keeping with my original discovery."

"Yes."

"But when you applied your four-dimensional model, future events were revealed. In my example, they would give us details about a future war. Am I on the right path?"

"That is correct. I could not have said it better."

"And the *plaintext*. I don't quite understand. Using my example, there are several references to wars throughout the Hebrew scriptures. How did you know where in the scriptures to apply the model?"

"You are absolutely right about that. It was a trial-and-error process. In some cases, we were just lucky. In other cases, we had to search through several passages before we found a match."

"But, Professor, I am sure you had a plan."

"In most cases, the correlations were sought through common sense. We tried to make those same common-sense correlations between events that happened several thousand years ago to those happening or about to happen."

"And I suppose you are not ready to share the model with me yet."

"No, I am afraid that I cannot do that."

"I cannot blame you for that."

"It is a dangerous weapon in the wrong hands."

"And possibly a temptation to use it to promote—might I say—an agenda for even those with good intentions."

"Rabbi, I made a promise to my father that the codes would not be used for personal gain."

"Which you do not seem the type to do."

"That promise was made before the discovery was made."

"I don't understand. Are you saying that you now have intentions to use the information the codes reveal?"

"After we saw what the codes revealed—their awesome power—we realized that it was no longer enough just to commit that they would not be used for personal gain. They must be hidden."

"Where, if I may ask, did you find the reference to the *Appointed Time* and the *Appointed Place*?"

"Exodus, where the *plaintext* speaks of the Ark of the Covenant," replied Neil.

The rabbi pulled out his Torah, which he always carried in his inside coat pocket, and flipped to the reference of the ark. He read out load in Hebrew. He set the Torah down and rested his elbows on the table. He tapped the table with his fingers as he contemplated the passages.

"The ark…the ark…the Ark of the Covenant." He repeated the words. His eyes widened and seemed to brighten as if he alone had the only key that could unlock this mystery.

"You look as if—"

"I know where the *Appointed Place* is located," the rabbi blurted out. "I know where to hide the codes. The *Appointed Place* is the Ark of the Covenant. This information is to be hidden with the Ark of the Covenant."

A young man interrupted the moment as he placed food on the table.

"Now we eat," said the rabbi, smiling broadly.

CHAPTER 31

It Gets Ugly

Steve Gold was getting frustrated. He had tried all morning to contact the rabbi but to no avail. There was no answer at the rabbi's office or his home, and the rabbi's trustworthy, always-reliable secretary did not answer either. There was not enough time to sit back and wait for an answer. It was his time to dictate the course of future events. He would try one more time as he put on his coat and headed for the one place where he expected to find the rabbi.

The caller ID on the rabbi's phone identified the call was from Steve Gold's cell phone.

"Yes, Steve, is that you?"

"Rabbi, I have been trying to reach you all morning. We must meet. It is extremely important."

"Not to worry, Steve. The professor will show up. It is not like he is an international terrorist."

"Rabbi, I received a call from the prime minister saying that you were observed meeting with the professor at the King David Hotel."

The Rabbi hesitated for a moment to collect his thoughts. "I am sorry that I misled you, Steve. That is correct. I did meet with the professor today."

"That is not my biggest concern, Rabbi. I know that there is always a reason for your actions and that you would not mislead me unless you thought it was in our best interest."

"Then, may I ask what your biggest concern is?"

"My contact with the security office of the prime minister said that the American, Larry Haggerty, met with the American ambassador upon his arrival from the United States."

"Oh."

"After that meeting, the prime minister received intelligence that the American was observed buying a K2X from an underground weapons dealer. He also bought a silencer."

"I am at a private patio just behind the Michael Andrew restaurant, Steve. We need a plan soon before this gets ugly."

The rabbi was unaware that Steve was just minutes away.

*****

Steve Gold was not one to waste time. Things were getting out of control quickly, and he did not have a good feeling about it. If Haggerty was already in Jerusalem, he only had a limited time to make his move.

Steve proceeded through the restaurant to the private patio. The patio, located behind the restaurant next to an alley, was surrounded by a brick wall that had just enough openings to allow some breeze to flow through. Its privacy was important, especially for those epic meetings between the rabbi and the prime minister. Given the rabbi's propensity for secrecy, Steve felt confident he could take care of business without anyone aware of his actions.

The rabbi slowly and painfully stood up as he entered. "So glad to see you, Steve."

The person sitting in the chair with his back to the entrance also stood up.

"I think you remember the professor."

"Yes. It has been some time since we last met. It is my pleasure to see you again, Professor."

"Likewise."

"It was my understanding that your daughter and one of your students are also visiting our country."

"Yes, that is correct. They joined us for dinner with the rabbi, but they left to go back to the hotel to take care of some matters."

"Please sit down, Steve. I was just telling the professor that I had been less than honest with you. The professor did contact me yesterday. I had hoped that my meeting today with the professor would have remained confidential. But the prime minister and the ambassador have made this into quite an international issue."

"I was contacted by the prime minister a few minutes ago, asking why you have not returned his calls."

"This is a matter of total insignificance. The professor felt it necessary to deliver a personal message. If it is okay with the professor, I would like to relay that message to you and the prime minister."

"I have no objection to you sharing my news," said the professor, knowing that he and the rabbi had previously collaborated on the story they would tell regarding the professor's research.

"Steve, the professor, with the professional courtesy fitting someone of his high moral standing, has come to give us a message."

"Yes?" Steve's heart quickened with anticipation.

"The professor's message is simple. Neither he nor his team has made any significant discovery beyond what I had discovered many years ago."

Steve could feel the blood draining from his head. This was not the news he expected.

"I must admit that I am more than a little confused by your comments, Rabbi. Then why travel halfway around the world? The professor could have delivered that message over the phone."

"He only came to Israel so that I may intercede on his behalf. He did not know where to turn. His father has been killed, and he feels like a hunted man. Now we find that it is not just an ambitious American capitalist after him. It is two countries. What must the professor do to get his life back to normal? He is an innocent party in a misguided grab for power."

"I am sorry, Rabbi, but your comments do not match with the intelligence services from the two countries. There are many in high places of at least two governments who believe that the professor has made *the* discovery—the discovery that has alluded us for many years—and that he has come to our country to share the news with you."

"That is preposterous. He has absolutely nothing of value to share with me or with anyone."

"Then you will have to convince the prime minister that the meeting at the hotel was not as it seemed."

"I will have that conversation with the prime minister right away, Steve."

"Rabbi, I must warn you before you go off promoting a lie: The meeting between you and the professor at the hotel was recorded. Everything that was spoken about is now in the hands of the prime minister."

The professor looked intently at the rabbi for an answer. It appeared that this news did not surprise the rabbi.

"I see. And this recording that you refer to, have you listened to it?"

"No. And frankly, I don't need to. I have already formulated my opinion."

"And that is?"

Steve's head was spinning. He had heard enough and knew he did not have much time before Haggerty would be arriving. He stood up and backed against the patio wall overlooking the side alley. He clumsily pulled out a gun and pointed it in the direction of the rabbi. His hand began to shake.

"If the professor told you that he has not made any breakthroughs in the research, he is lying. Your son, he knew the professor had made these discoveries."

"My son, my son. He is not here to question about such matters."

"Your son is dead, Rabbi," Steve blurted out.

"No. You don't know what you are talking about. My son is not dead."

"If you do not believe me, ask the professor. He knows your son is dead."

"How do you know that?" asked the professor, wondering if he had discovered Shimon's body after Jimmy left.

"I saw his SUV at the bottom of a drop-off near your cabin."

"It is true that we heard a crash, but we had no idea it was the rabbi's son." The professor breathed a sigh of relief that he did not have to tell the rabbi what really happened to Shimon.

The rabbi's eyes swelled as tears began to roll down his cheeks. He dropped his head into his hands as the combination of sadness and pain grieved his soul. "I should have never gotten him involved with this…with the Americans. They must have filled his head with opportunistic thoughts. How could he attempt to gain on something so sacred?"

"You are wrong, Rabbi. That is my motivation, but that was never your son's motivation. Shimon wanted the codes for one purpose and one purpose only—to destroy them. He saw the codes as sacred. You must believe me, Rabbi."

"And how do you know this, Steve?" asked the rabbi.

"He called me when he was on his way to the professor's cabin. He was going to get the program, then destroy it. He had no intentions of hurting the professor or his family, and he definitely had no intentions of profiting from the professor's discovery.

"Rabbi, I was already in the mountains the day you called about Shimon. I followed Shimon to the cabin that same day. My plan was simple. Once Shimon got the research, I was going to make my move."

"To get the research from him before he destroyed it."

"That's right, Professor."

"How do you explain what happened to Haggerty's men? He said he killed them."

"That is correct. He killed the two men in the street. He was afraid they would get to you before he could. And if they could gain this vital information, Haggerty's men were instructed to kill all of you."

"We had worked out a plan. I was to meet up with him after he got the material from you. He wanted to destroy it on the spot. I told him we should take it back to Israel to make sure that the professor could never take credit for the discovery. Believe me. We had it all worked out. The only difference is that I was going to take it from Shimon before he would do something stupid with it."

"Like destroy it."

"Yes."

"He could have destroyed it, but we had the model. We could have duplicated the process. You are not telling me..."

"Yes. My plan was to eliminate all three of you. Unfortunately, I would have had to eliminate Shimon too. It would have been very easy to blame the American."

"But, Steve, you have always been like a son to me. Why are you doing this?"

"Rabbi, I do not share your view of the world or your view of God. My world is different from yours. Mine is the here and now. It is what I make of it. Life only presents so many opportunities, and this is one of them. I intend to seize it."

"But, Steve—"

"We have talked enough. Now, Professor, hand over the program or—"

Thanks to the silencer, no one heard the bullet leave its chamber until Steve slumped. From short range, the bullet hit its intended mark. Steve was dead before he hit the floor.

Neither the rabbi nor the professor moved, both paralyzed by fear. *Were we the intended target? Would we be next?* For sure, they were easy targets. They were defenseless, except for the gun that lay next to Steve's body, which the professor reached down and grabbed.

Motionless, they waited. There was no one to call for help. They couldn't call the police. How could they explain the body on the floor? The next few minutes seemed like an eternity, but miraculously, there was no follow-up from the shooter.

Finally, the professor spoke. "Rabbi, they are getting close."

"By *they*, you mean Haggerty?"

"Yes. I can only assume that Haggerty had to eliminate Steve first. I suspect we will be next, and no doubt very soon.

*****

The professor gave Lisa the address and some crude directions to the rabbi's home. He knew that the rabbi was in no condition to be bothered with this detail.

Before their meeting with the rabbi at the King David Hotel, the group moved from the missionary's home to a local hotel. It was part of their plan to constantly be on the move. The professor gave specific instructions to them not to check out of the hotel, even though they would not return there tonight. That would draw too much attention.

The rabbi arranged for them to stay at his home in the Me'a She'arim village of Jerusalem, less than a mile from the Old City. The rabbi assured them there would be a greater amount of protection there.

In the meantime, the rabbi did what he could to clean up the situation. It required that he report what had happened to the two members of the group he could ultimately trust. His story was that the Americans were obviously on a plan to destroy all competition for the codes, including Steve for now. He saw no need to relay Steve's intentions for the codes to the other members. That would all be sorted out at a later date.

The military strategist called in some favors to have the body removed, supported by a creative explanation that even the rabbi was not made aware of. The rabbi decided not to call the local police. How could he explain the death of one of Israel's up-and-coming entrepreneurs and the son of a respected Israeli family? After all, who could he trust at this point? The professor agreed. It was hard to tell who was on your side and who might be the next to put a bullet through your head.

The flurry of activity and the adrenalin that it produced had momentarily served to delay the rabbi's confrontation of the news of the death of his son. It wasn't until their drive to the rabbi's home that the reality started to sink in. The news of his son's death was almost more than he could bear.

The professor was relieved that he did not have to tell the rabbi the real story of Shimon's tragedy. For now, the story would remain that Shimon was involved in an unfortunate accident.

THE REDEMPTION CODES

The rabbi repeated the words that Steve had told him. His son had not been an opportunist mercenary, just looking to make money from the codes. Instead, he had remained consistent to his faith right up till the end.

*****

The Me'a She'arim village was originally built in the late nineteenth century as a semifortified agricultural community. The courtyards were originally designed to defend against marauding Bedouin tribes. Today, the village is predominantly populated by Hasidic and ultra-Orthodox Jews, mostly of East European origin.

As the rabbi and the professor arrived at the rabbi's home, the professor's initial observation was that the modest size of the rabbi's home did not seem to match his position and prestige. Not only did the home appear small, but it was also shoehorned between houses on both sides with only small courtyards separating each home.

The rabbi and the professor pulled into the small driveway only a few minutes before the cab with Lisa and Neil arrived from the hotel.

The rabbi, wanting to be alone, excused himself as the professor greeted Neil and Lisa at the door.

"Could you tell if anyone followed you from the hotel?"

"No, I don't think so," replied Lisa.

"But the cab driver appeared to be very interested in what we were doing and why two Americans were going to the Me'a She'arim section of Jerusalem," said Neil.

"Did you walk to a cab?"

"No. We had the hotel call one for us," said Neil, realizing before he had finished the sentence that, by now, he should know better. This was serious business, and he knew he had to be more careful.

"The research?"

Neil removed the backpack and opened the zippered part. The files were just as the professor had left them.

"Good."

"We don't have long to plan," said the professor as he sat down at a table overlooking the small courtyard with a fountain and several potted plants. "The visit earlier illustrates that they know where to find me. If they followed us here, they could have this place surrounded within hours."

"You had a visitor? That sounds ominous," said Neil.

"Yes, someone apparently bent on doing us harm. I can share the details another time. Unfortunately, the rabbi knows about his son, Shimon." He would wait until later to tell Steve Gold's version of Shimon's death.

"He must have been devastated," said Lisa.

"It was hard for him to make sense of it. I know how he feels. Lisa, I will be glad when it is over. There has been too much pain for everyone involved."

Lisa was not about to argue that point. She had already learned an important life lesson: Every major discovery comes with sacrifice. This one just had a higher price tag than most.

"Dad, I received a call from the missionary."

The professor winced at the thought that the missionary could get caught up in their dangerous game.

"He is okay but is very shaken up. Several men came to his home this afternoon. They knocked on the door, but he did not answer. They went to the back door and knocked as well. He was convinced they were going to break down the door when one of them received a call, and they left immediately. He decided to go to the home of one of the families who attend his weekly meetings until this whole thing dies down."

"That is a good idea. Any association the missionary has with us could mean instant eviction from the country for the missionary, if not worse. There have already been enough casualties of innocent victims who have only tried to help us."

*****

After about an hour, the rabbi walked back into the room where the three were huddled together. It was obvious by the pain still etched on his face that the news of his son was difficult for him to process.

"Professor, when you heard of the death of your father, did you want to just quit...to just give up?"

The professor knew where these doubts were coming from and tried to weigh every word. "At times, yes. Well, if I am to be totally honest, there were several dark moments—even now—almost every day when I cannot reconcile his sacrifice for me. For what? For a discovery that he would never know was ever made. But in the midst of those dark moments, I believe he would want me to persevere—to not quit."

"Then persevere we must, Professor. For your father and for my son. I will make us some coffee, and we will start where we left off."

"Rabbi, at the restaurant, you were confident that you knew that the *Appointed Place* is the Ark of the Covenant and that the codes were to be hidden in the Ark of the Covenant," said the professor.

"That is correct."

"What makes you so confident?"

"You found the word *Jeremiah*."

"Yes. How did you know?" answered Neil, looking at Lisa incredulously.

"I also found those words hidden in the codes."

"It is good to know that we are at least on the same page," said the professor.

"We are guided by the same divine hand, inexorably on the same divine path, serving the same divine purpose. I don't think any of this is an accident."

"I am confused, Rabbi. I can understand why Lisa and Neil found certain references of the ark because they were looking for them, but it is somewhat of a mystery that among all of the things you could have searched for, you chose to search references of the ark."

The rabbi had the same facial expression that the professor had seen when he heard that his son was dead. It took the rabbi a few seconds to compose himself enough to speak. "My wife, her name was Naomi. She died in the spring of last year. We had just celebrated our fortieth wedding anniversary. She became ill and died within six months. As a famous biblical archaeologist, it was her lifelong obsession to find the Ark of the Covenant. In fact, she was considered an expert on the subject. Her articles about the ark appeared in newspapers and magazines all over the world."

"I vaguely remember my father showing me her article about the possible locations of the ark," said the professor.

"A little history lesson is in order. The ark was last seen as part of Solomon's Temple—what is often referred to as the First Temple era. The ark was not even a part of the Second Temple. But it has been a tradition held by many, and I should say hoped by even more that the Ark of the Covenant still exists. Many believe that it is located in Ethiopia, perhaps in a monastery. Neither my wife nor I ever subscribed to that theory. If it is there, it would be a secret held by a few individuals. Secrets can only be kept for so long. Eventually, someone will tell. That's human nature. No, if it were in Ethiopia, we would know.

"Presently, there are three main theories concerning the location of the ark, and at varying times, each theory has been held as the right one. One is the location at the south end of the Temple Mount. Of the three, this theory has had only limited support. Another theory is that the ark is located at the north end of the Temple Mount. This location, as with the south end, could support an archeological dig without interfering with the Dome of the Rock. The predominant theory, and one held by most of the respected archeologists, is that the ark is buried underneath the Doom of the Rock. But in any of those locations, it would be easier to obtain a permit to dump nuclear waste in the Amazon Rainforest than for a Jew to have access to dig for the ark on one of the holiest of Muslim sites.

"Naomi was convinced that the ark was located underneath the Dome of the Rock. That all changed the day I found the name *Jeremiah* in the codes in the same location as the ark. You see, I was looking for something in the codes that might give me a hint as to the location of the ark.

"Well, when I found the *Jeremiah* reference, Naomi immediately embarked on the most ambitious study of her entire, illustrious career. She read and researched everything related to the ark and Jeremiah. You see, Jeremiah was the prophet during the time of the Babylonian conquest of Judah. She became convinced that Jeremiah and the ark were somehow connected. After extensive study, she reached the conclusion that Jeremiah must have been involved with the Temple implements in an attempt to save the various articles so that they could be used in the future."

"If the Temple were ever rebuilt," said the professor.

"Exactly. Basically, Jeremiah attempted to hide the implements. You can imagine that when the Temple was destroyed, the gold value of these items was worth a great deal."

"I could see hiding bowls or other implements, but hiding the ark, well, that is a different matter altogether," said Neil.

"Maybe, maybe not," said the rabbi, gesturing with his hands. "You see, Naomi had been convinced, even before my reference to Jeremiah, that there were a series of tunnels underneath the Temple Mount. Maybe in the days when the Temple was active, the tunnels might have been used for a variety of reasons. She had done extensive research on one of the tunnels."

"Do those tunnels still exist?" asked Lisa.

There appeared a slight glimmer in the rabbi's eyes. "Yes, Lisa. Those tunnels still exist today."

"But how does that relate to the ark, Rabbi? Are you suggesting that Jeremiah might have moved the ark away from the Temple through an underground tunnel?" asked the professor.

"Yes, it must have been his intent to hide the ark from the invading Babylonians. Anyway, Naomi was able to obtain some very sophisticated equipment that enabled her to trace a major tunnel from the location of the Dome of the Rock to the south end of the Temple Mount. To her surprise, the tunnel appeared to end abruptly. The area where the tunnel ended was an area that had not been previously explored."

The professor was sitting on the edge of his seat. He could sense something of cosmic proportions was about to be divulged.

"One day, near the end, when I was sitting beside her bed, she motioned for me to come close to her. It took all of the energy she had to talk. She whispered to me, *'Ark, I see the ark. Please find the ark.'* She was in so much pain right before she died. In her mind, she probably did see the ark. Then she mumbled something about entering from another direction. I had no idea what she was talking about and more or less assumed it was some delusional thought that came with the illness. She motioned to me that she wanted to write something down, so I got her some paper and a pen. It turned out that she did not want to write something down. She wanted to draw me a picture."

The rabbi reached into a drawer beside a sofa and pulled out a piece of paper. "Professor, you might have your fancy models that can show the future, but I have a treasure map."

Lisa, Neil, and the professor closed around the rabbi and the drawing.

"See this long double line? This is the original tunnel that Naomi discovered. Now you see a space, and then the double line continues. What Naomi was trying to show me was that the tunnel started again. Originally, the tunnel had been one long tunnel, but the middle section had collapsed, probably from an earthquake. She was telling me to locate the end of the tunnel and then work back in the direction of where the other tunnel would have connected."

"And the *x* between the two tunnels, am I to assume..."

The rabbi grabbed the professor's hand. "Yes, Professor, that was the area Naomi was convinced the Temple implements were located."

"And the ark?"

"Yes, and the ark."

The professor looked at Neil and Lisa in disbelief.

"But you need to know something that has remained a mystery to me. Right before Naomi died, she mumbled some words to me in Hebrew. You must understand that Hebrew was not spoken except for very holy occasions. Our conversations were in English or an occasional Yiddish. I knew what she said was important, so I wrote it down. One day, I prayed that I would understand what it meant." The rabbi reached into his pocket and pulled out his wallet. A torn piece of hospital stationery was folded. He took it out and unfolded it. "In translation, she said, *'Bury the future with the past until the end of that Present Day.'* The future obviously makes reference to the power of the codes. She believed that the codes would someday reveal the future."

"Did you speak with her about the power of the codes to predict the future?" asked Lisa.

"Yes, many times. She was confident, even more than myself, that the codes could reveal the future. But she also felt that the power of that knowledge was too great for mortal man to possess."

"Bury the future with the past sounds like an instruction to bury the codes—" said the professor.

"The *past* reference is the ark," interrupted Neil. "You are to bury the codes in the ark."

"I agree with your conclusions. Since you told me you made the discovery of the codes and we identified the *Appointed Place* as the ark, I understood that part of what she was saying. But what do you make of the phrase, '*Until the end of that Present Day*'?"

Lisa and Neil looked at the professor, who was stroking his chin. "I think *Present Day* is another term for the Present Age. If a day is like a thousand years and a thousand years is like a day for God, I guess it would be reasonable to equate an age with a day. So what she said could be rephrased *until the end of that Present Age.*"

"Tell me more about this *Present Age.*"

"As you know, Rabbi, the history of man, as chronicled in the Scriptures, is divided into several ages. Ages were periods of time in which certain factors or characteristics dominated. For example, the antediluvian age was the age prior to the Great Flood. The age up until Pentecost might have been referred to as the age of Israel or the Jewish Age. The Present Age is another way of saying the age we are living in now. My father referred to it as the Age of the Church or the Church Age."

"The Church Age?" the rabbi questioned.

"The time after Jesus died when it is believed that the Christian church became the beneficiary of God's kingdom. Another name would be the Age of the Gentile or Gentile Age."

"By beneficiary, I assume you mean they replaced the Jew as God's chosen people."

"Temporarily, yes, you could say that."

"But what do you make of the phrase, '*Until the end*'?" asked the rabbi.

"That would be the end of the Church Age," replied the professor.

"But how do we know when it is the end of the Church Age?"

"Do you remember when we were discussing the future of America, and I told you that many Americans suddenly disappeared?"

"Yes. What you people refer to as the Rapture. You had another fancy name for it."

"Correct. Another way of looking at it is that those two events, the Rapture and the end of the Church Age, occur simultaneously, I believe. The Rapture is evidenced by the mass disappearances, which also signifies the end of the Church Age. In other words, the church is raptured—gone. No church, no need for a Church Age."

"I think I understand."

The professor stood up. "Rabbi, your wife's request was quite straightforward. Bury the codes in the ark until the Messiah returns. I believe sometime after the Messiah returns for the church, the Rapture, the Jewish people will rebuild the temple on the Temple Mount and reinstate the sacrifice. When the Temple is rebuilt, there will be the discovery, or should I say, rediscovery, of the ark."

"And when the ark is discovered, so will the codes," said the rabbi.

"And when the codes are rediscovered, it will serve to reconfirm the Jews' faith," said Lisa.

"Rabbi, what your wife knew that day in the hospital was what I needed to discover for myself. That is why I was to travel to Israel. We were instructed by the codes to hide them at the *Appointed Place*. Thanks to you. We now know the *Appointed Place*."

"I can understand that you believe, with very strong convictions, that the ark is located at the south end of the Temple Mount. But, Rabbi, there is no way that an Israeli Jew could get approval to have an archaeological dig on one of the major Muslim holy sites. That would cause an instantaneous holy war," said Neil.

"And even if you were ever to get such approval, it could take years to complete such an excavation," said Lisa.

"And unfortunately, Rabbi, time is not on our side," chimed in the professor.

"I cannot disagree with you on that matter. Having access to the Temple Mount was not an easy thing to obtain. Let there be no doubt. I know it was an act of God."

"What are you saying? It sounds like you already have some sort of approval," said the professor.

"I don't actually have an archeological permit to dig on the Temple Mount. That would have generated too much public outcry. The politics would have eventually destroyed any attempt by a Jew to dig on the Temple Mount. No, but I do have a letter signed by the prime minister and the then-acting director of the Temple Mount authority. It was part of a trade between the two parties that was never made public. I don't even know what the director received in exchange. I suspect it had something to do with one of the director's sons who had been involved in an embarrassing episode. The truth is, I don't care. The only thing that mattered was that I have at least limited access."

"But, Rabbi, act of God or not act of God, for a Jew to dig on the Temple Mount, that is a little much for me to believe," said Neil.

"After what you have seen from the codes, I am surprised that anything is hard to believe from God. But let me finish. There is more to the story, which may help you understand how this happened. It turns out that a main water pipe near a public restroom on the south end of the Temple Mount was leaking. The public restroom, as providence would have it, was near the tunnel that my wife had drawn. The argument was made to the acting director of the Temple Mount authority that it needed to be fixed before it caused serious erosion that could have long-term effects on the sacred Muslim buildings."

"Is that true?" questioned the professor.

"It is true that some erosion has occurred in that area due to some underground leakage. But not significant and certainly not one that merited excavation or repair at this time. The prime minister knew what I was up to and convinced the agency that has jurisdiction of the Temple Mount to have a plumber do repair that required only minor digging. After all, you see, there was that messy situation with the son of the director."

"So there was a trade."

"Yes, the prime minister would make an embarrassing situation disappear for the right to pick the plumber."

"And you were the plumber?"

"Yes, in a manner of speaking."

"In a manner of speaking? I have a feeling there is more to this mystery," said the professor.

"One of my students is married to a Palestinian woman whose father is a plumber. We used his license to get approval for the repairs through the Temple Mount authorities."

"And they weren't suspicious of your actions?"

"Not at all. In fact, I convinced the prime minister to intercede in the whole affair by claiming that this ground should not be unduly disturbed without an archeologist's oversight."

"And you happened to be that archeologist?"

"That's correct," said the rabbi, managing a smile.

"And have you started on these…so-called repairs yet?" asked the professor.

"Oh, yes. I have been working on this for several months."

"And your efforts, Rabbi, have they yielded any results?" asked the professor, eyeing the rabbi intently for any tangible reaction.

"You are carefully weighing your words, Professor. What you are dying to know, as are Lisa and Neil, is whether I made any significant discoveries while fixing a water pipe?"

The rabbi went over and took a picture of his wife off the shelf. He placed the picture against his chest. Two nights ago, at around three in the morning, I dropped to my knees, and with this picture in my hands, I told my wife what I would say to you now. *I have seen the ark.*"

No words were spoken for several minutes. Finally, the rabbi walked back to the shelf and carefully placed the picture back on it.

"Now there is one more matter. You were instructed to hide them not only at the *Appointed Place* but also at the *Appointed Time*," said the rabbi.

"I assume the *Appointed Time* is now before we are all killed," said Neil somewhat humorously.

"You are right, son, that the *Appointed Time* is now, but not for reasons that you think. You see, I received the okay to start the repairs almost twelve months ago. A small earthquake occurred where we were digging, which forced us to stop for several weeks. Then when we were ready to get started again, the weather turned bad. I was getting frustrated. It was raining every day."

"Had the weather, or should I say, acts of God, not have held you up, would you have been finished by now?" asked the professor.

"Yes, there is no doubt about that. I would have finished months ago."

"I guess God had a different timetable," said the professor.

"Yes, you are right about that. So, my friends, we have the *Appointed Time*. It is now. Days ago, it would have been too early. Days from now, it will be too late."

There was a silence when words were not necessary. They had witnessed one of those moments in life that they could not fully explain, could not fully understand, and would never forget.

"So my efforts to locate the ark was not to reveal it to the world. It was so that I could place the codes there," said the rabbi.

"That is right. I don't think the world is ready for either the codes or the ark, at least not yet," replied the professor.

"Does that bother you, Rabbi? You could have been a national hero if you would have discovered the ark," said Neil.

"As much as I would like to think that our nation would benefit from the discovery of the ark, I'm afraid the professor is right. This is not the time."

"But from what we know about the future of America, it will not be long," said the professor.

*****

As the four loaded into a somewhat dilapidated and faded blue van, the professor could not help but notice several shovels and wheelbarrows stacked in the back of the van. The rabbi insisted that the professor drive the short trip from the rabbi's home, located just a few blocks north of Jaffa Road in the Old City, to the southern end of the Temple Mount. The rabbi, sitting up front, did not say a word during the drive through the Old City except for an occasional instruction as to where to turn. His hands were folded on top of the Torah, which lay across his lap.

Night was falling upon the Old City, and the tourists and worshippers who had been so prevalent were now replaced by a security force of young men and women with rifles strapped across their shoulders. Even though the professor had long ago reconciled himself to his fate and mission, as he drove past the Western Wall, he wished now he was just a tourist. The trip through the Old City was inspirational, and more than anything, he wished his father was here to share this moment.

The trip to the Temple Mount took just a few minutes. Neil and Lisa sat quietly in the back, occasionally glancing at each other with a mixture of fear and anticipation.

Finally, the rabbi broke the silence. "I forgot to ask, but you have the zip drives, Professor?"

The professor tapped the backpack sitting beside him. "Yes, they are in here, along with references for each of the future events. They are in an envelope."

"Do you mind if I see it?" asked the rabbi.

Neil took the backpack, pulled out the large envelope, and handed it to the rabbi.

The rabbi turned on the inside light and looked at the envelope. When he turned it over, he saw some writing on the front of the envelope. As he started to read it, he stopped and handed the envelope back to Neil.

Neil read the inscription: "On behalf of Rabbi Benjamin Breuer – 2024."

THE REDEMPTION CODES

"Professor, Lisa, Neil, you are much too gracious to this old man. I do not deserve this. After all, it was you who made this discovery, and it is you who should receive the credit."

"Credit? This is way bigger than an individual achievement. What I have seen and learned throughout this process is greater than all of the credit or accolades the world could offer," said the professor.

"Yes, I guess you are right about that. Just think of it. We have both made a discovery, either which would be the greatest discovery of the last millennia, and we will be long gone before it is rediscovered."

"Maybe, Rabbi. But if our calculations are accurate, it will be sooner than you think."

"The envelope. Did you enclose how you arrived at your predictions along with the zip drives, you know, the model…the calculations?"

"No. Just the future events. We did enclose a graph of the events in the sequence we expect them to occur."

"Are you worried that by the time this is discovered, or should I say, rediscovered, all of the events you saw would have already occurred?"

"No, Rabbi. This envelope will be discovered when the ark is discovered. When we talked about the future of Israel, I did not specifically detail the sequence of events. After Israel wins the initial war that I told you about, Israel's border is pushed out to the area originally promised to Abraham. One of the side benefits of her victory is that Israel will take back complete control of the Temple Mount. This victory will usher in a short period in which Israel is very secure, and her enemies will be gone. How long that period lasted, we could not tell. But it is long enough that the Third Temple is rebuilt."

"Oh my. My son was very active with the Temple Institute. If he were only here to see that day."

"Rabbi, the ark must be discovered before the Third Temple is built."

"Who am I to argue with one who has seen the future? But we have a long-standing tradition that the ark cannot be revealed until the day of the coming of the Messiah."

"Rabbi, do you remember when I told you about the sudden disappearance of the Christians, what we found in the codes as the Harpazo? That *was* the coming of the Messiah."

"Yes, I remember. So you believe that after the disappearance of the Christians, we will soon build the Third Temple?"

"No, I don't just believe that. I saw that."

The rabbi appeared to be deep in thought when he realized that they were close to the southern entrance to the Temple Mount.

"Park right there," said the rabbi, pointing to a flat section of pavement just a few yards from the road. "Each of you, bring a shovel and a wheelbarrow from the back of the van so that we can complete our work tonight. Follow me. You have shown me your discovery. Now I will show you my discovery, but I must be the one to place the envelope on the table. I believe it to be the table of showbread."

A chill ran down the professor's back as he looked at Neil and Lisa. Their odyssey that, for the professor, started when his father issued that first challenge may be over faster than they had thought.

The rabbi presented his credentials to the guard and his letter of authorization from the prime minister. It was a formality he had done dozens of times. He wondered what it accomplished at this point, but he did not complain because he knew he had been given a special privilege. He was not going to make waves, at least not at this point. The true mission that he did not fully understand until the professor arrived was almost finished.

"Go ahead, Rabbi," said the young soldier, his Uzi assault rifle lying across his cupped hands. He lifted the rifle so that the rabbi could proceed. He dropped the rifle in front of the professor.

"This is Professor Lange," the rabbi said to the young soldier. "Present some identification to the soldier, Professor."

The professor did as he was instructed and showed the soldier his passport. The soldier lifted his rifle again to let the professor proceed.

"These are the two students who are included in the approval letter." The soldier waved Neil and Lisa through as well.

"I am amazed that you were able to accomplish such an approval in the short period of time since we have been in the country," said the professor after they had walked beyond earshot of the soldier.

"I didn't."

"Then how could you possibly know to include me on your list?"

"After I first met with you in New York, I had a feeling we might meet again. I realized that day that it was more than the codes. Something inside me said the codes and the ark were somehow inextricably connected. So from the beginning, I added your name to the list of approved diggers."

The professor did not know how to respond.

"But how about us?" asked Lisa.

"When I found out that the professor's daughter and a former student had joined the professor, I went back and had the approval letter amended to include two appendices of my choice. The condition was that the apprentices could not participate in the repair, only observe."

"That is amazing," said Neil, shaking his head in disbelief.

"Follow me," said the rabbi. "We only have nine hours to finish our mission."

About a hundred yards from the entrance gate, the group arrived at a small building with signs in several languages indicating public restrooms. Next to the small building was a large hole and one smaller hole. The rabbi unlocked the gate of the small fence that surrounded the two holes.

"Follow me, Professor, and I will show you my discovery. But there will be a point where I ask you not to go any farther."

The rabbi slowly and, at times, painfully descended down the side of the larger hole by virtue of a wooden ladder that leaned against one side of the hole. Reaching the bottom, the rabbi signaled for the professor to follow. Lisa and Neil followed the professor. The flat surface at the bottom of the hole was barely large enough to accommodate the four of them.

The area outside the hole was encompassed by a darkness that appeared impregnable. Inside, the rabbi shined his flashlight on a small tunnel that proceeded out from the bottom of the hole in the direction the professor assumed was the Dome of the Rock.

"There." The rabbi focused the light on the opening of the tunnel. The professor could just see enough to know that the light appeared to hit a back wall of the tunnel.

"And you are absolutely certain that you have found the ark?" asked the professor.

"Yes, I am absolutely sure. Two days ago, I confirmed the ark's length to match exactly the specifications of the Torah. I also found some writing on the end of the ark. And"—the rabbi hesitated as if he was trying to gain some composure—"I found the menorah."

"It appears from the light that the ark is in a room," said Neil.

"Yes, I believe that the ark is protected by four solid walls. I believe it was Jeremiah who decided to hide the ark. He went to great links to make sure that it was protected."

"Can I see the ark?" asked the professor.

"Out of respect for the sacredness of this place, I will shine a light on the exposed sections of the ark and the menorah, but I request that you do not enter the room where the ark is located."

The three nodded as the rabbi shined the light in the direction of the ark.

"Well, I guess this is my lucky day, Rabbi," came a voice from above the entrance to the hole.

The voice startled the group that had been transfixed on the ark. They looked in the direction of the voice, but darkness obscured the identity of the person. Only a silhouette of a man appeared.

"Who is this? Identify yourself," demanded the rabbi as he raised his light. No response was necessary as the light made contact with the figure, Larry Haggerty.

"How fortunate can one man be? It appears that I came for the goose, and now I might leave with both the goose and the golden egg," Haggerty said arrogantly.

"I am not sure what you are alluding to," said the rabbi, his voice starting to crack.

The light showed the gun Haggerty had in his right hand. "Climb out of the hole and make sure you bring the codes. Perhaps we can make a deal."

As the rabbi reached for the side of the ladder, the professor realized he had to come up with a plan quickly.

"Quick, Neil, give me the envelope, and then you and Lisa slowly follow the rabbi up the ladder so that I can have some extra time," the professor whispered.

Neil took off his backpack and handed the envelope to the professor before he slowly exited. The professor reached the tunnel and carefully laid the envelope on top of a table before following Neil.

The rabbi stood at the mouth of the hole between the professor, Neil, and Lisa as Haggerty positioned himself so that all four of the group were directly in front of him.

"It is unfortunate that we were not able to work together. We would have made a great team," said Haggerty.

"My greatest regret is that we ever had anything to do with you," said the rabbi.

"In the end, that will be your loss."

"You never had the intellect to make the discovery you were seeking," said the rabbi.

"Maybe the professor made the discovery, but after tonight, it will belong to me. When you have other means to get what you want, what does it matter about my lack of intellect?"

"You are not worthy to have this information."

"Worthy? Rabbi, you sound as if this is sacred."

"It is sacred."

"You can take that position if you like that this is some noble—some sacred discovery. But my worldview is not your worldview. Sacredness is not what fuels the world. Money, finance, and maybe a dash of greed—power and control. That is what rules the world."

The rabbi looked around nervously, realizing that there was no one who could come to their rescue. A sense of hopelessness was sinking in for the rabbi.

"If you are hoping that the security guard will come to your rescue, then you must think that I am a fool. He has been silenced and cannot help you now."

"What do you want?"

"I came for the code programs from the professor. But maybe we can make a deal."

"A deal?" asked the professor.

"You give me the code program. I will hold the codes until you bring me the ark. When I have the ark safely in my possession, I will return the codes."

"That is preposterous. Now you must think that we are the fools. Plus, you are not worthy to hold the codes," said the rabbi.

Haggerty raised the gun and pointed it directly at the rabbi. "You don't have much of a bargaining position, now do you?"

"The ark has no value in the open market. It would be like trying to sell the *Mona Lisa*. The only ones to have an interest in the ark are the Jews," said the rabbi.

"What you say is correct. I deliver the ark in exchange for one billion dollars, and you get to keep the codes. It is simple."

"How did you know about the ark?" asked the rabbi.

"Steve Gold told me that you were involved with something on the Temple Mount. He said it was somewhat strange that an academic, much less a Jew, would all of a sudden have an interest in digging in an obscure location, not to mention how you were able to get approval. It was Steve who put the pieces together. At the time he told me, I had all but given up on ever discovering the mysteries of the codes. But the ark, now that was a different matter. He wanted the codes, and I wanted the ark. The plan was very simple until Steve met an untimely death this afternoon."

"Untimely death. Yes, and I suppose you had nothing to do with that," said the rabbi.

"That is right. I did not. Why would I kill my partner?"

"Somehow, that sounded insincere. After all, you were not bothered by killing my father."

"Professor, that was an unfortunate miscalculation on my part."

"So killing us will be another unfortunate miscalculation," said the professor.

"I don't intend to kill you as long as you provide me with the codes now and then follow it up with the ark."

"I don't understand. Why would the Jews pay you one billion dollars for the ark?" asked the professor.

"There is a group who wants to rebuild the Temple. They will do anything to achieve this."

"I know of these groups. They don't have that kind of money," said the rabbi.

"But the Israeli government does. Don't you understand what this discovery means to them? And all that I need is right here in front of me. I am getting impatient. We have talked enough. Give me the codes."

The professor knew he had to act quickly.

"We don't have the codes. They are locked up in Tel Aviv. Tomorrow, the codes will be published in the *Jerusalem Post*. That is why I came to Israel. The cat's out of the bag, Haggerty. The codes are no longer of value to anyone. The rabbi and I agreed they should be made public. If you don't believe me, you can call the editor."

He started reaching for his phone to advance the charade when he realized Haggerty might think he was reaching for a weapon.

Haggerty looked momentarily confused. No one was prepared for Haggerty's response to the professor's challenge. The darkness obscured the gun as he lifted it, and the silencer muffled some of the sound. The results were apparent as the rabbi staggered from the bullet, which hit flush against his chest. His knees buckled under him as he fell back into the hole.

"We can make this easy, or we can make this painful," said Haggerty. "I came for the codes." He lifted the gun again, this time in the direction of the professor.

No one saw the figure that had approached from behind Haggerty. There was no silencer to silence the sound that punctuated the night air. The bullet met its target. Larry Haggerty staggered and fell to the ground.

When the professor turned to look at the figure who had just saved his life, he thought he had seen a ghost. It was Shimon.

Shimon ignored Haggerty's dead body lying in front of him and ran straight to the hole. He scurried down the ladder. Dropping on his knees next to where his father was lying, Shimon lifted his father's head and lowered his ear to the rabbi's mouth. The professor could not see or hear what the rabbi was saying. He could only see the tears rolling down Shimon's face. After a few seconds, it was over.

"He is dead. My father is dead."

Chapter 32

The "Appointed Place"

And he said, "Go thy way, Daniel: for the words are
closed up and sealed till the time of the end."
—Daniel 12:9

My father will get a proper burial. Shimon exclaimed as he carried his father out of the hole that had so unceremoniously swallowed him. After determining that Haggerty was dead, the professor and Neil dragged his body and carefully lowered him to the bottom of the utility hole next to the main hole. Shimon insisted that Haggerty's body could not be buried in the main hole. The professor assumed that Shimon must know the sacredness of the contents in the main hole. Haggerty's disappearance would have to remain a mystery, at least for a few more years.

The wooden ladder was removed, and the holes were filled back up from the stockpile of dirt next to the holes. The makeshift, chain-link fence around the holes and the sign that read *Utilities Under Repair* were removed and discarded in a nearby dumpster.

Shimon would tell the prime minister that the rabbi's calculations were wrong. The Ark of the Covenant was not located on the southern end of the Temple Mount where the rabbi had thought. The prevailing wisdom would remain for a while; the Ark of the Covenant must be under the Dome of the Rock, after all.

Though there would be some questions and suspicions, the rabbi's death could be explained very easily. The prime minister and the group were aware that doctors had given the rabbi only a few months left to live.

Several revelations came out that night in the heavy, damp air on the southern end of the Temple Mount. For one thing, Haggerty was telling the truth. He had not killed Steve Gold. That was the work of Shimon.

Shimon desperately wanted to believe that the intentions of his long-time friend were the same as his—to get the code research from the professor for the purpose of making sure the professor never took credit for the discovery and if everything went according to plan, to make sure the research was never made public.

Even though Shimon had lingering doubts about Steve's motivations, he had not planned to kill him when he followed him to the courtyard that afternoon. Standing outside the wall listening to what Steve was saying unfortunately confirmed his worse suspicions.

Whether it had been Steve's intentions that day to kill his father and the professor, Shimon would never know. In his heart, he had his doubts, but when he saw the gun in Steve's hand, Shimon's decision was made. He could not take that chance. Nor could he allow someone to profit from the codes. They were sacred.

Shimon told the professor that Jimmy most likely died from a car accident leaving the airport. The newspaper read, "He rolled over and hit a tree. The driver was exceeding the speed limit and weaving through traffic. Drugs and alcohol have not been ruled out."

It was a clear day when Jimmy dropped them off at the airport, and he was a careful driver. The professor suspected there was more to the story than he might ever know. The one thing he knew for sure was that drugs and alcohol were not part of Jimmy's life.

Shimon showed the professor the hole in his shoulder, which was still heavily bandaged. It was one of those unexplainable injuries that appeared a lot worse than it was. It was the shock of the injury and the sight of the fire poke sticking through his shoulder that caused him to pass out. It had been several hours before he awoke in a damp, cold cave inside the mountain where Jimmy had laid him.

The most amazing thing they heard that night was the story of how Jimmy saved Shimon's life. Its message was one of incredible love shown for someone who, by his previous actions, didn't deserve it.

When the group was on their trek away from the cabin, Jimmy returned to make sure that no one followed them. Looking into the cave, he saw that Shimon was moving but in a great deal of pain. Without hesitating, he rushed to find some alcohol to pour into the wound. Shimon could not bear to look, but somehow, Jimmy sawed off the fire poke's tip. He removed the fire poke and bandaged up the area. He gave Shimon some blankets and told him that someone would come to take him to a local doctor.

Shimon also revealed on that terrible night in the large room that it was not his intent to shoot Jimmy. When Jimmy charged him, he tried to drop the gun, but somehow, the gun discharged. He regretted not telling Jimmy he was saved on that night. He would have to live the rest of his life with that confession.

Shimon recalled Jimmy's last words to him. *I don't think you are a bad or a dangerous person, except maybe to yourself. I could tell by the way you acted that you wouldn't hurt the professor. And I don't think you killed Biltmore either. I hope I'm not wrong about that. Now stay here until I can get you to a doctor.*

"It wasn't long before someone who said she was Jimmy's cousin arrived and carried me to a local country doctor. I think that doctor was somewhat suspicious of the injury but did not say anything."

For a second, the professor remembered his father's words. *From life to death and death to life, what a frail veil that separates the two.*

The professor never found out the rabbi's last words. That would remain Shimon's secret. He was just thankful that the last person the rabbi saw was his son—a son who he was told had died so ungraciously, a son who understood that nothing of real value could come from something that caused so much death and destruction in its wake.

The professor confessed to Shimon what he already suspected. They had discovered the model that unlocked the full power of the codes to reveal the future. Unlike his father, Shimon did not wish to pursue the details of what they had found. The professor assured him that he had given the rabbi some good news about the future of their beloved country. That was enough for Shimon.

"And where is your research now?" asked Shimon.

"Thanks to your father. The file that contains our research has been hidden at the *Appointed Place* and will be there until the *Appointed Time*." He waited for Shimon to question what he meant, but there was no response. The professor suspected that the rabbi shared those secrets with his last words.

In the meantime, Shimon would be the trustee of the incredible secret that the words dictated by God to Moses several thousand years ago contained the codes that would someday reveal the future.

For now, the professor knew that the world was not ready for his discoveries. Even if every prophetic event revealed by the codes was distributed to every household in America, it would only be a matter of time before its message was rationalized away. *The prophecies of the Torah and the Bible have taught us that much.*

It is true that the codes reveal again, for a different generation, that there is a God. But the professor's father was right. If you want to know whether there is a God, open your window and look outside. He is revealed daily through His majestic nature and through the love so expressed by individuals such as his father, Biltmore, and Jimmy.

The professor asked himself again whether the search for the holy grail was worth it. The scorecard said no. Eight dead. *Death and destruction always chase greed.*

If you could ask the professor's father whether it was worth it, you might get a different answer. He would never know how reaching out to connect on his son's turf played out, but he would be happy to know the effort led to a path of redemption. And for that alone, he would say his sacrifice was worth it.

The professor learned three important life lessons along the way. The redemption was discovered in the journey, not the destination. It wasn't what the professor discovered that mattered. After all, there were only three people who knew the key that unlocked the secrets to the future, and they were not talking.

And the future is not always a pretty sight. But in the end, it was not about finding out what the future holds, as it was who holds the future.

Maybe the greatest lesson of all is that there are those whose love is so great that they are willing to give the ultimate gift—their lives.

"Greater love has no one than this that he lay down his life for his friends."

The professor's promise that they would not profit from the codes was partially fulfilled. After all, no one could quantify how much the professor, Lisa, or Neil had profited from the journey individually, especially spiritually.

Any of the events that had occurred tonight or over the past week were beyond comprehension, but when you consider the sum total of all of the events, it took on cosmic proportions.

With little discussion and no disagreement, the three agreed that none of the revelations would be shared with the world. The codes were buried along with the ark, its *Appointed Place*. The professor knew that at the *Appointed Time*, the ark would be rediscovered. When that day occurred, the world would be in disarray, chaos the likes of which had never been seen before.

Perhaps at that time, the code research could confirm, to a select few who would listen, that there is a God, and He is in control.

Epilogue

The snow was piled high around the cabin. It had stopped for an hour or so, but the forecast was for it to continue snowing for the next several days. A fire roared in the fireplace as the two sat closely on the couch. There was no place for words. Finally, a smile came across her face, and it assured him that everything would be alright. They had shared a lot over the last few weeks. *A little triumph, a lot of tragedy, sacrifice, and redemption.*

Had they made a difference for humanity? Perhaps that would not be determined until the codes were uncovered. There was definitely a difference in their lives.

He finally started to grow up right before her eyes. What had seemed important to Neil Coles just a few days ago now seemed so trivial. Not that life itself was to be taken too seriously, but death surely was. He now realized those he had taken for granted could be gone quickly and forever. Not even goodbyes were guaranteed.

He held her hand tightly as if letting go was like a balloon flying from a child's hand. He had lost her once; he was going to make sure that never happened again.

"I found an old deck of cards in the drawer. Do you want to play blackjack?"

"No, not really."

"I bet I can beat you."

"I doubt that," he said, smiling.

The professor walked into the room after sleeping for what seemed like a week to him. Rest was certainly something that he needed, but true rest continued to allude to him. There were those moments when he could not distinguish between nightmares and reliving the still-fresh horrors of the previous days. His mind constantly reminded him of the ones who gave their life to protect him. He thought a lot about his father. He was sure his father would be proud of the way he handled the codes and the revelations that he saw of the future. But in his heart, he wondered if his father had seen what the codes revealed, particularly about America; he might have second-guessed getting his son involved. Then the same thought returned: *Sometimes, it is more about the journey than the destination.* The true lesson he learned was now clearer than ever. It was the journey where he found redemption—not the code discovery.

I am a changed person. Now what do I do?

The professor remembered the stories and sermons that his father would tell about the warnings the Israelites received from the prophets. The message was always the same: *If you don't change your ways, destruction will come.* Maybe that would be where this journey would lead. Maybe he could warn America and change the course she was inexorably heading. But he was no prophet, and without disclosing the codes, would those warnings be heeded, or would he be marginalized like so many others who tried to warn America? Deep down, he was not sure, even with the revelations from the codes, that the nation or the civilization would change the path it was on. Could he be a watchman on the wall, warning America about what is just ahead—a modern-day Paul Revere? He would think about his role for a little while. According to the codes, he did have a little amount of time—but not much.

Science had been his god for many years. It was what he had relied on to explain everything. Now he was not sure it could explain anything.

Although technology had helped him discover the holy grail, it was the miracle of the discovery itself that spoke to him. Yes, there is a God. Yes, He knows the future from the beginning. Yes, He is available if you seek Him. Even scientists can seek Him.

The knock at the door served to wake up the professor from another unrelenting bout of daydreaming. The visitor did not wait for an answer to enter. Limping into the cabin with a walker and a cast on his arm, the visitor was met with friendly smiles and hugs.

"I thought you were going to be in the hospital for several more days, but you don't look the worse for wear," said the professor.

"I think that I got on the nerves of the nurses and doctors, and they finally decided to let me out."

"Jimmy, we will never forget what you did for us. Biltmore would have been proud of you," said the professor.

"You know, a promise is a promise."

The professor reached over and put his hand on Jimmy's shoulder. "Jimmy, what you did for Shimon was an amazing act of kindness and forgiveness."

"Yeah, I was surprised that he was still alive. I think I did what any decent person would do."

"Yes, maybe. But you had the uncanny sense to know that his heart was in the right place, even in spite of his actions."

The professor continued, "Jimmy, you might be surprised to learn how saving Shimon's life actually played out in the end. Without Shimon's help, the last few days could have ended tragically."

Jimmy could sense that all eyes were focused on him, and the compliment and attention made him uneasy.

"Unfortunately, my truck is mashed—totaled."

"A truck can be replaced. I am just glad you are okay."

"Speaking of my truck, I got a buddy of mine, and we are going to try to get the black SUV pulled up from the ledge. Do you suppose if I pull it out, I could keep it?"

"I don't see why not. The people who owned it will not be coming back."

Jimmy smiled. "Say, Professor, are you a hunter?"

"No, I am not much of a hunter. I prefer fishing."

"Well, what say we go fishing tomorrow?"

"Isn't it cold for fishing?"

"Yeah, you're probably right. Never mind."

"Now that I think about it, Jimmy, let's go fishing tomorrow."

*****

"I seek to do the will of God. I trust you will too."

About the Author

Daniel Brown lives in North Carolina with his wife, Karen; three sons, Nicholas, Alexander, and Christopher; their wives; and eight grandchildren. Daniel is presently completing the sequel to *The Redemption Codes*.